Medium Dead

Richard Kennett

A Novel

Special Thanks: to the following who helped make this book happen:
Terra Kennett, Karen Inman, Brenda Moore. (Story Editing and Beta Reading)
Hot Pockets, Chipotle, Michelob Ultra, and Coffee. (Lots of coffee.)
The Write-On by Kindle Community, and Insomnia.

Available from Amazon.com and other book stores

For Terra
The one who stole my heart.

1

IT STARTED LIKE a normal day.

For the twenty-six years I have been alive, I wake up the same way. My eyes open and I get out of bed. It's that simple.

For these past few years, the years I have lived on my own, the first thing I see when my eyes open is a digital clock beside my bed. It displays the exact hour and minute of the day. It sets the pace. Without it I'd be lost in time and out of sync with the rest of the world, it's the one thing I trust is always right.

At exactly 6:25AM, every Monday through Friday, the alarm starts in.

I'm usually in a half-awake, half-asleep state of mind, and just finishing up the tail end of a dream. This particular morning it just so happens to be a dream about work, which is unfortunate. I haven't even clocked in yet and it feels like I've already been there for an hour or two.

It's always something with time and I struggle with it on occasion. My body and mind need to get together with the clock and figure this shit out—I'll either stay in bed too long, then end up in a rush to get out the door, or I'll get up too early and end up watching television to kill the time while I'm waiting to leave. My system for waking up and starting my day is not quite there yet—but *I am* working on it.

I have quite a long life ahead of me to figure it out. I know I may never be rich or famous, but I'd like to think I'm doing pretty well for a guy who washes cars at a fairly popular car dealership in Ohio. It's what makes me get up in the morning—knowing others are counting on me to get *my job* done today.

By the time I roll out the door, it's always just enough time to make it to work and clock in with roughly three-minutes to spare. That part, thankfully, has been pretty consistent. I am hardly ever late, unless something major happens along the way.

THE PEOPLE I work with are really not that exciting to be around, just ordinary, vanilla, plain people—but after working with them for over six months, something has formed between us. A bond I guess. I might even say that they were my friends if someone asked.

Cathy Barlow is a hardworking married woman; she needs this job to help feed her family. Her husband is pretty much a career bum who stays at home and collects checks from the government each month for some sort of post traumatic disorder he has. Not that there is anything wrong with that if it's true. Every time I've seen him come into the shop (which is almost always on a Friday), he looks completely normal to me. He's always coming in to get something from Cathy—like money. Then he runs off to pay some past due bill.

Cathy is a very caring person with a big heart, but can sometimes be very unreliable, and only has two speeds when it comes to getting her work done—*slow* and *stop*. One thing unique to Cathy Barlow is that she has a strange body odor that is quite noticeable as she passes by you. If she were to walk down an aisle at a grocery store—any aisle within the past twenty-minutes, I would be able to identify that she had been there without physically seeing her. It was that noticeable and unique, but after a while you got used to it.

Then there is Joe Meadows. Joe started the same day I did in the detail shop. So we had that in common. That's about where all the similarities in our life ended. Joe had, what at the time I thought to be a complete set of front teeth. That was until he opened up his mouth to say something. He did have *something in there*, but it looked more like black jelly beans stuck up and hanging from his gum line. Until you get used to seeing that, you really don't listen to a word that he says. You're still trying to figure out what all that business is in there. Other than that slight cosmetic flaw, he is a really nice guy. A hard worker, a heavy drinker at night, and a heavy smoker all day long. The bad teeth were probably just a byproduct of his lifestyle. I did get along with Joe fairly well; we sometimes would team up on big wash jobs. I would enjoy hearing his long drawn out stories about all sorts of interesting topics from all the wild women he has slept with (hopefully back when his teeth were not completely black), to his favorite brand of bourbon—I just tried my best not to stare directly at the bottom part of his face. Not easy to pull off when he would be talking directly at you, but as time went on, I got the hang of looking at his eyes whenever he opened his mouth to say something.

The coolest cat and most interesting person in the shop by far is a man who ironically goes by the same name as I describe him—Cat. I have no idea what his real name is. He does not look like a cat at all; he is an older black man, probably in his sixties or very close to that. He has a full head of frizzy gray hair that sort of sticks up a little and not just in the morning—*all day long.*

Most of the time when Cat talked, it was about the lottery. I'd say over half of what came out of his mouth was about the lottery. He talked extensively about it to say the least. He knew all the Ohio Lottery games there ever was it seemed: Pick Three, Pick Four, Lotto, Buckeye Five, and all the seasonal scratch off tickets. He kept accurate records of every nightly drawing.

"Pick Three last night was five-five-five!" Cat would say writing the number "555" on his calendar that hung up in his work area at almost the exact second he would walk into the shop. If you wanted to know what the Pick Three number was last night, or any other night for the past eighteen-months or so, you could just look on Cat's calendar.

The last man on our three-man and one-woman crew is me, and my mother named me (get ready for it) Guy.

Yes, my name is Guy—Guy S. Bishop *the Third* to be exact. I can't actually believe that there were two others before me with the same name, my dad and his dad too. It could have been worse, I could have been named John Jacob Jingleheimer Schmidt, we all know there are a shit ton of people with that name out there (or they wouldn't be shouting at each other all the time). "Hey, that's my name too!" It's not that I don't like my name, I just wish my parents could have come up with something a little more creative.

WE USUALLY START the work day by standing around or leaning up against the worktables, just bullshitting with each other for the first fifteen-minutes or so that we are clocked in. This is really normal protocol for blue collar type of people like us. I guess we're not really blue collar per se, but we do wear blue shirts and they have a collar.

We also have nice logos that bear the name of the automobile dealership we work for *Bill Bradley Chevrolet,* and our first name stitched in nice embroidery on the other side—just in case our co-workers forget our name.

The place we all come to work at is a small car dealership in Paris, Ohio. It's one of those little cities along a north-south river, and right along a major north-south highway. The people who first settled here back in the eighteen-hundred-somethings must have had no imagination or creativity when naming their new city. So they just named it after a major city in France.

Joe stood there with us leaning up against a car in his stall. His black jelly bean teeth shining in the morning sunlight. He had just finished up cigarette number three of our daily twenty-minute-long morning bullshit session. He certainly does get his money's worth out of those things, I'd say he got a little bit of the filter on that last drag for sure. "So, Cat, did you say the Pick Three was a triple five last night?" He said.

Great, get him talking about the lottery, that's all we need—I need an extra few minutes this morning, why not.

"You can't miss with a number like that huh?" Joe said kicking the now crushed butt into the middle floor drain.

"Ah, rah, oh hell yeah, Ida got it too if Ida played that number now, ah rah, that five-five-five come up three times in five years now." Cat rattles this off with a stumpy old toothpick that he's been chewing on for at least an hour hanging from his lip.

It was Thursday, and everyone is pretty much tired of being at work and probably tired of even coming to work at this point in the week, not to mention pretty much flat broke. Payday is tomorrow, on Friday! *"The Eagle flies on Friday!"* That was one of Cat's sayings, he always had these weird phrases he would say, and I understood what most of them meant. The one I never really got was whenever it was time to leave for the day he would sometimes say "*—time to go grab some hairy!*" Not sure I want to really know the origin of that one, I think it might be an old black man thing. Either way, he always had a smile on his face when he said it, so *grabbing some hairy* must be something really great that you do to end your day.

"What's the good number for tonight Cat?" I said just to keep him going. If you ever wanted to extend the daily *do nothing but stand around and talk while getting paid thing* in the morning, just get Cat talking about numbers, that will get you an extra five to six minutes easy, every time.

"Oh deyz some muffuckers be playin' eight-five-oh tonight, but if you playin' that make sure you get that fifty-cent back up, that way you—"

Cat continues on with his monologue. He is very knowledgeable when it comes to this particular subject. The toothpick he has in his mouth that is bouncing up and down with each syllable he speaks is just about done. At about the halfway point in the ramble, he flips the last remnant of the saliva soaked wood pulp stick into the drain, right alongside Joe's butts.

He went on for about another six or seven minutes about how the numbers come up and how it's not random at all, that something makes certain numbers come up—something other than random plastic balls coming out of a machine? What? I never really figured out the point he was trying to make with all that, and I didn't really care, I just wanted to stand around a little longer and finish my morning pop before going out and grabbing a big van to wash, that's actual work, and I prefer to do nothing for as long as possible, especially first thing in the morning.

Cat finally finishes up, pulls out a fresh toothpick from his pants pocket, sticks it in between his teeth, and we were all off to begin the actual work day. This is about the time Cathy Barlow, the only woman on our crew and always twenty-minutes behind life itself, shows up for work.

You could set your watch to Cathy's chronic tardiness, twenty-minutes behind, it's just the way her universe works. It's always something to do with either her kids, her old man, or for no other particular reason at all—she just can't go anywhere and be on time.

"Good morning! Glad you could make it in today!" That was my standard greeting to Cathy just about every morning, at least on the days she made it in at all, she was also the type that liked to call in sick for whatever ailment of the month that may be affecting her health.

"Hey, Guy—goooood morning! Damn kids again! The six-year-old made a mistake and put my anti-itch cream on her toothbrush, *again!*"

"Geez!"

Cathy heads to the time clock to punch in for the day. Things like anti-itch cream being used for toothpaste is what makes Cathy a very memorable person. You could tell Cathy Barlow stories to others, just so that we can all appreciate our lives better. Everyday there is another story of why she is late, and out of the three things that are the most common, her kids and the stupid shit they do make her late the most. Makes me never want to have any. I don't know how she even has them herself, she is not that attractive at all—not ugly, just wouldn't think twice about her if I didn't know her and she walked by. Plus, that funny smell, you know the one that seems to linger around. That.

2

THE DAY WINDS down, almost five o'clock and *time to go grab some hairy* as Cat would say from time to time. I wonder if he'll say it today? I should ask him sometime before he retires or croaks, what the hell that means—then again maybe not—I really think I should just leave it up to my imagination as to what this *grabbing hairy* is all about.

"T'morrow I'll drive—we gonna go up to Toto's for lunch," Cat said to me as he sweeps and squeegees the wet floor so we can get out on time. "They got that new Keno game an' we can play while we eatin', I'll show you muffuckers how to play too."

Every once in a while we would treat ourselves to *real food* for lunch, instead of the mystery meats of Ariella's Canteen, which is just a mobile meals-on-wheels wagon that stops by our shop every day. More commonly referred to as a *roach coach*, but really they had some decent affordable food to eat, and I was thankful for that. Typically, on Fridays we would venture out into the *real world*, go out, and maybe have a little fun too. Everyone except Cathy that is, she always volunteered to stay behind, just in case one of the salespeople needed a car washed down real quick. She always needed to make up her time from being late in the morning too, so it really wasn't that big of a deal for her.

"Toto's huh?" I said.

"Yep."

"Last time we had lunch there the guys from the body shop showed up too, you remember that?"

"Ah rah, not really."

"Well they were. Sitting right behind us on their lunch break, just like we were, and in addition to the pizza, pop, and pretzels on the table, they were pounding a pitcher of Bud Light."

Cat started to chuckle a bit. "Got-damn, them some crazy fools!"

"It was kind of embarrassing don't you think? I mean they all had their uniforms on with the big *Bill Bradley Chevrolet* logo on it for all to see."

"I remember that, about three weeks ago," Joe said, bringing in an empty trash can. Smoke still coming out of his nostrils from cigarette number five-hundred or so for the day. "I didn't get embarrassed, I was jealous that we weren't pounding our own pitcher!"

We all head to the time clock to punch out, it's been a long draggy ass Thursday. But now it's quitting time, and it feels great.

"See you later!" I said.

"See you muffuckers tomorrow, gotta go grab some hairy!"

Ahhh, he said it today!

We all left for the day, heading our own ways to the place each of us called home—for me it was a ten-mile trip to the north, up the highway, the next city up the map. About the same size as Paris but with more of a redneckish population—Belle City, or just "Bell" as we locals called it.

I get home, throw in a microwave meal and watch some TV, nothing much more exciting than that. Like I said it's Thursday and I'm flat broke. Tomorrow is payday! Plus, lunch at Toto's with the guys, life does not get any better than that! It's not much of a life I guess, but it's my life as I know it for now.

Well, time to hit the sack—I'm getting tired. I think, and off to bed I go.

Tomorrow, a new day. There is one extra event that will happen tomorrow that I don't even know about just yet. One minor, very small detail, trivial to some, but a profound impact on one's future for sure. An event in your life that you really shouldn't even know is coming, because if you did, it would paralyze you in fear and you couldn't live normally. Yep, tomorrow is the day—tomorrow is the day *I'll die.*

3

My car is a piece of shit.

There is no other way to explain it. It's an '89 Geo Metro, the first year they were made. It's a very *small* compact vehicle. However, it is very good on gas and that's why I drive it. The great gas mileage is because the engine only has three cylinders. Most small cars have four as the minimum, a nice even number. If one cylinder fails, you would have three more as a backup and could possibly continue on to your destination, albeit limping the whole way home. But, at least you'd keep going down the road.

Because of that three-cylinder inline design, the failure of just one could lead to a complete and catastrophic engine failure. The other two cylinders can't keep the dead jug's piston moving (without the proper internal combustion needed for said, *now dead,* piston) and the cheap iron forge that the manufacture uses for the cam shaft—*just snaps!*

I only know this because (of course) that is exactly what happened to me about a month ago. Just driving along on the highway going to work one morning, at highway speed, plus ten (the Metro could do seventy-five on flat land). Then it happened, I hear a *Snap! Bang! Pop!* Or something like that. I was able to pull over into the breakdown lane without pissing off too many people—just one big rig semi that I had to veer in front of suddenly while my car was slowing down. I really don't think he saw me though, the Metro could have easily driven underneath the trailer part of that semi, that's how tiny it is.

Well fuck me, this sucks! I thought to myself after sitting there and now listening to a hundred or so cars and trucks whip by me.

What in the hell do I do now?

I *was* on my way to work, now I'm definitely going to be late. I only give myself three-minutes to spare and that will be up in about one-minute and thirty-seconds from now.

I don't have one of those new fancy portable cell phones, they are expensive to have. I only bring home maybe $200 a week on my check. That only gives me about $860 for the month for income and that's before taxes are paid. My rent alone is $300, so you can see that anything extra is very limited. I don't really need a cell phone anyway. I have very few friends, and my mother still lives in the same city as me, so I can go visit her (when I'm hungry and need laundry done) and I can talk to her then. I never really needed a cell phone you see, until now—this very moment while I'm sitting here trying to think what my next move is.

I am almost afraid to open my door, to get a change of scenery other than the dashboard of my dead car—don't feel like getting whacked by a semi-truck or other moving vehicle coming down the highway—not today, not ever.

I think to myself: *I just really need someone to stop, let me use their fancy new portable phone so I can call into work and get someone to come rescue me. When I get back to work I can send a tow truck up here to grab this piece of shit and take it back to our shop so it can be repaired. I'll just have them take the money it costs to do all this out of my paycheck or something.*

I sat there staring off into space. Just thinking about my shitty luck and my shitty life up to this point. As I'm sitting there, I notice a couple of white crosses planted into the ground about twenty-five feet up from where my car decided to stop at. It's those crosses that someone plants into the ground along the highway to mark the spot where someone has passed away at—a roadside memorial.

Eewww, kinda creepy, someone died close by, I thought to myself noticing them. Which is kind of stupid really if you think about it. Humans have been around for so long on this planet that someone has probably died just about everywhere at one time or the other. The main priority is to make sure what these poor unfortunate people leave behind, like their rotting corpse, is taken care of in a timely fashion.

You never know really *what* happened or even *when* it happened, you just know that something very tragic must have taken place and that someone's life was taken from them. And, it all happened *right there,* at that very spot where the cross is stuck in the ground. I get an uneasy feeling sometimes knowing that something so bad happened there and that the ultimate price was paid. I really try not to look at them very long or read any words that might be written on them. I'm sure they mean something very special to whoever put them there—a family member, a friend, or a spouse—a loved one who wants to be reminded.

But, when I pass by one, I'm just as bad as the people whizzing by me while I'm stuck on the side of the road here. *I'm just glad it's not me.*

Tap! Tap! Tap! "Jeezus!" That scared the crap out of me! I didn't even notice the state trooper that had pulled up behind me; I was still in daydream mode. He had sort of snuck up on me, from behind, and tapped my passenger side window using the butt end of his beater stick thing, *with authority!*

"Hello, anyone in there? *Hello. . . I can see you.*"

Thank God! I thought—as a shot of adrenaline went through my body from being startled—I was suddenly out of my semi-depressed state of mind and ready to get life moving forward again.

"Hello Hello! Officer sir, so glad you stopped to help me out!" I said after leaning over and rolling down the *passenger side* window, revealing the face of this somewhat small statured, but very stern looking law enforcement officer. In Ohio, the state troopers wear these broad brimmed hats with a chain wrapped around it. Similar to what a drill sergeant would wear in the Army. A *Campaign Hat* is what they're called, or a *Lemon Squeezer.* Call it what you want, it was a pretty big hat to be wearing on such a small faced man. It made him look *really angry* too, since the hat pushed down so much on his brow. He was standing on the edge of the grass—on *the passenger side* of my vehicle.

"Oh, no problem at all. That's what we're here for," the tiny faced state trooper said. "So what happened here do you think? I see some oil kind of leaking over here under your front fender. . ."

"Well I'm pretty sure the engine took a crap, these little engines you know, I should have had the oil changed about twenty thousand miles ago, but I just never got around to it, that's probably the problem, I would say, that's, yep. I'm sure that's what happened."

I always seemed to fumble my words around when put under a little pressure. I was nervous too. Talking to the cops will do that to you. Even though this was certainly a non-criminal, non-confrontational type of situation, I still go back to the days of my youth and the juvenile delinquent that I was. Talking to the cops was never something I liked to do, but today in this situation, I did feel good about it. I should, this guy was about to save the day for me.

"You need me to call in a tow truck for you? We always have some on standby. I can just radio my dispatcher and she'll send one right out."

"No, actually I just need to call my shop at work, I uh, I work up there at Bill Bradley's in Paris, I was on my way to work and then this—this happened."

"Oh, sure no problem, so you need to use my phone then?"

"Yeah, sorry, is that cool? I don't have a cellphone, I'm sorry."

"Oh no, that's fine, lots of people don't have cellphones, I see it just about every day. I know from being out here so much, that anybody who is just sitting in their car staring out into *never never land* is probably incommunicado." He stood there still talking to me through the side window, his tiny face seemed more pleasant now. I was getting used to his presence. He seemed more like a friend now, a friend that was going to help me. "And if all you need to do is make one phone call and I can get this vehicle removed from my highway, then I'm a happy man, let me go grab my phone out of the cruiser and I'll be right back. Don't go anywhere!" He kinda had a half-assed laugh at the end there. He took off in a jolt, towards his vehicle, obviously making light of my situation.

"Don't worry— I'm not going anywhere," I said to myself.

He got back in almost no time at all carrying the cell phone, it wasn't the newer portable kind though, it was the kind that came attached to a huge bag and had a shoulder strap so you could carry it almost like a backpack. It must have been his own personal phone I had guessed.

Even though I knew I should just get this over with, my curiosity about those crosses that I had been staring at earlier in front of my car was getting to me. I'm sure this dude had to know the story behind them since this was *his* highway, and before I knew it, before he had time to ask me what number for him to dial—the words just came out on their own.

"What's the story about those white crosses in the ground up there?" As if he would certainly know the full story, and what exact circumstances led to the tragedy that unfolded there.

He looks up and over at the two crosses for a few seconds. "Oh yeah those, that incident happened before I started working this area. I just transferred over here from Akron about three months ago."

I figured that would be it, if this guy just recently came to the area, but he still stood there staring towards the crosses. I couldn't tell if he was looking directly at them with his aviator sunglasses on, but then he lifted them up, and you could see his little squinty eyes that went along and matched his tiny face looking that way.

"Ok, the one on the left says *Trp. Chapman,* he was a State Trooper from this area. We were all made aware of that accident, even up in Akron, statewide actually, that was about five or six years ago I believe."

Ok, so he does kinda know the story—I just sat there and listened.

"It was a bad bad deal, he had pulled over a speeder, was just going up to get the citation signed. A semi-truck hit the rear end of the pulled over car at fifty-five miles an hour, missed the cruiser altogether, but slammed right into the rear end of the stopped car. If *Trp. Chapman* had just waited thirty-seconds more to walk up, there would only be one cross there. Major change in policy statewide after that, that's why you see my cruiser back there parked at a slight angle, to deflect any forward moving energy away from us if something should come our way, and why I'm talking to you on the passenger side of your vehicle now."

"Man that sounds terrible, I bet that had to hurt something awful, geeze fifty-five miles an hour?"

"Oh, instantaneous death for both—you probably have never seen anything like it before, but I have. Back in Akron, I was coming on scene for a minor accident—little fender bender type of deal—but the two parties involved didn't move into the far right breakdown lane. Instead, they were up against the cement barricade, inside the yellow line, the left side of a three lane interstate highway, way more dangerous place to be. I was getting closer and the first thing I was going to do was get these guys over to the right, when all of a sudden a truck—" He looks down and sort of shakes his head side to side. "Well I'll just say you can believe me, it was instant. I can't even go on to describe the damage of what an eighty-thousand-pound semi-truck going forty or fifty miles an hour can do. But hey, here we are right? And we're safe, right?" He had a half-cocked smile after he said all that, but I could tell he wasn't lying about that day in Akron.

"So anyway, how about that phone number so we can get you out of here?"

I sure am glad my registration was good, my driver license valid, and no outstanding warrants were issued for me at the time. Even though Mr. Tiny Face State Trooper didn't ask for my driver license or social security number, I'm sure he probably knew who I was well before he walked up to my car. Luckily for me, all that was good, and after a quick call up to the shop on the trooper's personal cell phone. I was rescued.

4

TODAY IS FRIDAY. Payday. *The Eagle* flies today! I'm broke as broke can be, not even any loose change in my pockets. I know I said I'd go to Toto's today to have a little fun, but I sure hope this doesn't break me even more. I really would like to eat some of those great tasting chicken wings, instead of that mystery meat shit I get on all the other days of the week, so I guess I'll figure it out somehow.

This morning during our twenty-minutes of *stand around do nothing, but still get paid time,* we were getting an education. It was on how to play the latest lottery game sensation, Keno, and directly from the Cat Man himself.

I could understand him quite well today. I think since this was something he was so passionate about; his stuttering was (for the most part) non-existent. It was quite amazing really, his everyday profanity laden vocabulary stayed in check, all the while as he talked about the ins and outs of a basic Keno bet slip.

Here's a summary of what we now know:

You fill out your Keno card bet slip, checking the boxes on how many "spots" you want to play. You can pick these spots, or have the computer pick them for you. You go up and turn in your filled out card, and then pay *the man.* Your ticket prints out. *The man* hands the ticket back, then you go back to your table. While you're just sitting there enjoying life, and the great food, your eyes constantly look at this big screen that lights up some randomly selected numbers. Hopefully, you have some of the numbers you already picked on your bet slip that show up on this screen.

Sounds pretty easy to me, and pretty fucking boring too. But, I'll play along, it's not about me today. I like the Cat Man and all his crazy talk that comes with him. I'm one of his *muffuckers,* and I like that. Besides, I already got this figured out, I can just buy one ticket and pay the two bucks or so. Then *act like* I'm playing for an hour on the *one ticket*. They will never know! I will just keep walking up to *the man*, then ask him something stupid like "When is the next game coming up?" I'll then sit back down with the same ticket I purchased to begin with (even though it's completely worthless). I'm sure I can find two bucks by lunchtime in seat cracks and ashtrays alone. So I guess. . . *I'm in.*

Before I knew it, it was about time to head out for lunch. Almost straight up noon. I hit a pretty decent honey hole this morning in a blue mini-van and found $3.58 in coins, which is pretty damn good I might add. Mostly pennies, but a few dimes and quarters were sprinkled in the mix as well. One of the quarters I pulled out was pretty nasty, had some gum stuck to it or something. The gummy like substance was now more like black tar. You could still make out that it was a quarter, George's outlined head was clearly visible as was the date the coin was minted—1979.

I was only eleven years old when this coin was made—I wish you could rub the coin, say some enchanted spell, and then you would somehow go back in time to the year the coin was born, *oh the stories it could tell.* I would definitely go back and give myself some good advice like:

"Don't buy that '89 Metro from Uncle Jason in a few years, for it will leave you stranded on the highway someday…"

I then began to wonder if this poor coin had been stuck in the crack of this mini-van's seat since 1979 too, it sure did look like it.

"You muffuckers ready to go! We gone go eat some chicken wings and play some Keno!" Cat yelled as he was punching out for the lunch period. Joe and I were right behind him.

Oh, I guess it will be fun to watch, look at him, he is a nut!

"You guys have fun! I'll be here as usual!" Cathy Barlow said still working, standing on a ladder, and spraying some suds off the top of a full size G-20 van.

"Did you want me to get you anything while we're out?" I asked.

"No, that's ok—my husband is supposed to stop by and get my check, then go pay the water bill. He said he would bring me something in from home to eat so I'm good, but thanks for asking."

"Okee doke…see ya!"

We walk out the door and head into the parking lot. It might be for the last time ever, who's to know.

My life, and everyone else's life around us, moves along on an unknown path that changes every second you breath or take a step in one direction or the other. Do I want to go with these people and let them steer my future? Let them make the decisions that control my fate in this world? Those are just choices, one of a hundred or more you make every day. Sure, some choices can make our life better or worse, but some things—*some things just happen. And, sure enough something will happen today.*

5

I HAVE ONLY been a passenger in Cat's car one other time. Usually, on our periodic lunchtime adventures we would take my Metro. Joe and Cat could fit *somewhat* comfortably, just as long as Joe sat in back and Cat in front. There was slightly more legroom up front in my super sub-compact car and Cat, being an older and slightly taller man than Joe, made it the most efficient way to travel. But not today. Today was Cat's idea to go to Toto's for lunch.

We all walk up to the tan Buick Park Avenue, a four door vehicle with nice silky smooth leather seats all around, clean rims, and a waxy shine that stood out from the rest of the cars it was parked beside. You could tell Cat took care of this vehicle like it was one of his children.

"You can have shotgun Joe, I'm cool in the back."

"Sounds good man, thanks."

Joe is now desperately trying to finish up a cig that he just lit up walking out the door not ten-seconds ago. His constant fast paced drags one after the other never allow it to ash up. The cigarette from the filter up is just one hot cherry, and a long one too. You call that *hot-boxing it*, and nobody could hot-box a cigarette better than Joe Meadows. Not even the kids over at Paris High School were as good as him. If the administration over at the school wanted to curb all the smoking in the restrooms between classes, they should shorten the time allotted between them. Those delinquents can easily suck down a Marlboro Red in sixty-seconds flat. Joe could do it in thirty. That's just how much better he was at it.

He just *had to* get that last one in before the ride to Toto's, didn't he? We certainly don't want him going into any sort of nicotine withdrawal on the way there, it could get ugly in here quick. Joe finishes up, at just about the same time the car doors open. He flips the cig butt across the parking lot and the three-inch-long fire cherry smashes into a hundred pieces when it hits the ground. It looked like a firework going off, but without the loud explosion.

I nestle myself in the backseat for the ten-minute ride up the highway. Wow, I absolutely love the smell of Cat's car! It smells like fresh cut flowers in here! I need to find out what he's using to make it smell so good.

As soon as Joe (the human cigarette) hops in the front seat, the aroma of a dirty ashtray suddenly fills the interior. We need to get rolling down the road, and get that fresh air circulating in here, *as soon as possible!*

Here is the thing I suddenly remember about Cat: *He does not drive on the interstate highway.* I am reminded of this slight issue he has as we roll by the on-ramp to I-25 north, the main highway around here. Oh, I remember the day he told me: *"No sir, not ever, with them big muffuckin' trucks getting too close tryin' to run me over, so my ass don't be driving no highway..."* Cat will just avoid the interstate at all costs, no matter what, including extra driving time. I must have forgotten all about that.

"Ahhh shit Cat! I forgot you don't drive on the highway."

That will be an extra seven minutes to Toto's.

"Oh, don't worry now, I got a good route picked out—we'll be good!"

THE ROAD WE are driving on at the moment, would most likely make you sick if you happened to be looking down, reading something, or just not paying attention to the wild ride your body is about to take, as the forces of gravity pull you from side to side. There are some parts of this road—right before you cross the county line—that are just ridiculously ill planned. What has happened here is that about fifty-years ago, when some of the county roads were first being planned out, certain property owners would *refuse* to sell their land to make way for the new roadways. This was all farm and cattle as far as the eye could see back then, and that's how everyone made their living—from the land. Less land, less money—and nobody wanted to give it up.

So instead of fighting with these people and just seizing the property to do what is needed in the name of public safety—the county engineers simply *bent* the road around all the farms and houses.

Problem solved—so they thought.

Sure, problem solved. If you still lived in the 1940's.

Speed limits have changed over the years, automobiles got faster, people needed to get to places and they needed to get there fast. *Time is money.* Back then, if you were going over forty-miles-per-hour, or had recently just traded in your horse for a car; you were living life in the fast lane. Most of these curvy roads wrapped around farmhouses and their respective property lines. You needed to slow down. If you didn't do that, you would more often than not, end up in someone's living room.

As we whip around one of these corners, my body slides over to the other side of the car. This is due to the super-smooth leather seats that Cat likes to maintain. I don't usually wear a seat belt when I'm sitting in the back seat of a car. The law says only front riders have to wear them. The polyester dark blue work pants I have on are not helping the matter at all, it's like an ice skating rink back here!

The one thing that some property owners have done out here (which is quite noticeable on just about every hairpin curve) is strategically place a huge tree in their front yard. I'm not sure how these trees grew in such a convenient spot, more than likely they were planted there on purpose a long time ago. It's a smart move; you never know when someone will be distracted, or just forget that the curve is approaching before it is too late.

I notice something strange here as well. I'm not sure why this even sparks my curiosity. Possibly because I have nothing else better to do right now. Anyway, on the second sharp turn (there were always two in a row since you basically travel along the property line), I notice a pretty solid looking structure right where you would normally see one of those big-ass humongous trees.

It looks like a large garage, or storage space area for all your lawn 'n garden tools and whatnot. If we come back this way (and I'm sure *we will* be coming back the same way), I will be able get a better look at this thing and figure out why it's even there. Seems like a weird spot to build such a huge outbuilding.

Maybe if Cat will allow *me* drive his car back so that we can take the goddamn highway back to work, we won't have to worry about any of that. I've really about had it with these nausea inducing backwater roads, so when the time comes, I'll at least ask.

After that last sharp curve with the odd-looking and out of place structure in the property owner's front yard, we cross the county line, and its straight roads for the rest of the way—we're just about to Toto's now.

"I hope those assholes from the body shop aren't there today," I said poking my head up front so Cat and Joe could hear me better, "you just know they'll be drinking again if they are, what a bunch of alcoholics."

"What's wrong with being an alcoholic?" Joe said, "I'm an alcoholic, my dad was an alcoholic, my grandpa was too. I'm just trying to carry on a family tradition that's passed down from generation to generation, nothing wrong with that is there?"

"Yeah yeah sure—but at least you don't drink when you still have to go back to work, or at least I've never seen you do anything like that before since I've known you—and we both started the same day, and so far you've been good."

I just had to add in a little something about the smoking too.

"Although I guess if you did nip on the bottle a little at work, we would never know since you smoke ten packs of cigs a day and that would definitely cover up the alcohol smell."

"Oh no no no— I only smoke about *three packs a day*," Joe said. "Once again I'm a product of my environment man, everyone in my family smokes, it's just what we do—I've been smoking since I was thirteen years old, and now I'm almost thirty and I feel just fine."

Really, thirteen years old?

"What about all that lung butter you cough up every morning and stockpile in the drain at work? What about that? Are you *sure* your health is fine? That's not right all that crap coming out of you. What's your doctor say about all that, huh?"

"You muffuckers shut up now, we almost there, I can smell them wings!" Cat interrupted with. Now pulling into the parking lot of Toto's Bar and Grill, home of the twenty-ounce Manic Margarita. That's what Toto's is well known for, a mixed drink they seem to have figured out how to make really really well. One other thing that is well known about Toto's is that it's not too family friendly at night. It attracts a pretty rough crowd when the sun goes down, and it wasn't always just because of the mix of bikers and rednecks either. In fact, those folks seemed to get along better than others. Something just seemed to change here after dusk. The evil demons came here to play and they didn't always play nice.

We walk in and get a seat—its self-serve seating, so you just pick out your seat, and then hope you get a good server who is prompt and courteous. We technically only have about forty-minutes left for lunch now, and that will have to include the drive time back.

"Good, don't see anyone from the body shop, just us today—we're the only ones wearing blue uniform shop shirts in here, so let's make sure we all just order pop or water to drink ok?" I said taking a visual survey of the customers that were already sitting down inside.

The place was about one-third full—enough for Toto's to have a reason to be open for lunch and make a few bucks I guess. Their food wasn't bad at all—it wasn't a mainstream place like a Buffalo Wild Wings, but they had some decent tasting local wing sauces, in all different flavors and level of heat to satisfy anyone's comfort zone. I always order a ten-piece in the *Asswarmer* flavor, in my opinion the best sauce that their wings come in, very tasty and not too crazy hot. If I wanted to go nuts and live on the edge I might order a ten-piece in *Rocketfuel*, that's the next one up the scale. The absolute highest level they make are called *Chernobyl's,* a flavor of wing sauce named after the Russian nuclear power plant that melted down in 1986, anyone who puts in an order for these stomach liner eroding things must sign a liability waiver *before* they were brought out. I don't really think they could actually hurt you, the waiver thing was just part of the hype to get you going—but one thing was certain—you never went to take a piss after you handled a *Chernobyl* flavored wing without thoroughly washing your hands first. Even some of the wings that were below the *Chernobyl* level of intensity (which was pretty much all of them except teriyaki through mild), would put a mighty *sting on your thing*.

"Well, that didn't take long," I said to Joe, pointing my head towards the area where the lottery terminal was. Cat was already up there filling out his Keno bet slip, even before anyone had come to our table to greet us.

"He is on it—you going to play? Do you even remember how to play from what he was telling us this morning?" Joe asked.

"Yeah, I'll play at least one time I guess, I did find a bunch of nasty looking coins in that blue mini-van I was working on this morning, I was able to scrounge up almost four bucks!"

We sat there for a few minutes. The server came over and got our drink orders, Joe played nice and just ordered an unsweetened tea, and I ordered a Pepsi for Cat and I. A few more people were showing up now in the bar for lunch, mostly older folks who liked Toto's food, but are too scared to come here at night—and a few other oddballs here and there. Overall a pretty decent turnout for a little after twelve-noon on a Friday.

A Friday now turning into the afternoon and that will eventually turn into the evening, then the morning again—it's a cycle, and a never ending one. The earth will keep turning and turning, day after day, and night after night—that's time. You can't stop time, it will catch you no matter how fast or wherever you go in the universe—it just keeps moving along no matter what—but someday *we will not, we will stop—in time, forever.*

6

WE ALL THREE settle up with the server before we head out. As far as that Keno game went—well, I of course didn't win jack-shit, but Cat somehow ended up with a seventy-five-dollar winning ticket. He is without a doubt *the luckiest man alive.* We step out into the parking lot. Joe, getting ready to do his usual thing, lights one up almost before we even exited the building.

"Hold on guys, I gotta get this in—I need a smoke something fierce—only take a minute."

"Hurry up, we only have about fifteen-minutes to get back, and that's going to be pushing it, since we have to take the *no highway* route," I said trying to give someone a hint that we were pressed for time. "I don't suppose you would let me drive Cat, would you? We could get back quicker and I have no problem taking the interstate highway."

"Oh hell no!" Cat snapped back. "Ain't no muffucker drivin' my car sept' me!"

"Oh, that's what I thought—it was worth a shot I guess."

We both just stand there by the car. Cat and I looking at Joe in utter amazement. I do believe he is attempting to break the world record for the shortest time it takes to smoke a regulation sized Marlboro right now. Once again, the entire front end is a flaming red hot cherry, but this time splitting into two distinct branches. It actually looked something like a miniature volcanic lava snake tongue at this point. Did he say he needed a minute? Joe finishes off this thing in just twenty-five seconds easy, not sure what the record is, but I think he got it that time. He throws the butt up in the air, the wind picks it up and carries it off twenty-feet away into the middle of an empty parking lot. The end of the useful life for that cigarette was just twenty-five seconds, but *seven minutes* will be deducted from Joe Meadows life.

That's what they say those things take from you each time you light one up and that really doesn't seem like a fair trade at all.

Let's see, three packs a day—for about seventeen years, that's sixty cigarettes a day multiplied by 365 days a year—umm, that's about 22,000 cigs a year, for a grand total of a whopping 374,000 cigarettes that have passed through Joe's lungs during his smoking career. What a lifetime achievement that is for someone! That's if he started doing the three-pack-a-day thing from the first day he started when he was thirteen—not likely, but this is Joe Meadows we're talking about.

"See now you shoulda played the numbers I told you to play Guy, you could have won like me!" Cat said, obviously still thinking about his little lottery game that he almost tripled his money on in less than an hour.

"Shoulda coulda woulda—you're the best man, I should have known better!"

We get in the car—close the doors and off we go—Toto's is now a memory of the past.

7

ON THE WAY back to the grind now, cruising at a paltry fifty-two miles an hour along the nice straight-lined county roads. My stomach is as full as it's been in a long while. The *Asswarmer* wing sauce is usually my friend, but I'm thinking I'll probably chew down a couple of Tums when I get back to the shop, just out of an abundance of caution. I start to settle into the smooth feel and soft textured leather back seats of the Cat Man's car; *wow, this is really nice.*

The full stomach, lack of conversation, and soothing white noise coming from the tires rolling down the road put me right out for a few moments. I even go into that first layer of *dream mode*. The same state-of-mind that happens in my wake-up routine, which is sort of in-and-out of reality.

My mind replaces the tire noise with the sound of the ocean. I now find myself sitting on a beach and a gentle breeze blows on my face. There is a slight whiff of smelly fish and the sweet aroma of suntan lotion wafting around me. The two contrasting scents sort of offset each other in perfect balance and harmony. I jump in the water. What a great scene this is. The ocean is so refreshing, and the waves that approach me are ever so gentle. I float on my back in the saltwater and just take it all in—*ahhh, maybe someday this will really happen. . .*

The once gentle rhythmic waves quickly turn into massive swells. I stand myself up, turn around, and look toward the horizon. A growing crest of particularly large size approaches me and I can't get out of the way! The sound it makes is deafening! The massive wave collapses into an angry wall of whitecap water, but before it ever reaches me I hear Cat's voice scream out *"Got-Damn!"*

I snap out of my micro-nap in an instant. The sound of Cat's voice was real; he has seen something he fears the worse. The one thing that prevents him from driving on the highway, *those big semi-trucks.* Quite a few, all in a line and heading in the opposite direction that we are traveling now. Each one going by with the same sound as that angry white-capped wave in my dream.

"Where'd all these muffuckin' big ass trucks come from! They be wantin' to run me off the road now!"

"Relax man—probably a wreck on the interstate and all the semis are taking the alternate route now—which is 25A, the road we are on now. The 'A' stands for *alternate*, so we're just going to have to deal with it." I tell him this as matter-of-fact and clearly as I could. He needs to realize this is nothing to be afraid of—*but you should see the look on his face now*—he is truly frightened by all this.

Most of it is big-rig traffic. It is a bit intimidating if you happen to stare at the front grill of these trucks when they whiz by. This is just a little ole' two lane county road, with a double yellow line in the middle and white edge line. It does sort of look like they will hit you *head on* if you're not extra careful to stay on your own side of the road. Which is what Cat was so desperately trying to do now.

"Don't worry Cat, look at the white edge line to the right side of the road and try not to focus too much on the oncoming traffic, that should help." Joe said now trying to coach Cat through all this. His fear of big trucks is real. This is definitely a disorder of some kind, there might even be an actual name for it. If there isn't one, I'm making one up when we get back to the shop.

"Ok, muff—" Cat stops talking in mid-sentence.

"You OK man?"

"Yeah yeah, I'm alright—*but my mouth is dry-as-a-muffucker though*, I'll be cool, I'll be alright. . ."

I sure hope so, I want to make it back alive to the shop.

Cat is handling it remarkably well up to this point. He is keeping cool as the Cat Man can keep it. Not saying a whole lot and with a death grip on the steering wheel. I'm not sure if that's good or bad right now. We are fast approaching the county line, and the ill planned roadways that follow. This first one is a real doozie too, the one with the fortified structure built in the front yard.

The trucks, still coming at us in full force one after the other, create such a wake when they pass you—they can *really* push some air, and the car shakes side to side each time one goes by. They must have shut the highway down completely and re-routed everything for it to be this bad and congested.

"Doing good man, don't forget that sharp curve up ahead at the county line," I said.

I thought I might have heard Cat say *cool,* or was it *fool?* Another big truck whipped by right when I thought I had heard him respond. It was perfect timing with the passing of the truck and an anticipated response from Cat. It was definitely his voice. I just wasn't *one-hundred percent* sure what he had *actually* said. I went with what I thought he most *likely* said, and *to me* it was *cool.* That might have been a mistake to assume, but assume I did.

As we approach the curve—I can confirm my theory as to why someone would build that huge outbuilding in such an unusual spot. There is a big farm house just beyond in the distance. They must have built this solid structure in that spot as a first line of defense, to prevent anything that might exit the roadway from hitting the house.

Looks like the garage doors are open today, how nice, just in case we have to plow through it—one less thing to hit.

"*Getting closer—now is the time when I would probably start to slow down Cat.*"

"*But not happening yet…ok still some time here….*"

"*How about now?*"

"*Ok definitely now…*"

"*Oh shit!!*"

8

I AM NOT exactly sure how we got to this point.

I do have a good idea though; first thing was Cat's state of mind. I think he was so focused on watching that white edge line along the road, he just went into *auto-pilot* mode. Unaware of anything else around him. He just held the course. *But he got stuck*—stuck fixating on that white line a little *too much*. All the other factors too: the late departure from Toto's, the closing of the highway, and the truck that passed us at the same moment that Cat was supposed to give me that reassuring answer. I thought he did. *I was so certain of it.*

Just the perfect ingredients. . .

Cat held it steady along the edge line. Once that line disappeared from his view to follow the curve—the message never made it to his hands to turn the steering wheel. Even if he turned the wheel to follow around the curve, at this point it would have been too late. Our excessive forward speed would have sent us off the road anyway. So, we just continued forward. Full speed ahead.

I could see the inside of this garage, and oddly enough in great detail (things were slowing down in my mind). I noticed a very nice array of tools along with a peg hole board to hang them up on. Someone really took the time to make this garage look nice, and they really did a fantastic job. But, right now I'm not really thinking about tracking down the owner to commend them on such an awesome project that surely took many weekends to complete—I'm thinking about how bad this is going to hurt slamming into a solid brick structure held together with cement, wood, and more cement. This is about the time I felt an electric jolt go through my entire body (we still had not penetrated the building yet), I assumed that this was my brain sending signals to various parts of my body telling them to prepare for the worst.

Everything turned white in my field of vision. As fast as that happened, probably no more than a second or even shorter—there I was just standing up beside the car—still inside the garage.

That was a great reflex; I never knew humans could do something like that. The nervous system is a beautiful and complex thing. Just turn off, then wake up again and you're fine. I didn't even notice that any time had passed. Am I the first to discover this?

The car is still in the garage—and it looks fully intact. It's as if Cat must have snapped out of it, hit the brakes hard, and slid inside this garage at just the perfect angle. Not hitting *a thing*. He is *the luckiest man alive* if he pulled this off! I am going to give him every penny, dime, and quarter I find in a car from now on! I might even name one of my future kids after him for this!

"Jezus!" I yelled. "That was awesome Cat! How the hell did you do that?" I was looking around at this garage now, and like I said before, what a nicely laid out and very organized place this is. I would really like to applaud the person who owns this building, if I find them that is, but not until I properly thank the man who just saved my life and Joe's too. The absolute *luckiest man alive in the world* as far as I'm concerned.

"Yo, Cat! —Joe? What the hell man! You are one lucky son-of-a-bitch Cat!"

I bent down to look inside the car. Nothing. Nobody in there.

"Hmmm—I must have been out longer than I thought. These dudes are nowhere to be found." I said this out loud for nobody in particular to hear. They must be outside, trying to figure out who Cat has to pay for all this. I look around to survey this garage, sliding in like that surely must have caused some sort of damage somewhere, but nothing that I could tell was even touched.

I walked outside the garage, looking for Cat and Joe, still nothing. I yell their names out loud a couple times, just trying to get some idea of where they may have walked off to. Things start to get weird—I start to feel strange—like I do in the mornings when I wake up to my radio, half-awake and half-asleep. I can control my actions and think about what I want to do, where I want to walk, and when I want to talk, but everything seems to be going slower in my mind.

This could only mean one thing; I must have hit my head pretty good back there. The symptoms are starting to show and I may need some medical attention after all. There is no blood that I can see or feel anywhere. I'll need to find a mirror. I need to see what my face looks like.

I walk back into the garage, hop back into the Buick Park Avenue, and just as I was about to poke my head up to look in the mirror, I hear a voice coming from behind me. A woman's voice—a very soft tone. I could understand the words so clearly:

"Guy, wait."

The woman spoke only those two words.

Who's here that knows my name? And is asking me to wait? Wait for what? I didn't even get a chance to look in the rear view mirror to see how bad my face looked. I'm probably about to be blamed for all this, so I quickly jump out of the car. Surely this must be the person who owns the building—and with Joe and Cat fleeing the scene and leaving me to deal with everything now—I'm going to have to do some fast talking.

"Oh, so so sorry!" I stumbled over some junk lying on the ground and also stumbled over most of my words at the same time.

"Umm, I wasn't driving mam'. . . Uh, this wasn't my fault. . .It was the older black gentleman outside who was the driver. I'm sure you must have seen him? And the other man with him as well? Probably smoking a cigarette by now. . ."

I could see her outline now as I looked towards the direction where her voice was coming from. I can't tell yet for sure what she is thinking here. Is she going to just assume this is all my fault? I walk towards her and hope for the best. Hoping she'll give me a chance to tell my side of the story. She spoke again, and just as before, the words were very clear to me.

"Guy, I don't have much time here to talk to you, most of this will not make any sense to you yet— so you need to listen to me carefully." I could see her face now and what a beautiful woman she was.

"When the time comes you're going to need to make a decision, don't think of anything else but walking through the door, just remember that okay? *Walk through the door. . .*"

"Ok, walk through the door, I got it." I replied with sort of a confused look on my face.

"And uh, why would I need to do that?"

"It will allow you to move on," she said, "it will let you see things from beyond this point in time. It's going to happen very quickly when you see it—if you don't walk through the door Guy, you will have to wait for another one. Don't think of anything else, there will be a lot of distractions, just clear your mind and walk through."

Well she's right about one thing, none of this makes sense. Why is this woman giving me advice on how to walk through a door? Is she selling them? Is that what this is all about? I've just been involved in a fairly serious automobile accident here, and now I'm being solicited to buy some doors?

I begin to think. I rewind the tape in my head. Back to that part where we're going *really fast* around the hairpin corner in the car, not slowing down, driving on the grass and right into that building. Yeah, that part right there. The impact and sudden stop had to be pretty forceful. I'd say some internal organs were certainly displaced in the process. Yet, I don't feel a thing wrong with me. I keep thinking about it and replaying the whole sequence over and over again. Then it hits me, the one thing it could only be—*I'm dead*. Yep, I'm dead. Got to be— I probably never even made it out of the car; there was no way out of that situation now that I look back at it. The flash of light wasn't a reflex at all, it was just the death setting in and nothing more—swift and quick. Just like the tiny faced state trooper was telling me the day I was stranded on the highway. He had witnessed a situation like that himself, and it wasn't pretty. I guess it would be a lot worse to see it happen right in front of you and see all the carnage that happens after the fact. I feel sorry for the owner of this garage, coming home and seeing a vehicle smashed into his nicely laid out area here, then watching the authorities pull three bodies out. My God what a mess that has to be. I truly am sorry about all this.

Now that I've come up with my own likely explanation, I feel the question I'm about to ask should not be of any surprise to the woman who stands before me.

"Ok, just a second here, I have a quick question here before we talk more about this door thing—*am I dead right now?*"

She looked at me. It felt warmer when she looked directly in my eyes, and I could already tell what the answer was going to be before she even said anything. I am pretty good at figuring out things, and this was a no brainer to me. So many questions to ask. I'm sure things are going to get a lot worse before they get better, I can already see that happening.

"I can tell you now since you asked—*yes, Guy Bishop died back there in that car accident,*" she said. Each word rang inside my head with pure clarity. "But your journey is just now beginning here, and you can still move on—I'm going to help you as much as possible before I have to go, but I promise I'll come back when I can."

"So I'm really dead huh? Geesh, I was actually hoping you would tell me I was wrong. So you're not trying to sell some doors then? What exactly do I need to do again? I want to keep moving. . . moving on if I can, just like you said..."

"Yes, whatever you get out of this remember the door, *get through it,* no matter what you see, think, or feel—just get *through the door.*" She said, looking directly at me. It sent warm feelings through my being. It made me believe that every word she said was true. Somehow I got the feeling this lady really wanted me to pay attention, with the emphasis on *the door* since she has now mentioned this no less than six times.

"Also, Guy, this is important too—there are others here—others just like you in the middle looking for their own door, you will see them, and they may try to misdirect and lie to you. Don't let them, it's that simple. *Don't let them.*"

And with that she was gone. I don't know how to describe it other than it's just like you see in a movie. She just ceased to appear before me. No smoke screen, no curtain, or trap door—just gone. That by far was just the craziest thing I have seen today. The only other thing that probably tops it was finding out I was killed in an automobile accident about twenty-minutes ago.

My new journey begins.

9

TIME TO GET my mental notebook out here—I am trying to process all the things this beautiful woman (who just vanished in front of my eyes into thin air) just said to me. She never even told me her name. Of course this all sounds too familiar. In my now former real life, beautiful women would often vanish into thin air without telling me their name all the time. So nothing has really changed in that department at all. I assume she is some sort of angel or a part of the New Member Welcome Committee to the world I'm standing in now. I'll just call her Angel for now.

Angels are supposed to be beautiful, and this one certainly was all that and more. Let's see, Angel said I needed to go through a door (six times she tells me this), so I think I got that—and that there will be others here too. That sounds interesting and scary at the same time. I wonder where I'll find these *others* she talked about? Speaking of others, I wonder where Cat and Joe ended up? Why are they not here with me now? Those guys were up in the front seat, they surely kicked the bucket too, they were wearing seatbelts, but still, that had to have been a pretty solid hit we took.

I step outside the garage to look around. Nothing really sticks out to me just yet; I do notice that it's very quiet except for a really faint sound in the distance that I catch every couple of seconds. It sounds like a merry-go-round of all things, the carousel music is unmistakable. I used to love those things when I was a kid. That has to be it! That's probably where I'm supposed to be headed. Go toward something you're attracted to, just like a bunch of bugs going toward a light. I guess I'll let my instincts take over for now, I don't see why not.

I really don't know where else I would go. It looks like nothing works or even moves around here, very quiet, no wind blowing around or anything. I go back into the garage one more time to see what is up with the car. It's just there, you can't even make it move by pushing it. It's just stuck there frozen in time, my time I guess, the exact moment I entered this new place. What did Angel call it? *The middle?* Sounds about right to me—I'm stuck in *the middle* of the world I was in, and wherever you go after this place. Then according to Angel, I'll need to go through some door to move on. *Remember, six times she said that to me.*

I try to ponder then if I'm *medium dead* or *medium alive?* Halfway between being completely alive and completely dead. I'd prefer *medium alive*, but I'm sure there is no going back to being *actually alive* (since my physical body is likely not in such great shape now) so really the next step is to be *fully* and *completely dead*, so I'll go with *medium dead*, just makes more sense that way. I never thought I'd want to be dead, but that's the world I'm in now.

I LOOKED OVER at the old farmhouse. I wonder what would happen if I just went over there and walked right in? Would I get in trouble for trespassing or breaking and entering? Hell no, I'm dead! What's the worst they can do? Kill me? That's already been taken care of! This might actually be fun for a while, until I get bored with it I suppose. There are all kinds of doors in a house, and maybe the one I need to walk through. I should at least go take a look.

But what about that merry-go-round sound I keep hearing? It sure as hell sounds like it's a few miles away at least, and there is a perfectly fine house sitting right here. Shouldn't take long to go poke around a bit. I'll just go up and see if I can even do something as simple as open the door. I need to figure out all the basic *Dead Guy 101* anyway before I go on any further, or before I run into someone else. It just seems like a good place to try some things out, to see what I'm even capable of doing in the current state I'm in.

10

A PRETTY BASIC looking old farmhouse here, nothing special about it really. I get on the porch and knock on the door. I have no idea why I even need to knock, but I do it anyway. I guess it's that I don't want to feel like a criminal when I try to open the door and walk into this house uninvited. Ok, so here it goes—I put my hand on the knob, turn it, and it opens right up. No transparent *hand through the solid wood door* or any type of ghost trickery here, no nothing like that. I just opened it right on up, it wasn't even locked.

Well, that mystery is solved. I can touch things and move them. Should have realized that when I knocked on the door in the first place.

"Hello?" I said. "Anyone home?" I walk inside, just inside the foyer area. Still uneasy about the whole prospect of entering someone's home uninvited while they are not there, but then again maybe they are home. I don't think anyone can see me, or me them at this point. I'm surely in a totally different plane or dimension than they would be, at least that's my theory.

I start to think. . .*should I abort this mission?* Nahh, I have to keep reminding myself that I'm dead *(well technically speaking, medium dead)*, and there is not much anyone can do to me now to make my life, or the lack of my life, much worse than what it is now.

"Cat? Joe? You guys in here?"

No response at all.

It's the same thing being inside as being outside, no sounds of any kind, except the ones that I make on my own, like the knocking on the door, and when I move things around. If they can even be moved at all, some things are just "stuck." I can also hear my own footsteps, so it's not always completely quiet. You just don't hear the normal everyday things like, air moving, appliances kicking on and off, or the ticking of a clock.

I walk all over this house. Every once in a while I might call out Joe and Cat's name, but after a while I just give up—they're not in here. I stop and look at some of the pictures on the wall. Nice looking old people—*at least they got to get old*. That was the first time in my short *middle of the after-life* that I kind of felt sad and a little more emotional than I normally am, things are starting to sink in. *Will I ever see mom again?*

I finally had enough of this place. Not one of those doors (and I walked through about every door that I saw) made me feel any different. If anything, the excursion through this old farm house made me more sad and lonely—I'm actually looking forward to talking to someone else that will talk back to me. I don't even care if they lie to me, I just want to get some answers and move on to wherever I need to go. I step back outside, I can still hear the carousel music up in the distance, so I mentally prepare myself for this surely long ass walk that is about to take place.

THE MUSIC GETS louder as I get closer. I have been walking for about thirty-minutes now I'm guessing, just have to go with what I feel, since I have no way to keep track of time. I'm not tired or anything, just sort of bored from walking so much. I think of what might lie ahead here, and try to imagine what it will be like once I run into someone who can communicate with me.

I start to think of some pretty bizarre stuff while I'm walking. What if someone gets stuck in this world? Can't ever find a door. You could literally spend eternity here. This land before it was Ohio, was occupied by Native Americans for the most part. Before that, who knows. I would say dinosaurs, but that's probably going too far back in time. My guess is that I would see an Indian first before a dinosaur, and we know how all the Indians were treated way back when. Like I said, it was a *long walk*...

I AM FINALLY here.

It took a while, but here I am standing in front of the thing making all the noise for the past hour or so. It's your garden variety whirligig carousel, nothing too exciting at all.

When I was a kid, my mother would take me to our local amusement park, which was just down the highway—I remember you had to go through the *big city* of Dayton and then it was another twenty-minutes of driving after that. We would go at least two, maybe even three times a season, and I would always remember the merry-go-round. That was the first thing we hit when we arrived. For some strange reason it appealed to me, and was the perfect warm up ride before hitting all the other hard core rides, of which there are not too many around at all when you're just seven-years old and barely four-feet tall.

I never noticed this at first, but now that I'm closer I see that there are some kids riding on this ole' thing. Wow, real *other people* and they are right there! If it slows down, I'll go up and see what this is all about and try to chat one of them up if I can. I start to think, if they are here and I can see them, then they must be like me, and well, I'm dead. I try to think what this field used to be, it's pretty close to the shop. Just a big empty field. I have no idea what it was used for in the past. Could this have been an event or something from the 1800's? A scene of tragedy from years ago? Maybe an accident happened right here, and this is what it left for us to see—us meaning all the *medium dead* people that can see this sort of thing. The kids look happy though, I would think if this was a tragic event that took place a long time ago, we would see some pretty fucked up looking faces on these kids. . .but that's not the case here today at all.

Looks like it's slowing down a little—I can start to make out some faces now. A pair of people go by and I think: *That looks like me right there as a small child, just like the pictures mom has on the wall when I was about three, I'd recognize that terrible bowl haircut anywhere. . .*

Well if that's me, then who is sitting on the white pony right beside me? It's probably mom. I had to wait for it to go around again to make sure.

Nope, that's not my mother—it's dad!

That's pretty interesting. I don't ever remember my dad taking me to the park. He died when I was *three years old.* I have seen countless pictures of him, and that is without a doubt Guy S. Bishop Jr. (my father) sitting next to me on that merry-go-round.

What is this all about? *I've got to talk to him!* I try to run along with the merry-go-round, but it's just not slow enough for me to keep up with it. I try shouting out his actual name— which is my name too— so that was weird. I even shout out a very loud "DAD!" But still nothing, they just kept going round and round without even looking over at me. I don't know how this is happening, but really today has been just full of surprises. I just assume this is par-for-the-course around here to see this.

My dad died when I was three. It wasn't an accident, he just got sick and died, at least that's what my mother told me. Is he stuck here too? Stuck in the middle? With me? I need to find out more—*where the hell is Angel?*

11

I LOOKED UP and there it was.

Nobody had to explain this to me. It was the door Angel said I would need to walk through to move on. It was cracked open slightly, a warm inviting light beamed outward around the edges, it felt good on my skin, or whatever they call this stuff that's holding all my energy and internal innards together. I had a sensation of peace and relaxation. It felt good knowing that this was it, my time here is done.

The dilemma I face now is this: *I'm not so sure I'm ready to go in that door right now.* I know that I absolutely should, since Angel was very specific about that. But still, I might be needed here, with my father; to help him move on too. I needed to make that decision—*and fast!*

I looked at the merry-go-round and then back at the door. It really drew you in—it wanted you in there and right now—*but that's my dad out there.* A man I hardly knew, but owe big time for making me who I am or I guess now it's *who I was.* Wouldn't it be so great to go talk to him? I really only know him from pictures and a few videos. Most of the time he was behind the camera so I never even got to see him speak to me directly.

Just then the decision was made for me in my mind.

I think I'll stay. As soon as that thought entered my head the door vanished.

Not only that, but everything else disappeared too. No merry-go-round, no little kids enjoying themselves, including me as a young boy. Also the one thing that made me *want* to stay. . . *my dad.*

Well this is bullshit!

It was gone. All of it. Back to the lonely silence and empty spaces.

I'm in hell aren't I?

Was it something I thought? I suppose you can't even have a private thought to yourself around here! That door disappeared the second I thought about not walking through it, I don't even think I spoke the words—*I didn't, I know I didn't.*

I PUT MY head down and start to walk away from this empty field. There's nothing there but lost hope and sadness now. I'll need to head to the east, I want to go back to my shop, but which way is east?

Everything is so—*so fucking dull.* I can't even think of a good word to describe how dull this world looks to me now. As I walk (in the place that was once my mind), I picture the inside of our shop from work: the drain, the hoses, and the big cabinets. I'm picturing Cathy Barlow standing on her ladder, she always had to use the six-foot aluminum one because it did a much better job of supporting her portly little body. She's probably still spraying off the same van that was in her stall when we left for lunch a couple of hours ago too. That's where I wanted to go. I just concentrated on that space.

I looked up, and I was in the middle of our shop.

Holy shit! I just poofed myself!

Why couldn't I have figured that out before I walked all that damn mileage today? That wasn't hard at all—*son of a bitch!* Next time, I'll think of Hawaii, and spend the rest of eternity on a beach and just forget about waiting on this door!

Sure enough, I was in the middle our shop—back at work! I had finally made it. It seemed empty and stale, but it was definitely our shop. I recognized the bays, also some of the cabinets and storage bins that were along the walls. All dark and dingy too. This is the way the shop normally looked on any given day in the *real* world, so it made me feel alive again, which was nice.

I walked along the drain that runs down the length of the building. I start to kick a few things around, try to inflict some real damage to the place. I don't have to pay for any of this so why not? I found that I can put dents in things very easily. I was really enjoying this, and it felt good.

As I'm doing all this kicking and breaking stuff, I start to feel—well, as if someone was *watching me.* You know that feeling right? I take a cursory glance around and identify immediately what's making me feel this way. It's most likely those four, dark, shadowy looking human figures standing up towards the front of the shop. Yes, most definitely, that's probably the cause of all this uneasiness I'm experiencing at the moment. I was about to get my wish; *real live dead people* like me to talk to—*but*. . .

They sure as hell know how to make an entrance don't they? Not speaking. Standing thirty-feet away so I can't see their faces, acting all stealthy, and starting to make me feel a bit *unwelcomed*.

I chicken out. I don't really feel like doing this social thing just yet, so I start to move away. For some reason my legs wouldn't move fast enough. Every time I gave my legs the command to move, they seemed to move just like I wanted them to. But, so did the potential lynch mob up there. They move right along with me and are getting closer with each passing second. Finally, I gave up. I just figured I'll engage them and just get this over with. I have to keep reminding myself: *I'm dead, so who gives a rat's ass!*

They stop and sort of gather around me in a semi-circle. Not even saying one word. I thought I could start to see some faces now, but they were still a bit blurry and unrecognizable. I'm hoping at any minute now, these punks are going to remove their masks and yell something like "gotcha Guy!" As if this was some sort of big elaborate mega-prank being pulled over on me. The hidden camera crew will run out and we'll all just laugh our asses off!

But that never happened. The faces come into a clearer focus and they aren't masks. It's definitely three men and one woman. I thought for sure they would start off by introducing themselves like normal human beings do, but since we're not actual human beings anymore, I shouldn't really expect that to happen. No, what they do is just start asking a bunch of stupid questions, all at pretty much the same time. Nothing like: "Hi my name is Billy-Bob and I'm stuck in *Purgatory* just like you. Welcome! Don't forget to check out the snack bar and have a great time!" No, just right straight to the point with the questions.

"Do you know Alex Girdner? Eight-seventy-five Morris Lane? In Paris? Girdner, that's G-I-R. . ."

"Never heard of him, sorry!" I answered.

I don't even know who asked this question. If I didn't mention this before, the lips don't move with what they say. Not as bad as an old

Japanese movie overdubbed in English, but real close. In fact, most of the time they don't move the lips at all, but I sure can hear them plain and clear. This group of four were *going to town* with the questions now, in rapid fire succession too, one question after another. Each one rattling off a name and an address, like I was the 411 operator.

"How about Sally Rutherford? Teddy Rutherford? Out of Silverton? Please tell me you know the Rutherfords. . ." I had no time to respond to anything they were saying.

"No, sorry. . .I sure don't. WHY DON'T YOU ALL JUST SHUT THE HELL UP FOR A SECOND!" I had enough. "One person at a time, and I'll point to you when you can talk! Now you over there in the blue shirt—you can speak—go for it!"

I pointed to the one person who I thought looked like they might have had it all together. One of the younger looking men. He was just sort of sitting there, staring around aimlessly ever since I blew my lid and yelled at all of them. I like the color blue and he had this really bright blue shirt on, so that's the guy I pointed to. He acted surprised and spoke. "You know you shouldn't yell at people around here, you will never get to see a door to move on."

"Oh?" I said. (*Is that how it really works?*) "Well, you all were driving me absolutely insane with those questions, so, sorry if I came across a bit curt."

"Well, we don't know how long you will allow us in to talk to you, so that's why we all ask our questions like that. You never know if you might know one of our loved ones, there is always a chance you might," the blue shirted dude said. It's like a direct connection to my head. His lips didn't move much, but I can completely hear what he is saying to me.

"By the way, since you are allowing *me* to talk—what about Horace Ford, do you know Horace? He was my uncle and he lived up on Pinehurst Avenue," blue shirt dude asks.

"Hmmm, the only Ford I know is Henry Ford out of Detroit, and he invented the automobile, or horseless carriage if you're from the nineteenth century and don't know what the hell I'm talking about (which if he hadn't invented the fucking thing I wouldn't be here right now), so no, I'm sorry, I don't know a Horace Ford."

He kept staring at me with the stupidest look on his face.

"Does that answer your question?" I said. He never answered me. I must have pissed him off with my lack of information. I really didn't care either.

None of these people were getting any answers, and it was making them frustrated. I could tell. They looked down and out, and I could start to understand why.

Let's say you get caught in this *middle of the road* world. No tastes, no smells, no sounds, no news, nothing at all. Time stops here, that's exactly what Angel said. Remember what she said happens when you walk through your door? *"It will let you see things from beyond this point in time."* So that must mean that nobody here has any idea of what has happened since the time they arrived here in this empty-space place. When they see someone new (like me), *I am the future*. I may even know one of their loved ones and could give them an update on how they're doing. I really wish I knew some of these names, I really do.

I start to feel some compassion now for these sad souls but not too much. I really don't know them that well yet, and I have no idea what I'm getting into here.

"How about I tell you my name, where I'm from, and my situation that brought me here, and you can take it from there. Does that sound like something that would work?" I said to them.

Nobody really said anything, so I just went ahead with my plan.

"Ok well, my name is Guy Bishop *the Third*, that fancy suffix at the end there just means my dad and grandpa have the same name. I am from Belle City, Ohio. My mother's name is Marion Bishop, I work, or I guess *worked* in Paris at Bill Bradley Chevrolet, in the detail shop. I cleaned cars and I was *damn good* at it too. The date was—ummmm, well not exactly sure. . .it was a Friday, October was the month, it was around the beginning, I just had to pay my rent the week before, so probably about the sixth or seventh? It is not my fault that I'm here with you now, I was in an automobile accident, and I was just sitting in the back seat, the person who was driving had some sort of issue."

One of them interrupted me.

"What year! What year is it now?"

"Oh, yes—it's uh, 1994. . ."

It was as if I was the bearer of bad news. They looked even more depressed now. If it isn't bad enough that they are a pack of aimless wandering souls, that little piece of info was definitely a buzz kill. It was at that moment that these folks realized that it was now 1994 on the other side of the fence, in the real deal world—and who knows how long they have been here—this has to be one of the saddest days in their non-living lives.

"So anyway, the man who was driving, he was...."

They started speaking again, right over top of me now. Very rude of them I thought. This time it was a lot harder to make out the questions they were asking. It was one after the other; each question contained a name, a city, and sometimes a date. At least that's all I could make out. This direct connection to the head thing was not pleasant at all, who's idea was it to communicate like this? I thought of what the blue shirt dude said to me earlier. He said, *"he didn't know how long I would let them,"* as if I had some control over all this chaos that was happening now. So what I did was just *look away*. Looked at the top of the building. All around, including the shelf by my old workstation. I see something familiar. A face I recognized from earlier today, it was Angel.

I tried to zone those babbling idiots out of my head, it was hard to do, but they did start to fade away when I walked over to where Angel was standing.

I tuned them out completely. Who knows for how long. I had about a thousand follow up questions to ask her, and one of them should have at least been *by the way, what is your name?* I really wanted to know more about the fake merry-go-round scene, and if that was really my dad out there. She never gave me a chance to talk, just handed me what looked like a small piece of folded up paper.

"Here, take this and try not to show anyone else. Don't read it until you're alone. Remember this—you can control a lot of what's happening around you just by knowing what they're trying to do *to you*—keep working on that for now. Don't worry, they can't see me, I can choose who sees me, someday you'll find your special gift that you'll be great at. Stay focused."

She didn't say anything about me missing my door. I'm sure she already knew that I blew it on the first try—she had to have known that. Just like before out in the field, she was gone again.

I took the parchment that Angel handed me and placed in my pants pocket. I didn't even think about it. I just put it somewhere where I thought it would be safe, but then. . .wait a second! I just put that in my pants! I know that may sound stupid, but up until now, I didn't even know if I had a head, legs, or even a body. It felt like I was *just there*. I looked down to see if I had pants on, or even legs, but I just can't tell. At least that paper is safe for now, I can feel it, it's hidden, I can tell.

I'm starting to develop my after-life skills, like a newborn baby learning how to focus his or her eyes on their mother's nurturing boob for the first time. I walk back over to that pack of talking heads; it felt like they never stopped either, just kept yapping and yapping.

I'll try to hone a new skill here. Turning the volume down again and maybe getting rid of them in the process! I'll try to keep just one of them around so I can extract my own information, but which one? The blue shirt dude was kind of a dick, so forget about him for now—how about the woman? I think women are easier to deal with and talk to here, at least it seems that way so far. Angel seemed eager to help me, so let me see if I can even pull this off.

This woman looks to be about my age, and I try to focus on just what she is saying to me. I close my eyes and just listen to her speak.

"Do you know a Joseph and Mary Banks from Paris? October 12th, 1979 is when I died, car accident like you. They lived at 632 Downing, please tell me anything you know about anyone with the last name Banks—please!"

Banks? Hmmm, 1979, well I was just thinking about the year 1979 earlier today when I was alive, when I found that nasty looking quarter in the mini-van. I was only eleven years old in '79, the year is sort of misty for me, about the only thing I can remember are some of the TV shows I used to watch back then.

I knew some Banks in high school later on, there was a Dennis Banks, who went by his nickname *Skeeter*—I'm pretty sure that Dennis was his real first name.

"I know a Dennis Banks, we called him *Skeeter* in high school and I think his parents were from Paris, does that help you any?" I now wanted to exclusively talk to this woman. I just kept my focus on her response. Everyone else was fading away, this was working.

"You're talking to me now, aren't you?" She said back to me, her face lit up, she looked happy now.

"Yes, you standing right there," I said.

"Oh thank you so much, can we go outside and get away from the others in here?"

"Sure, I don't care."

As soon as those words came out of my mouth, we were both standing outside, a big empty field, just me and the woman.

"How the hell did you do that?" I asked. "But wait, before I forget to ask you—please, tell me, *what is your name?*"

"My name is Reannon Banks, and you are Guy Bishop, I did listen to what you were saying inside there," she said.

"Ok, well hello Reannon Banks, nice to meet you, now how did you get both of us out here so quick? I really need to figure out that one, could come in handy someday!"

"I just did it. It's one of those things you learn to do when you're here. Have you figured out how to get yourself from place to place yet? Well it's the same thing, but you can take another with you," she explained.

"Well, it's pretty damn impressive I'd say! And yes, I figured out how to get around, that's how I got up here to the shop. The pisser was that I did end up walking three or four miles before I figured it out," I said.

"You'll find out more things you can do the longer you stay here, but let me tell you—*you need to get out of here as soon as you can.*"

"I already missed my first door."

"I know, we all saw that, I'm sorry that happened. Most new ones like you miss the first one. Only a few walk right through the first time with no hesitation. People like you and me who were so quick and violently brought into this place are the ones that usually have a problem. People who *know they are dying* are more mentally prepared for this so to speak. Older people too, they seem to know what to do, like an old elephant heading to their graveyard, they just know."

"Makes sense, makes total sense to me, thanks for explaining," I said.

WE SIT AND talk for at least an hour I would guess. Turns out I didn't quite know her direct family, but Dennis "Skeeter" Banks, who would have been eleven-years-old at the time of her death, was a second cousin on her father's side. We tried to mesh our timeline's together from the real world. In 1979 I was eleven, she was twenty-five—she is still twenty-five and now I'm twenty-six. Only thing we really connected on were television shows from that time like: *Three's Company, Dukes of Hazzard, Love Boat,* and *Fantasy Island* to name a few. Other than the TV shows, there's not much else that an eleven-year-old and a twenty-five-year-old had in common. Our paths never really crossed back then. It had also been fifteen-years ago for me since I had experienced the year 1979. Some of the memories had faded away of what was going on and who I knew back then.

"I hope I helped you out Reannon, I do like your name, it's like that Fleetwood Mac song right?"

"Yes, but I spell mine different. That song came out just a few years before I died, I loved hearing it on the radio, it was *my song.*"

"Let me ask you this—can we make others like us see something that's not there?" I'm thinking of that merry-go-round deal from earlier and my suspicion that it was all a rouse just to keep me here.

"Yes, some can do that," she answered. "You will find that the longer you are here, the more things you stumble upon that you can do. Once you know what others are capable of, only then can you block it away. But Guy, you're new here, so you're completely vulnerable to that sort of thing. . .and I'm so sorry about the merry-go-round, please forgive me."

"Why are *you* sorry?"

"That was all of us doing that to you, I feel so bad now since you've let me talk to you. I was the one who found the memory of the merry-go-round inside your head and how much you loved them. But, it wasn't my idea to put your father in there beside your young self. I just want you to know that, and I hope you at least *forgive me*."

"You can read my mind? Then what the hell do you need me to tell you that shit about the past? Just go in and get it yourself why don't you?"

"Wish it were that easy, but it's not. You can only pick out little things like childhood memories, things like that, otherwise we wouldn't have needed to ask all the questions. At least now you can block it out. I can't see anything now, totally blank."

"So, your group in there, you all were following me from the get go? I remember hearing the merry-go-round from when I was over at that old farm house, where the crash happened."

"We noticed right when you got here, yes. We went over to check you out, that's where I dug out the memory of the merry-go-round."

"Well, did you find anything else in there?" I said to her, trying to think of a few things that were hopefully buried way too deep to find, like the time I intercepted my mom's Fredrick's of Hollywood catalog in the mail and went upstairs to spank the ole' monkey meat in my room, how embarrassing would that be if she saw that?

"I saw you and your father. You have several memories of him, even though you may not be able to recall them. I found some sweet moments of you two together before he died. That really did happen what you saw out there on the merry-go-round. That was the first time you ever rode the carousels, and it was with your dad. That is probably why you loved that particular ride as much as you did."

So that's why mom took me there all the time.

"I didn't want to include that with the vision we put inside your head Guy, please believe me, I was certain that you would have stayed with the feeling that the merry-go-round would *have* given you—made you *not go through the door*. It was someone else's idea to put that in there, and I'm just one person out of four."

Seemed like a lot of effort to keep me here, just to find out if I may have known someone in their life. The more that time passes, the worse the odds are that you can find some sort of link to the real world. Still though, I wonder if she can pull some of those lost memories of Guy S. Bishop Jr. who is *my* dad, out of *my* head. It would be nice to remember those. I wonder what it was like when he was sick? I have no memory of him being sick. The only way I know anything about his death is the stuff my mother told me. It's possible, I suppose, that she may have not quite told the truth about it. Being sick seems like an easy way to explain how someone dies to a little three-year-old boy. Maybe, if I let Reannon Banks in again, she can *dig them out* and let me see what really happened, but for now, they ain't nobody getting inside my head and pulling a damn thing out.

12

I DON'T KNOW how long I stood there with her. There is no time to keep track of here. It's no wonder the first thing someone wants to know when they run into a fresh kill is what time, date, and especially what year it is. There is obviously no night here either, I feel like I have been in this place for at least twenty-four hours or more, and it's all day-daylight. If you want to even call it daylight. It's more like a pale grey gloom overcast with no hint of a sun.

I figure I must be in a vast expanse of the universe reserved exclusively for the storage of *used up stuff*. Shells of what used to be. Then if you're lucky (like me), you can walk around it freely with Reannon Banks and get even more and more depressed with each passing hour.

I never thought of this either—it just crosses my mind—*I may not even be dead yet!* I could be all laid up in a nearby hospital. Possibly in a deep coma, on life support, each breath possibly my last, and this whole world is just a fabrication inside my brain. If so, I hope all this action I'm doing now is showing up on some sort of medical instrumentation. We don't want them to pull any plugs prematurely. I should remain as active as I can here, *just in case*.

"What about you? What's your story Reannon?" Thinking I should at least ask about her own situation, and why she has (according to my calculations) been here for over *fifteen* years wandering around this barren world of cumulus grey colored clouds and silence.

"It's a sad story, but I'll tell you if you want," she said.

"And why haven't you moved on? How many doors have you seen and *not* gone through?" I asked.

"Thirteen, I've counted them all."

"What the—?" I said. "Thirteen? Why so many?"

"I know, I always want to walk through them, but something always tells me to stay here, and as soon as you have just that *one thought* of staying here, it goes away."

"That's exactly what happened to me—of course you know all this because you're partially responsible for that, since you helped hijack my mind back there."

"I told you I was sorry."

"Yes, you did, I suppose I do forgive you. I don't know about the others though. I guess I'll see how I feel about it when I meet them."

"All you have to do is *turn them back on*. Let them in again. That's how it works," she said. "Would you like to go try and find them now?"

"We can do that later, I'd really like to hear about how you ended up here first, do you mind?" I asked.

"No, not at all."

She sat there and began to tell me her story. As I listened to it, I felt as if I was inside her head re-living the same events with her and in great detail. Even if she left something out; if *she knew*, so did I.

I could see the entire backstory. Exact dates. If it was hot or cold outside; it was a pretty interesting and efficient way to communicate between people. This would be very useful in the real living world. Just think how much time could be saved.

She was definitely *letting me inside her head* on this. I started to notice more things about her presence in front of me as well—the little tattoos on her ankles, scars on her arms and legs, and her hair and eye color. (Is that burnt orange maybe?) Little things like that were coming into better perspective. The once blurred and unrecognizable face was much clearer now. The more you looked at these people the more their true appearance started to show outward.

Reannon Banks

REANNON BANKS, a twenty-five-year-old mother of one and her daughter Lilly lived alone. Little Lilly was born six years earlier. The kid's biological dad, Chad Groves, had stuck it out for the first month after she was born, but soon became disenchanted with the thought of being a father and all the responsibility involved with such a thing.

Reannon and Lilly had been doing just fine for the past five years and eleven months, living on their own and making it work. The once outgoing Reannon Banks had been living the life of a responsible parent this whole time. The part-time job she had cleaning houses, some modest government assistance, and every so often even a child support payment from Chad Groves (via the court ordered garnishment coming out of his paycheck every other week) is how they made ends meet. Reannon's parents would help out whenever possible too. Joseph and Mary Banks had Reannon late in life and were well into their sixties now, but they did whatever they could for their daughter and granddaughter.

One day out of the blue, the phone on the wall rang. It was Cherry Dearwester. An old friend from high school, she was calling to check in on the girls and also to share some news. Bonnie Millhouse, another classmate, was getting married in a couple of weeks and a few close friends were going out to yuck it up one last time before she tied the knot—it was going to be a bachelorette party like none other this century according to Cherry.

Reannon had not been out like that for a really long time; well before Lilly was born at least. She thought about it and had given a *definite maybe* on attending. But, the longer she thought about it, the more the needle would swing towards *go*.

Reannon called her parents and arranged for Lilly to stay overnight. During the conversation, Mary Banks had to remind her of Cherry Dearwester's bad girl reputation in high school. Mary went on to say that she saw Cherry at K-Mart, about a month ago, and that she was all covered in tattoos now. The desecration of one's body was not something Mary Banks endorsed at all, and in her eyes Cherry Dearwester was going straight to hell whenever her time came. *"Oh mom!"* Reannon said with that tone that daughters give their mothers when they think they are being a little over the top about something. *(There was a secret Reannon had been keeping from her mother for years now, she had several tattoos herself!)*

Mary agreed to watch Lilly next Friday night, she felt that she had expressed enough concern for the company that Reannon would be around, and hoped that her daughter would make responsible choices. She was after all twenty-five years old now, not sixteen. Besides, she really was looking forward to spending the time with little Lilly.

THE NEXT FRIDAY evening around seven-thirty, Cherry Dearwester, who had borrowed her brother's prized possession VW minibus just for this special occasion, pulls up into the driveway at 632 Downing. Reannon says one final goodbye to her mother and Lilly then walks out the door. Bonnie Millhouse and Wanda Hill are seated in the back of the minibus, and the four young women greet each other with long hugs and sweet kisses on the cheeks. After a few brief comments between them on how great each one of them looks, they were soon on their way.

The plan was to hit *The Lost Sea*, a sort of dance club and bar that sat just outside the city limits on County 25A. The scene at *The Lost Sea* wasn't disco like most of the other places that you could dance at. It had more of a country and western vibe going for it, and that's just what the girls were in the mood for.

The night was going great. The young women had let loose and were really enjoying themselves, this was something they hadn't done together in a really long time. Reannon tried to contain herself the best she could, but all those years of unintentional sobriety did not do her any favors in the containment department. She was drunk. Eventually that all caught up to her and soon she found herself in the bathroom bringing it *all back up*—most of which made it into the toilet bowl.

Reannon had recovered nicely (with a little help from her friends), she soon sat back out with the others. Nothing but crackers and soda water for the rest of the night. *Should've known that would've happened,* she thought.

Two-thirty in the morning—it was time to head home. A mock field sobriety test was in progress beside the VW minibus to determine who was the *least drunk* and could drive everyone home. Reannon took no part in this. She headed directly to the back bench seat of the VW minibus and then promptly fell asleep.

Cherry passed the test *the best*. She walked the imaginary straight line better than anyone else and retained her driving status. Besides, this *was* her brother's van and he probably wouldn't have appreciated Cherry letting anyone that he didn't know personally drive his precious VW minibus. It was hard enough convincing him to let her borrow it in the first place.

The best plan possible was conceived, considering the circumstances. In order to drop off Bonnie Millhouse, the bachelorette who lived directly on the other side of town, an alternate route was needed. This would be the best way to avoid any other traffic, and also to avoid any law enforcement officers that might be lurking around.

It was decided to head out of the city. The girls would use only country back roads to get Bonnie home. The one problem with all this was that it had been almost ten years since anyone had been out this way, and nobody could remember the names of the roads they had to turn on. Regardless, it still seemed like the best option, so they all loaded back into the VW minibus and proceeded toward the black abys of country roads that lie ahead.

THE SHERIFF'S OFFICE dispatcher for the night, Fawn Francis, had just received the third 911 call in the past two hours reporting the same thing. Several stop signs in the county were missing, most likely stolen by teenagers driving around in their cars with nothing else better to do. This had happened before about eight months ago. But, there was only one sign stolen then, and it was quickly replaced by the county road department that same night. A missing stop sign wasn't really considered an emergency, but it surely was an elevated situation to deal with. Per the county guidelines, anytime a stop sign was reported missing or destroyed, the superintendent must be notified immediately, and they would have to send a crew out to replace it regardless of the time.

Fawn had sent the signal that activated the county superintendent's pager almost two hours ago, and was still waiting for him to respond back. The last time only one sign was stolen, now there had already been three reported missing; perhaps even more. A much more serious situation than before.

The super finally checked-in. He apologized for his tardy call back, blaming it on his recent bout with a head cold. He told her he took some NyQuil before bed and was out like a light. Fawn Francis knew that the super was a well-known heavy drinker, if you didn't believe her, just ask anyone who was at last year's Christmas party and they would say the same. If he wanted to call the booze and beer that he likely drank all night long NyQuil, that was fine with her, she was just glad he finally responded to her page. This was a serious situation as one of the stop signs taken was at the intersection of County 25A and Belle-Paris Road, or more commonly referred to by the locals as *Dead Man's Curve*. Why these stupid kids would remove the sign at that particular place was anyone's guess. That is a very dangerous area to have a stop sign missing from view. The notorious corner was well known for several accidents over the years—some fatal.

The ladies had done a fairly decent job of navigating around the country block so far. Cherry only had to make one turn-around in someone's driveway, plus one other unscheduled stop in the middle of the road for a quick pee break. The scene of three squatting women urinating alongside the road would have been quite a sight if anyone had been around to see it.

Things were coming into better perspective now, and Cherry actually was starting to remember some of the road names that they needed to turn on. The ladies zipped up and were on their way again. On County 25A and soon approaching—Belle-Paris Road.

This was a well-traveled thoroughfare during the day, County 25A was an alternate route, a road you could use instead of the interstate highway, which connected Paris and Bell. Some people just preferred to use it for their daily commute between the cities. Anyone who regularly drives this way knows there is a stop sign at the upcoming intersection. It is programmed into their subconscious memory; they don't even have to think about it. Their eyes take in the scene, the brain recognizes the pattern and knows exactly where it's at. The autopilot in their mind takes over control of the feet and hands. They could be thinking about all sorts of things other than driving and they would still stop. That's how good the human brain is at automatic recall.

If you don't stop, you will go around the corner too fast and go off the side of the road. But, perhaps more dangerous is that another road crosses here and combines into the corner, so drivers need to stop and look for any traffic coming from the crossing road as well. In other words, *you have to stop no matter what!* What these teenage numb-nuts have done by removing the stop sign here is downright unconscionable, if not lethal, and it will be hours before anyone from the county can get out here to replace the stolen stop sign.

Cherry and the girls approach the unfamiliar intersection, completely unaware of the missing stop sign. All the women, except for the passed out Reannon Banks in the back seat, eerily talk about some of the stories behind *Dead Man's Curve* which unbeknownst to them, and also ironically they are approaching at this very minute and at a high rate of speed.

At approximately 2:58AM on October 12th, 1979, the VW minibus blows through the intersection at County 25A and Belle-Paris Road. The first hurdle would have been to avoid any crossing traffic, and luckily for the girls there was none at this time of night. A potentially major disaster was avoided. The second obstacle to overcome would be negotiating the corner itself and unfortunately their luck ran out. The minibus flies around the corner too fast; the curve is impossible to navigate and the minibus careens off the side of the road. The vehicle rolls three times before finally coming to rest in a corn field on its top. Cherry Dearwester, Bonnie Millhouse, and Wanda Hill all survive with serious injuries. Reannon Banks, who had been laying down asleep on the back bench seat, was ejected from the vehicle during the second rollover as the back door was wrenched off of the VW minibus. She was dead at the scene.

"THANKS FOR SHARING all that with me," I said. "I can't believe how vivid it was in my head too, how do you do that?"

"It just comes with practice I guess—we call it *projecting*. We came up with a word for it so that if someone really does not care to experience what you're talking about, they can tell you to *stop projecting*. It does bring you right into my mind, like the raw film of what happened—a home movie *projecting* on a movie screen, but I can talk about it as we watch it. You can let me into yours someday, *if you want* that is. I know you're probably keeping things locked up for now and I don't blame you one bit."

She was right about that. They already bamboozled me once and I'm not going to let that happen again if I can help it. I get it. I'm a rookie, so I have a weak (a *very weak*) dead mind. But, I sure don't want to go through this all by myself. I thought about Angel and where she fit into all this. I decided not to even mention her just yet, and I still have that parchment in my pocket. I need to make sure they don't find it and get some alone time to read it.

"Well, I don't mind if we go find your friends now."

"Ok, are you ready?" She said. "Just close your eyes and click your heels three times and say. . . *actually I'm just kidding!* Whenever you're ready, so am I, just say the word."

"Hey, you have a sense of humor now, I like it. . .Ok, I'm—"

Didn't even get to finish my sentence, or my thought. We were both standing back in the middle of the shop again.

13

I WOULD REALLY like to learn how to do that moving around thing without overthinking it so much. Reannon is good at that, and also moving more than one being at a time. I wonder if she can take three? What about four?

"So, where are they at?" I asked.

"They'll be here. Just open up your mind again and start thinking about what they looked like earlier—they'll come right back in."

"Ok, so the blue shirted dude, even though it was kind of fuzzy at first—he looked like he had a little boy's face on top of a grown man's body. That's how I remember him—wearing that bright blue shirt, pretty normal looking for the most part except that his face really didn't match his physique. . ."

"That's me?" The little man-boy said, now standing directly in front of me.

"Well there you go, how about that." I said, now looking at three faces, not fuzzy images like the last time, they were just people I had never met before. The only two I recognize is the blue shirted man-boy of course and Reannon, who was still standing beside me.

"Everyone, this is Guy—why don't you introduce yourselves to him—I have told him everything about myself, and I also told him about what we did to him earlier. So needless to say—we have some work to do to get his trust back."

First person to speak was that little man-boy. "Hi Guy, my parents named me Austin, like the city in Texas. That's where they met see, and Austin Kimball is my full name, parents are Mike and Patty Kimball. It's nice to meet you, sorry it's under these circumstances but let's try to make the best of it. You said 1994 huh? Us Kimball's lived up on Spruce Avenue, you wouldn't have happened to know if they are still around there would you? I believe the phone number would have been *four-nine-two-one-five-two-oh—*"

Here he goes again! This guy won't shut up and let anyone else talk! He went on for at least ten minutes! Someone probably murdered his ass; got tired of all the hot air coming out of his mouth and just shot him! No doubt about it. He's trying to get in all he can with me. I finally had to cut him off when he started talking about his cats.

"All right Austin, I get your point—I'd like to meet the others now, let the other's speak and me and you—we'll talk more later, sound fair?"

He looked a bit surprised, nodded his head up and down to indicate a *yes*, and then to my relief, the next person began to speak.

"Eric LaRoche. You just need to call me Eric LaRoche or Eric, don't need no nicknames. Sorry about that merry-go-round thing. We're all starving for info here, besides you looked like you wanted to stay anyway."

"Ok, no problem calling you Eric, no problem at all," I said.

No, you're wrong, I really wanted to go.

My impression on Austin was that he is sort of an offbeat goof-ball, but this guy Eric LaRoche, he seemed a bit grumpy and irritated. I got a real uneasy feeling about him when he spoke. I'll tread lightly around this guy for now—*hopefully I didn't think about that too loudly, I certainly wouldn't want anyone to hear it.*

"And I'm Edward Chapman, you can call me Ed, or Eddie once we get to know each other better I guess—or shoot, you can call me Eddie now! Makes me no difference!"

Now this guy seems tolerable for sure. A man who doesn't mind you calling him Eddie right away! Usually, it takes a while before you add any type of "ie" or a "y" to the end of someone's name. It sure does make it more endearing, brings your friendship closer together. It never worked for my name, it already ends in a "y" and it doesn't work on other names either, *like Eric.*

14

IT DIDN'T TAKE long for me to figure out who wanted to plant the vision of dad sitting next to my young self, riding that merry-go-round back in that field. Had to have been Eric LaRoche's idea. I don't even need to try and get into his head or ask Reannon, I can just tell by the way he introduced himself:

"—*you looked like you wanted to stay anyway.*"

Sounds like a man with issues to me. How can you assume someone wants to stay? You can't. Still, his story should be interesting to hear, all of theirs really. I wonder if it will be like when Reannon told me her story, that was awesome, it put you right there in the action.

"Well Guy, they would love to share their stories with you, do you mind?" Reannon said.

"No, let's do it, can I get some popcorn and a pop?" I said, but really I haven't even been hungry for any food since I've died, it's just an old habit I guess to hear some crunching inside your head, after all I figure this is going to be just like going to the movies, only difference is that it all really happened, and each story ends with some sort of grisly death. *I can't wait!*

"Ok, I'll go first!" Austin Kimball said.

"Why does that not surprise me?" I said, "Ok, go right ahead. . .let's try and stick to the highlights too—try not to get off subject too much—but first, I want see if my suspicion is right—*Were you murdered?*"

Austin Kimball

DENNY BADCOCK WAS accidentally dropped on his head when he was just a baby.

This happens more often than you think, and most of the time there is nothing to worry about—baby's heads are designed for that sort of thing—the bones are still soft and pliable from just recently coming through the birth canal. His parents, Reginald and Judy Badcock, have decided to bring this up between them now as they make their way to pick up Denny, a little shy of thirteen years from the day this accidental dropping on the head took place.

They have finally determined that their son, Denny, may indeed have brain damage from the event that happened so long ago. They still could not believe the phone call received twenty-minutes prior telling them to come down to the police station as soon as possible. Denny, now sitting in a police holding cell, with his head hanging low, and one hand handcuffed to a bench; had decided about an hour and a half earlier to steal a car that was parked on the side of the road. With the keys still hanging from the ignition of the green '85 Honda Prelude, and nobody else around; it just seemed like the right thing to do at the time.

What other people, including Denny's parents didn't know, was that Denny had a demon—and it gave *really bad* advice to him. For many years Denny just ignored his demon, but thirteen years of ignoring it finally caught up to him. After all, today was his birthday! Finally, a teenager! Something changed in Denny that day, *thirteen years is long enough—time to go have some fun!*

Denny had driven a car before, just for a short distance in his Uncle Jerry's long driveway, and out away from any other objects, people, or property. He remembers the feeling he got pushing his foot down on that accelerator, the power rush it gave him, and he wanted to feel it again. Denny Badcock should have walked right by that Honda. But, that voice in his head—*his demon*—told him to do something: *Stop, get in, and get going!*

He did just that. *The demon got its way and won today.* It was time to hop in the sporty two door version of an Accord and see what this baby was capable of.

It started right up.

Denny dropped it into drive, hit the accelerator, and was off to the races.

ACROSS TOWN, ABOUT seven miles away, Austin Kimball, a college student living at home and an avid bicyclist; was out doing the thing he loved the most—riding his bike. Today, like most days, he wore a helmet. On the days he chose not to wear a helmet, his mother would read him the riot act and explain to him that our human heads are easily crushed by very minimal force and could use all the extra protection it could get. Unlike a newborn baby's soft bones, a full grown human man's head is a little better than a thick taco shell, but not by much.

Today Austin decides to go on a longer route, around the river and ride along the new Tri-County bike path. He had just purchased a couple of new Adidas biker outfits for his long bike rides. It's that new design meshy stuff, and it's supposed to pull all the sweat away from your balls—but so far on this ride his balls are just as sweaty as they have ever been on any ride before this. One thing is for sure though, people—like other motorists—will surely see him riding on the road in this bright and almost blindingly brilliant blue top shirt. Life is still good for Austin, and despite the excess perspiration down below, he's living life the way that he always wanted to—at least for the next ten minutes.

The Tri-County bike path runs along the Big River (that's actually the name "Big River" just as original as the city name of Paris). The Big River got its name because it's BIG, no other reason, and in reality it's not really *that* big. About two miles of the bike path is along County 25A and runs parallel to the road. There is just no room for the bike path along that portion of the river. Also, this area is a designated flood plain, which in itself would not be too much of a problem, but the bike path planners decided they would like to use the bike path at all times; no matter what the water level of the river, even if it was in a flood stage.

DENNY BADCOCK CRUISES down Fairmont Blvd. He adjusts his seat forward as far as it goes to accommodate his very short legs. It's at that very moment he notices this particular '85 Honda Prelude (the one that he has just stolen for a joy ride), happens to have the Super Bose XL radio package with one of those new compact disc players installed.

Surprisingly, Denny Badcock, the city's newest juvenile delinquent, has done a pretty decent job of driving on the roadway and staying between the lines despite only being thirteen years, seven hours, fifteen minutes, and thirty-six seconds old. But now, he has noticed something else, the Super Bose XL sound system—and he wants to hear what it can do.

Fairmont Blvd. runs through the center of the city, and as you go out of the city limit becomes County 25A. It runs along the Big River for a few miles, right where the Tri-County bike path route is cut out of the shoulder of the road. The visibility there is great, plenty of signage to warn you that you're driving alongside a bike path, plenty of room for cars, trucks, *as well as bicycles.*

After placing his hand underneath the seat, Denny Badcock finds something to stick in the CD player. He takes a quick glance at the title and decides that a band called Loggins & Messina was just not good enough to listen to, so he digs around for another one. Denny was new to driving you could say, never took one lesson. Other than driving down that one lane dirt road at Uncle Jerry's, this was it. That's why he was just a little confused when some of the lines painted on the road were shifting to the side now. There were also two white lines along the edge, with a picture painted in between of some stick figure guy riding a bike. Denny wondered what that could mean? But before he could come up with his own conclusion, his demon explained it all to him: *"That's where you're supposed to keep your front wheel, just keep it in between the two white lines . . .it's for practicing your steering control, do that and you'll be the best damn driver ever Denny! Hell, you might even make it to NASCAR! Keep it up you're doin' great kid!"*

The kid really *was* doing a great job. The right front and right rear tire never left the inside lane of those two narrow white lines. If his Uncle Jerry could see him now he would be so proud—but Denny was still thinking of that premium sound system, couldn't get it out of his mind. It was after all a Bose system—one of the absolute best sound systems ever produced in the world.

"Doesn't the owner of this car have any decent music to listen to?" Denny pulls down the front sun visor and discovers a whole slew of

CD's stored in this area; the first one he sees is *Van Halen's Diver Down*. "That will work! I'll just get this out and stick it—"

THUMP! THUMP! Denny looked up at the shattered windshield. He concluded something really big must have hit him to make that God awful sound, and put such a huge hole in the windshield. He slammed on the brakes, got out, and looked over to see what it was— no demon needed to explain this one.

The first THUMP was the back wheel of Austin Kimball's bicycle hitting the front end of the Honda Prelude. The second THUMP was Austin Kimball's body hitting the windshield, smashing it, and launching him fourteen feet into the air.

Thank God Austin was wearing his helmet that day; it was able to contain his shattered skull and kept his brain intact so that first responders did not have to look around too long for it. Austin Kimball, college student and a beloved son, was dead at the scene.

"WELL I WAS close, not quite murder, but vehicular homicide comes in a pretty decent second," I said after seeing *and* hearing all that.

I do remember this Badcock kid, I don't remember Austin, but I did know the Badcock kid. We both attended Paris High School together for a short while and would have graduated together in 1986. But sadly, Denny Badcock took his own life when he was just sixteen years old.

The demon always wins.

15

I THOUGHT ABOUT how I should react to Austin's story. Should I tell him that I *sort of* knew the person responsible for killing him? I had followed the story in the paper, I wasn't sure if I should tell him that the little psycho shithead who decided to steal a car and drive around aimlessly without any regard to human life, only spent *six months* in juvie lock up. . .*six months!*

Six months was all that Austin Kimball's life was worth. *Six months for a life.*

I will admit something here—I was poking around inside Austin's head pretty deep. I suppose once someone lets you in, you can pretty much have the run of the place if you want. I was surprised at how much information was in there about the thirteen-year-old kid who ran him over *and* his family, *very surprised* how detailed it was. No wonder these people found that memory of my dad and used it to try and keep me around here longer.

I decided it would be better if I just didn't say anything about the Badcock kid only getting six months in juvie, or that he had committed suicide just three years later. There shouldn't be a chance that Austin would meet up with him again around here in our world. Everyone knows what happens to people who kill themselves, they get a direct one-way ticket to you know where right?

"I have seen and heard that story at least twenty-times, and I can't get enough of it!" Eric LaRoche said. You could tell he just salivated over every detail of the story.

I still haven't put my finger on it, but that LaRoche guy really seems to rub me the wrong way. Why would anyone enjoy hearing (let alone *see*) the graphic details about a person's death over and over again?

"So Guy, what did you think of all that? Anything you can add to my story that might help me sleep better at night?" Austin asked.

As far as I knew, we don't sleep here at all, in fact it's one big NoDoz all the time. Nothing changes. No sunset, sunrise, or anything that resembles or represents the passage of time—so why does Austin need to *sleep* better at night?

"Well, all I can say is—what a terrible way to die, so quick like that, and not even by anything you could have controlled Austin. Denny Badcock *was responsible* for your death, and I'm sure he was held accountable for the rest of his life." I answered.

"Yeah but aren't there laws about kids committing heinous crimes under the age of eighteen, I mean don't they get a free pass or something?"

"Sometimes, no," I said. "I can remember seeing on the news, kids only fourteen or fifteen being tried as adults and going to prison for the rest of their lives—the kind of places where you go in as a boy, become someone's pet, and get humped on nightly by some burly man-beast named Ivan or Bubbles—or both Ivan *and* Bubbles—I'm sure that's what became of Denny Badcock, he got what he deserved."

Actually, I think that they separate those little ones from the rest of the prison population or even send them off to *Junior Prison Summer Camp* until they get older, but I just wanted to let Austin think that the little boy with a demon had paid dearly for his actions the day that he killed him.

"I've been to prison," Eric LaRoche said. "It's no picnic for sure, but I wasn't anyone's bitch—they did try though—and if you ever want to see what I did to them, I'll let you jump on in here and take a look."

The thought of being invited into LaRoche's head makes me cringe. I bet there are visions in there that would haunt me forever, and I'm technically already something that is not alive but not really dead. *A ghost*. Ghosts being haunted by other ghosts, figure that one out.

I don't understand why he would still be here? I could have moved on the first day. If it wasn't for these people standing right here in front of me, some that I'm starting to actually like now, but that's beside the point. I wonder if he's been here longer than anyone else? He hasn't really told me when he arrived. It would seem the longer you stay here the weirder and more insane you get, most likely due to the constant pale overcast that filters through the sunlight (or whatever is sort of lighting up this world now), and the severe boredom that can set in— especially if you're *alone* for a while.

Every day is the same here, you don't sleep and there is no night— and no time. And, by now I'm thinking you don't even eat food, someone or something has just left you here and what for? That's why these people stay together, so they can keep each other from going completely crazy. They feed off of each other, become one with another, and share their old lives together while trying to find others to join them.

I think they might be afraid of what's behind the door.

16

REANNON HAS BEEN here for fifteen years. How she can even function with any sense of sanity is amazing. The effects of severe boredom can be quite debilitating to some. Why she has stayed so long and passed up on thirteen doors does not make any sense to me either. She seems like the mother figure here, and it's quite comforting hearing her speak. I'll take it. In this world—*I need it.*

These little stories that they tell and that you can almost participate in seem to help. They let you escape back into the old real world for a short time. The place from which we all came from and now are left searching for. Where do we need to go? That's what *the door* is for, according to Angel. I guess at some point I will have to let them in *my* head, let them look around *my* old world, and listen and live in my stories, but for now. . .no way.

"Oh Eric. . .we'll take a raincheck on the prison camp thing for now, they always make me queasy—did you want to tell your story next to Guy?" Reannon said.

"Nahh, I still don't know if I want to let ole' boy in there yet, not so sure he can handle it. It's pretty graphic and all—I'll let Eddie go next, I always like hearing his story, the war stuff, the accident on the highway—*this man has seen some shit!*"

"You would you asshole!" Eddie Chapman said. "I bet you wouldn't like it if it was your family in those crashes."

"Aww now c'mon Eddie, I'm just kidding you know that. I'm respectful of the situations and all—family is everything—that's why we try to keep these fresh kills like Guy here to stick around a while so we can pick their brain and see what's going on back home."

"I know, you can't help being what *and* who you are, we all can't—I still think you're stupid for not jumping in the last door you got, stupid

stupid stupid! Your next one comes, I'm going to try and throw you in whether you want to go or not."

"Won't be for a really long time, I'd say twenty-years minimum. . ."

"Not true, I'm due again any day now, and I might just throw your ass in mine."

"You would do that for me Eddie?"

"Look, I have grown to love these people—you tend to get attached after a while, and unfortunately that includes your sorry butt too, so to relieve these folks of your somewhat abrasive attitude, yes—I would." Eddie said while looking over at the others in this tight knit group of medium dead souls, each one he considered a member of his own family now.

"That's freakin' beautiful man, I love you too," Eric said.

"I mean, I would love to and all, but I don't really think I would go through with it. I'm really ready to move on. Guy says its 1994 already, that's six years for me, way too long to be around this dingy, damp, colorless world. I'm just being honest here Eric, I meant what I said, and even though I know your story and know the reasons you're the way you are—you're still quite the asshole sometimes—I say that in a loving, father kind of way, just so you know."

"Well at least your honest, I can appreciate that—umm *daddy*."

If I said I liked Eddie Chapman before, I really liked him now. Other than the part about loving Eric LaRoche like a family member, I couldn't agree more with what he just told him, especially about being an asshole. That really sums it up for me at this point too.

"Eddie, you want to get your story started for Guy?" Reannon said. "I know you have a long one to tell and it's great, but I'm going to sit this one out, so please *do not* project it to me this time, but I'm sure Guy will love it!"

Edward Chapman

ON APRIL 29TH, 1966 halfway around the world in a foreign land, thirty-year-old Cpl. Edward Ray Chapman stood at attention. His shift was almost over, and it couldn't get over fast enough for Cpl. Chapman of the United States Army's 44th Military Police Company. He was finally on the last day *and* his last tour in the Vietnam Conflict. Edward Chapman or *"Fast Eddie Chapman"* as he was known by his fellow soldiers was more than ready to go home. Three tours had taken a toll on him. The dwell time between deployments that the Army allotted was never enough time to get his feet re-planted back at home, but this was it—the last one, he would be going home for good.

It was the final hour, only fifty-nine minutes and thirty-seven seconds to go, then off to his barracks to pack up for the morning flight back home. He could hardly wait.

Today, Fast Eddie was stationed at the Charlie South Twelve checkpoint. Earlier in the day a BOLO alert was issued to all the checkpoints leading into the area. There had been some intel reports that Viet Cong suicide missions were being planned out, and that all units were to be on the lookout for anyone trying to gain entry with excessive bags or backpacks on their person. At fifty-two minutes and six seconds left on Fast Eddie's patrol shift *and* Army career, a young Vietnamese woman stood at the gate wearing a large backpack.

Eddie stood there and thought to himself. "This has to be what they are looking for. What the hell? Why the hell here and why the hell now? Why didn't these assholes pick tomorrow as the day they want to blow something up? I'm not even supposed to be here right now. I didn't even have to come in today, it's my day off, and I'm going home tomorrow—but I'm such a team player that I decide to come in anyway and let Pressley take an extra day off since I'm vacating the premises in less than twenty-four hours, what a stupid mistake that was—*I should have just stayed in bed today and let Pressley handle this shit damit!*"

But, no time for regrets, it was time to act.

Fast Eddie made a quick call on his radio and then approached the young woman. As he got closer, you could see that the backpack looked very heavy, it was sagging down below the middle of her back. Eddie thought if he could get her to stay in this area long enough for the others to get here, they could detain her, try to extract as much info out of her as possible, and find out who is really behind all these attacks.

There were already three attempted suicide missions carried out this year, two were thwarted successfully. One did manage to detonate himself, plus a small donkey. The poor thing (the donkey) had strayed unknowingly into the general vicinity of the explosion. There were no American casualties in that attack. The man who blew himself apart was Viet Cong and the donkey was, well, they never really found out, but most of the donkeys in the area were locally owned.

Eddie wanted to keep the casualty number at zero. He would have even liked to help with the interrogation on this crazy ass suicidal bitch once they captured her, *but he had a plane to catch in the morning.*

The young woman, who they later found out went by the name of Lien Chi Phan, stopped short of the checkpoint. Eddie raises his weapon and orders her to drop the pack and to step to the side. She immediately drops the pack and launches into a dead sprint down the road. Lien Chi Phan was skinny, she was young, and she was fast.

Now, here is why Edward Chapman is referred to as *"Fast Eddie"* by his buddies, the previous four-time letterman in track can run a forty-yard dash just a smidge over four seconds flat, in other words—he can run. . .*and fast!*

Even though Eddie had just turned thirty-years old the previous month, he still had some zing—and a lot more zing than Lien Chi Phan. Eddie was able to catch up, put her in restraints, and sit her upright before she even knew what had hit her. The other MP's followed quickly, scooped her up, and took her away. Later on after Eddie was home, he found out that the information extracted from Lien Chi Phan proved to be invaluable, the backpack that Lien Chi left behind was diffused and examined, several lives were undoubtedly saved—all because of Cpl. Edward Chapman—Fast Eddie *saved lives.*

NOW THIRTY-SIX-YEAR-OLD Ohio State Trooper Edward R. Chapman was on his normal patrol route that he liked to do at the 3AM hour along Interstate 25. He liked to start in the northbound lanes at exit 83 in Paris, go up to the 87 mile marker and then flip flop back down the southbound side. This was his *lucky* stretch of highway. So far this year seventy-five speeding tickets and twelve DUI arrests. Not quite his best year-to-date numbers at the halfway point in the year, which he always considered the Fourth of July. His best year was two years prior in 1970, when he was at eighty-two speeding tickets and fourteen DUI arrests on or about the same date. Still, not bad and on pace to break his own department record if he works an extra shift or two and kept his numbers up.

It really wasn't all about the numbers for Eddie Chapman, the Vietnam Veteran who after returning home received the Distinguished Service Cross (for his actions within the last hour of his active duty in the Army for chasing down a suicide bomber and saving so many lives), it was more about helping the people. The general traveling public—that was his passion.

Although, *he was* a stickler for speed limits.

The highway run between Paris and Belle City (Eddie's *lucky* stretch) has a posted speed limit of sixty miles an hour—and don't let Trooper Chapman catch you going over that limit too much. He once had a reputation for pulling over vehicles that were only doing *four* miles per hour over the limit. Most of these tickets were thrown out by a judge, just too much room for error with the older radar guns back then, so Trooper Chapman adjusted his style and only went for the big fish now—he came up with a saying, his mantra if you will. *Nine over you're fine. Ten over you're mine!*

At approximately four in the morning, the man formerly known as Fast Eddie to some, sat idle in his cruiser at the 87 mile marker. His turn around spot. Not much traffic at this time of the morning, mostly semi-trucks and an occasional van or two. A lot of dads preferred to drive through the night when traveling long distances, so that the kiddies would be fast asleep for most of the trip. Only problem with this tactic is trying to stay awake. A dark night, worn out eyes focused on the hypnotizing road, and quiet passengers with nobody to talk to. That makes for sleepy dads.

Eddie was catching up on a crossword puzzle, one he had been working on for three nights now. . .just finishing it up when a couple of headlights pop up on the northbound side. Eddie glances up at his radar to make sure it's still on. The lights are narrow—a passenger car or most likely a van, he thought. He looks back down to finish off the last three letters in twenty-six across—the only word he figured it could be, "PEPPERJACK" and it fit perfectly. Eddie looked up again to check the speed of the approaching vehicle, except now there was no vehicle, and no headlights to be seen either.

Before Trooper Chapman could even think about what happened to the approaching vehicle, a huge fireball appeared off in the distance that lit up the night sky. Trooper Chapman wasted no time at all— "Holy shit!" Eddie slams his cruiser into gear, hits the lights, and was off to see what had happened. It was full throttle ahead. Trooper Eddie Chapman held the accelerator to the floor. His special edition police pursuit packaged Ford LTD was doing over one-hundred-twenty miles an hour (and going the wrong way on the highway, no time to for being on the proper side). He knew exactly where to go, toward the fire and smoke up ahead. His heart rate hasn't been this high since back in 'Nam. The adrenaline was just coursing through his veins and he was now wide awake—even though just thirty-seconds ago he was so tired and bored that he had to start working on a crossword puzzle to keep from nodding off.

As he got closer to the scene, the light from the fire was not as intense as the initial explosion, but still quite a bit larger than your average campfire. On the way, Eddie had run scenarios in his head on what he might expect to find. The best one he could come up with was that the approaching vehicle's driver must have fallen asleep, went off the side of the road, hit something, and burst it into flames.

He expected the worse.

Now on the scene, Eddie looks over and sees a van, split into two pieces, one half still on fire, and the other that was about to be from the brush fire that started from this accident. It only took a millisecond to process what he saw and then to jump into action. He grabbed his flashlight and ran down the berm to the half of van that wasn't engulfed in flames. Through all this, Eddie (who hadn't been called *"Fast Eddie"* for some time now and coincidentally also ran a lot slower these days) just remembered that in all his rush to get to the scene as quickly and as humanly possible, had totally forgot to get on the radio and request backup and emergency equipment. Too late for that now, he would be on his own for all this.

Eddie yelled into the shredded half-sized van, smoke was starting fill in from the fire that was in progress outside. "CAN ANYONE

HEAR ME! HELLO!" No reply with words, but he could hear some grunts and moaning. That meant there is someone in there and they are alive! Eddie had to act fast if he was going to save lives today, the fire was getting closer. He manages to pull three people out and up to safety, one woman and two children, all had been unconscious from the impact of hitting the tree that snapped the van in half, but all three still breathing and alive. A trucker had stopped to see if he could help, Eddie yells over to him, "GO BACK AND GET ON YOUR CB, CHANNEL NINE! CALL FOR HELP!" The trucker reverses course and goes back to his truck to make the call. The woman that Eddie had just pulled from the van was coming around now. "You're going to be fine mam', your kids are fine too. . .help is on the way."

"Doug!" The woman screams. "Where's my husband!"

"Where was he sitting mam'? The van split into two pieces, was he driving? I'll go see if I can find him, it's Doug right? I'll go look—STAY HERE!" Eddie runs back down the berm to where the two mangled van pieces are. The fire was still burning, but now both parts were on fire. The half that Eddie had just pulled the woman and children out of still looked like he could manage a peek inside at least. He shines his flashlight into the burning van's gaping open side. "DOUG! DOUG! CAN YOU HEAR ME! DOUG TRY TO SAY SOMETHING IF YOU CAN HEAR ME, DOUG!" Nothing—and nobody inside the van. Eddie looks over at the more involved piece of van and thought, "If he is in there, there is no hope." As he starts his way over to at least give it a try, he finds Doug—laying on the ground, in between the two pieces of the van. He kneels down to check his pulse and to see if he was still breathing. He was. . .but he was in bad shape.

The fire seemed to be dying out some now, but Eddie didn't take any chances. He manages to pull Doug a little farther away from the flames the best he could, he would have to leave him here until the paramedics arrived, both Doug's legs were broken, Eddie could see the bone sticking out of Doug's right leg when he shined a flashlight down on his body.

"Doug, can you hear me? I'm going to go back up and let your family know I found you. Try not to move, help is on the way."

Eddie checks his airway and pulse again, both seemed fine for now. He didn't know if he had heard him or not so he grabs Doug's hand hoping for a response back—Eddie thinks he feels a squeeze—*nobody is dying today on my watch.*

"I'll be right back!" Eddie lays his flashlight on the ground next to Doug's body, pointing it upward toward the road so that when he and the paramedics come back this way, they can find him quickly.

On the way back up the berm, to where the rest of Doug's family were anxiously waiting for news of his condition, Eddie could hear sirens getting louder. "Thank God," he thought, help was almost there.

ABOUT SIX MONTHS later, Trooper Chapman is working the day shift. He gets a call on the radio to head back to the station immediately— and that there was no need to turn on his lights and siren, they just needed him to get back as soon as possible. Upon arriving he was surprised to see a small welcoming committee greeting him at the door. Trooper Edward R. Chapman was receiving the city of Paris's first ever Heroes Award for the bravery he displayed on the night of the van accident. Eddie knew this was just a bullshit award that the city council wanted to start giving out to create some positive news around Paris, things were pretty shitty in the city lately—factory closings, rising crime rates, etc., Eddie went ahead and played along. Humbly, he accepted his award presented by the committee in front of a standing ovation. *But, there was one final surprise.* Out of the conference room stepped Doug and Mary Henson and their two young children. Doug still walked with a cane, but Mary and the kids looked as if nothing had ever happened to them. They all looked great considering the hell that they had been through almost six months before in that horrific accident on the highway. This was the best surprise of all for Eddie Chapman seeing the Henson's alive and well, and he made it happen.

Trooper Edward Chapman *saved lives.*

THE YEAR WAS now 1988, and Lt. Cmdr. Edward R. Chapman of the Ohio State Highway Patrol's Paris post was in one hell of a bind. Budget cuts in the state this year delayed the hiring of three new troopers for his area. Eddie had been promoted to Lt. Commander of the Paris post about a year earlier and exclusively worked the dayshift now (like normal people do), and that was the way he would have liked to keep it. He was fifty-two years old—the word *"fast"* was barely in his vocabulary these days, and the thought of having to work an overnight shift again almost made him sick to his stomach. There was really no way around it. He was short staffed and really couldn't make someone work a double shift three days in a row if they didn't want to.

Juan "Dixie" Sanchez was always Eddie's man. Dixie would do anything for him, for anyone really, including working double shifts whenever asked. He was a *yes* man. But, one can only go so far on adrenaline, and one can only go so far without the proper amount of rest as well. Dixie was simply exhausted. He would need the whole next day *and* night off to recover.

Only *four more years* Eddie thought. Four more years and he'd be enjoying early retirement from the patrol and enjoying life somewhere in Florida, living off his pension and veteran's benefits for the rest of his life. Eating pizza and getting fat. Yeah, maybe he would get a part time job somewhere gathering shopping carts out of a parking lot or something if he got bored. You can only do so many crossword puzzles and watch so much cable television. As much as Eddie hated the thought of it, he would have to work the graveyard shift at least one more time.

Do you know how hard it is to try and sleep all day? Forcing yourself to stay in bed and not think about what you'd be doing right now if you weren't in bed? It's hard to do, pretty impossible for a fifty-two-year-old man who hasn't slept past seven in the morning in quite a long time. Eddie managed to get about an hour altogether of "extra" sleep in. Tonight he would need to stay awake until morning, and he would also have to get back into his super-duper-trooper cruiser and do some actual *highway patrolling*. That was about the only thing he was looking forward to, getting one of the new cruisers out that were recently delivered with updated radar, communications, and a higher output engine. Eddie has been wanting to put one of those new puppies through its paces ever since the units arrived last month, but it always seemed like he had something else to do—always something administrative.

Back at it again! Sitting at mile marker post 87. It was still twilight and not a whole lot of action yet for a Thursday evening that will eventually turn into Friday morning for Trooper Chapman. A thermos full of coffee and a new crossword puzzle too, it will be just like old times he thought. After fiddle-farting around for about twenty-minutes with the new speed radar and feeling pretty confident he could figure out which car he's tracking (the new radar system could check speed from the front and back now), Eddie decides to start fishing for speeders. It wasn't long before he caught him a wolverine doing sixty-six and tailgating. You can always count on a vehicle that has Michigan tags and is traveling northbound; they were the Ohio State Highway Patrol's best customer. It was easy to catch speeders these days, ever since the national speed limit was set at fifty-five, you could just pluck them out one by one. Nobody seemed to ever drive the speed limit, especially on this part of the highway as wide open and straight as it was. Trooper Chapman finished up his business with the wolverine, and then headed back to base for a quick piss and maybe to grab a snack or two.

He still had quite a long night to go.

Midnight—Eddie thought he'd try sitting at the 92 flip-flop for a change of pace, it's now officially Friday morning and only the entire wee hours to go. He just needed to stay awake a bit longer. He had started his new crossword puzzle only about an hour ago and almost had half of it done already. "Sixteen across, *General Motors Lux*," he read. "That's CADILLAC," but when Eddie wrote it in he was short by one letter. Even as an expert crossword puzzle extraordinaire, Eddie's spelling was not always the best. He was short one letter because he spelled it "CADILAC." "Damn it!" He thought.

A *ding* sounds off inside the cruiser. Apparently, when someone is really hauling ass, the new radar gives you this audible warning. It's especially helpful at night and when your head is down trying to figure out crossword puzzles. The approaching vehicle was easy to pick out, it was about a half mile away.

"I really like this new radar, it sure has some serious range! Better slow down there Speedy Gonzales, seventy-five, seventy-six, seventy-seven..." Usually the number *goes down* when you make visual contact with the offender, not up. It's not as if you can't see Eddie parked in the median cut-out, sitting idle in his state police cruiser, with the headlights *and* overhead interior light on.

Eddie puts the crossword puzzle down, throws his cruiser into drive, and just waits for Mr. Gonzales to pass. He's ready for him. "Eighty-two, oh baby—your ass is grass and I'm the mower!" Eddie has no idea where that saying came from, probably from his childhood, but it seemed appropriate for the situation now. Nobody speeds on *his highway*! The offending vehicle passes by; Eddie is out of the cutout and on the highway just as fast. "Let's see what this thing can do now!" Eddie puts the hammer down to the floor and the response is absolutely phenomenal. What a sweet sound a finely tuned eight-cylinder stock police pursuit edition engine makes at full bore power. They should make a musical soundtrack to this engine, it sounds like a purring cat to Eddie's ears—a cat ready to pounce on its prey, the big fish.

A FEW MILES back, Nathan Forest *aka* "Snowman" was on his last leg of a long-haul trip. He was a truck driver who would start at home in Ohio, drive his big-rig all the way to New Jersey, load up with a few tons of random cargo that just came off a boat, drive to Texas, drop it off—then load up again at a Ford plant, and back haul car parts to Detroit. You could do the trip safely in four days. But, if you really pushed it, three days would do it. This time Snowman needed to do it in three. He was delayed at the beginning of the week. His back was in terrible shape, and he had to get it *put back into shape* by his chiropractor on Monday. His appointment was too late in the day to begin the trip. The loading dock in Jersey would have been closed by the time he arrived, and he didn't feel like sleeping in the rig that night; not after he just got snapped and cracked. So he just stayed home, it would be better anyway on his back if he just slept in his own bed. Besides, he had done this four day trip in three days before, with no problems to speak of, he just had to fudge his logbook a little. Nobody really checks the thing anyway, so as long as he felt safe to drive, he did.

TROOPER EDWARD CHAPMAN caught him a good one tonight. Not only did he clock the perp doing over eighty-miles an hour in a fifty-five zone, the right rear tail light was out. A *two-fer* is what they call that, two citations for one stop. Amazingly enough Mr. Gonzales, whose real name was Linda Lyons from Toledo, lived in Ohio. Not the typical northbound speeding wolverine you would expect, but a speeder nonetheless. Sitting back at the cruiser with Linda Lyons's driver license and writing out the citations, Eddie Chapman sees exactly what he needs to see. The word "CADILLAC," Linda Lyons was driving one when she got pulled over by Trooper Chapman. "Ah ha, Cadillac! There's two L's!"

SNOWMAN WAS ONLY about two miles away now, going the same direction and heading toward Eddie and his pulled over Cadillac. Only about fifty-six miles to go for Snowman, the hardest part of the trip is now in progress—which is getting home and into bed—trying to stuff a four day trip into three days *is* hard to do, but it can be done. It just costs you your sleep that's all. Snowman hears some chatter come across his CB radio from a fellow trucker up ahead: *"Got a Smokey Bear with a four-wheeler on the side, lights on at the ninety-four-yard stick, northbound side, yuh huh. . ."* Snowman hears this, but it really does not sink in. He is fading fast, fighting to stay awake. He should stop and sleep in the back for a little bit, but he's almost home and its past midnight. He cranks up the AC to as cold as it goes and fires up a cigarette. He can do this, he thinks.

TROOPER CHAPMAN FINISHES up his tickets. He looks over at the crossword puzzle that he had thrown over to the passenger side seat right before he launched off to catch Ms. Lyons and her speeding Cadillac Deville. *"I should go ahead and erase all that out and put that extra letter in there right now before I forget, it will only take a half a minute. . ."* Eddie thinks, but he didn't want to keep Ms. Lyons held up any longer, she was already late for wherever she was speeding off to and now even later with this traffic stop, *customer service first* he thinks.

Eddie should have taken the extra thirty-seconds.

Only thing left to do is walk back up to the Cadillac, have Ms. Lyons sign her two citations, thank her for being cooperative, and send her on her way. Eddie steps out of his cruiser and walks up to the driver's side window. He stands with his back to the oncoming traffic. Eddie notices a light shining on the two tickets as he hands them off to Ms. Lyons. He looks behind to see where the light source is coming from, and two bright headlights shine in his face. It's Snowman and his big-rig, but really just the big-rig at this point in time—Snowman has momentarily checked out, and is fast asleep. He does wake up suddenly, but it's too late. The impact of hitting the Cadillac Deville and Eddie Chapman's body was with such great force that anything that could be broken apart, was broken, if not disintegrated. There was no discernable evidence that a vehicle even existed in the area, let alone two human beings after that collision happened. Just parts and pieces everywhere, and somehow through all this, Snowman missed the state trooper's vehicle completely—*if only Eddie had stayed behind and fixed sixteen across.*

Linda Lyons from Toledo, a wife and mother of three and Lt. Cmdr. Trooper Edward R. Chapman, decorated war veteran and a hero who saved so many lives throughout his career were both dead at the scene.

☩ ☩

"Now wasn't that some shit!" Eric said, "I told you he has seen some!"

I was still a bit taken back by Eddie's story. Wow, I thought, that was the most vivid and almost *as if I were there thing* I have experienced in my new world. Eddie was a great man, lived a great life, saved a lot of other lives. But, here he is now, with us.

Why?

This guy should be onto the next *wherever you go after the door place* in a heartbeat. This guy should be an Angel in Heaven looking down and protecting us.

"Wow, Eddie that was a great story, you are an awesome soul my friend! What ever happened to the other person you were killed with, Linda?" I asked.

"Not sure, it was like, well she just wasn't there anymore. I think I speak for all of us when I say this, the way we got here was a shock to our system, literally killed so fast that your soul doesn't know that your body just died. I think Linda must have moved on very quickly or she survived the accident. I'm just not sure. I never saw her again, even in the world we live in now."

I knew what happened. She was killed just as fast as Eddie was. I remembered the day I was stuck on the side of the road in my Metro. That tiny-faced trooper showed up and told me the story about the two crosses planted in the ground. He read the writing on one of the crosses, *Trp. Chapman*—I thought the story sounded familiar when Eddie was projecting it to me. I had been right there, at the same spot of the accident, and not too long ago. The crosses were still there to this day.

"I know what happened Eddie, I have been to the spot where you were killed and there are two memorial crosses planted there," I said.

"Two?"

"Yes, both of you killed instantly, by the truck."

"Hmmm, that's interesting, I never saw her again after I handed her the tickets. I sorta figured the big-rig probably did us both in at the same time, but like you and pretty much all of us here, when you first get here you have no clue or idea of what's going on until someone comes along and gives you the news."

"Same thing happened to me, I was with two other guys that I worked with," I said, thinking about Cat and Joe Meadows again and whatever became of them. Are they out here too? Did they survive the crash? "I have no idea where they are now, and it looks like I might never know."

"There are ways," Reannon chimed in. "Someone out here is different than all of us, able to go in between worlds."

"Really? How do you know that?" I said, "And uhh, how do you get a hold of this person?"

"Yeah, How?" Eric asked as well, "I want to know too, I got a few more things I need to gather to put *my puzzle* together, and it's not a crossword puzzle either Eddie. You been holding back on us Ree? This is the first I've ever heard of this shit, how do you know?"

"Austin told me."

"I'm only guessing though," Austin interjects quickly, "I think it's a woman too, she gave me something, at first I thought it was Reannon. It happened a while back when I was just sort of sitting there thinking about something when I was a kid. I was projecting it to Ree, showing her my first cat—Pickles and the litter of kittens she had one day and how cute they were and all—then all of a sudden I see the face of a woman I've never seen before around here, right in front of me, just for a split second—and she handed me something."

"Like a piece of paper?" I asked, but after thinking about it, should have just kept my mouth shut about a paper.

"Yeah, could have been. But, here is the thing, it wasn't Ree, and just as soon as she handed me this *whatever it was*, I dropped it. I'm still not good and putting things away here. I'm a bit clumsy in that department."

I seemed to have mastered the task of putting things away, must just be different for everyone out here. Some people must be better at things than others. Some can put strong images in your head and influence your decision making process, some can hold onto things like a piece of paper, and maybe some can move around better than others. We all seem to have pretty different strengths and weaknesses, and I suppose I'm just now finding out what mine are.

17

I'M PRETTY SURE Austin is talking about my Angel. She too gave me something to keep, and I still have it. I'm going to play dumb on this one, hopefully none of these souls can dig into my head and find it. I'll try my best to keep them out.

"So how do you know that this *whoever* can go in between worlds?" Eric asks.

I'm sure Eric LaRoche is up to something else other than helping his fellow lost souls find peace, love, and the pursuit of happiness. He just seems very self-serving, he's trying to put something together here—*his puzzle,* whatever that is.

"Ok," Austin said, "well, I just touched this thing she handed me, but even after I dropped it, I could see something new that happened *after* I was killed."

"Yeah, you're right. In your story, the one you were just telling to Guy. Denny Badcock, the little jerky kid that hit you, in the beginning you said he was at the police station handcuffed to the chair. That all happened *after you died,* yeah yeah I get it now. Did you get anything else?" Eddie said. The cop was coming out in him. He was good at figuring out crossword puzzles and figuring out little minute details that nobody else catches.

Austin stood with his head down trying to concentrate. "Not a whole lot more than that, I wish I could have found out what happened to him, would have loved to see him get what he deserved."

Of course *I knew* what he got. Nothing really—a slap on the wrist, six months away from home at a facility that housed other brain damaged juveniles just like him. He got three hots and a cot, then early release for good behavior I suppose.

All this talk about Austin's encounter (and possibly with Angel) has aroused my curiosity. I'd like to try and wander off somewhere by myself so I can pull this parchment out of my pocket. I'd like to see what it's all about. If you can get a fleeting memory of your life after you died just from touching the thing, I wonder what you can get if you sit there and stare at it. Maybe there is actual writing on it as well.

We are still in the middle of my old shop where I used to work, at Bill Bradley Chevrolet, lots of nooks and crannies everywhere. I always had my favorite bathroom I'd go to when nature would call upon me at work, it was up around the showroom, away from all the blue-shirted mechanics. It was for customer use only, but I could get away with going in there whenever I wanted. Nobody seemed to care. I needed an excuse to be alone for a little bit, but I just couldn't think of what to do or say. If I could just find my way up there somehow. . .

Then it happened.

"You feel that?" Reannon said to the others.

Eddie stood up ready for action. "Yep, feels like another new arrival, can't figure out where though, that's your department Ree, you wanna go check it out? Or do you want all of us to go too?"

I'm not really sure what they mean. I don't feel anything, but if I read between the lines, I'd say that there was just another accident, and there is another soul about to be *medium dead* in our world very soon.

"Let's all go this time again, but I want to leave Guy here. You might not like what you see. . .it takes some getting used to."

"Sounds good to me, I'll just—"

And with that, they were all gone. Poof.

18

I WENT AHEAD and found my way up to the customer lounge restroom. I figured might as well go into the one place that I knew so well. It sounds weird and strange to say this, but it felt good to be in such a place that gave me such pleasure and relief in the past, a comfort I haven't felt yet since I've been here. I sat down and pulled out the parchment that Angel had given to me earlier.

I looked down and read the writing on it:

DON'T TRUST ANYONE THAT LIES TO YOU.

USE YOUR NATURAL ABILITY TO HOLD AND HIDE THINGS, THAT'S YOUR ADVANTAGE HERE.

YOU CAN USE MIRRORS TO SEE THINGS MORE CLEARLY, THEY ALLOW YOU TO SEE BEYOND THIS WORLD, BUT THEY TAKE SOMETHING FROM YOU IN RETURN, USE THEM WISELY.

PUT THIS PAPER NEXT TO YOUR HEART AND IT WILL SHARE SOMETHING WITH YOU. IT WORKS ON EVERYONE.

LL

Interesting. The last two letters *"LL"* must be Angels real name. At least I'm getting closer to finding out who she is or at least what her name is. Now to break this letter down, let's see: *"Don't trust anyone that lies,"* well that's pretty much all of them, sort of, they all lied to me at the beginning, in the field, so I guess I won't trust any of them. Even though I probably like some better than others. *"Use your natural ability to hold and hide things,"* I knew I had that ability to hold and hide things. That's how I kept this parchment hidden away from everyone else for so long. The thing about the mirrors seems really vague though, I'll bet you that it's no real secret—and either LaRoche or that Kimball kid have poked their head in more than a mirror or two during their current tenancy in this place. They both definitely have had something taken from them, like their sanity. I'll bet Austin is using mirrors to see if his kitty's are doing OK, and LaRoche, who knows what he's looking for, missing pieces to *his puzzle* I'm sure. That leaves the last thing: *"Put this paper next to your heart and it will share something with you."*

If it's what I think it is—it's what Austin could have had if he would have held on to his damn paper longer. Some closure perhaps. A look beyond the actual time of your death, into the aftermath. The sorrow, the sadness, and the pain your friends and family surely felt by losing someone they dearly love. Oh my God, do I even want to see that? Am I ready for that? I will surely see my friends, the news stories with my name flashing across the screen, and I'd probably find out what really happened to Cat and Joe Meadows. What did Cathy do when we didn't show back up after lunch? What did my mother do when she found out I was gone forever?

I didn't know if I had the time for all that just now and I didn't want to see my cross just yet, but I will when the time is right. I can also use this for leverage if I so choose, it says *"It works on everyone"* and everyone here wants to know what happens *after* they died. For now, I'll hide it until I need it. That's what I'm good at.

19

SHOULD BE TIME for the others to get back I thought, and that's when I hear:

"Whaddya doin' in here?"

It was Austin Kimball looking directly at me with his goofy ass smile and his bright blue spandex sweat sucking biker top, standing up right next to me in this teeny-tiny two shooter bathroom, one stall and a urinal. Luckily I'm just standing up outside the stall at this point and getting ready to walk out, what happens next is just as scary as seeing those oily pores up close on Kimball's face. We were all now standing in my *personal* bathroom, just like one big happy family.

"Wow, hey guys. . .how'd it go out there?" I said, looking at Reannon, Eddie, Austin, and Eric's faces. Good thing we don't breathe or have any kind of body odor, because I'm sure we would be sharing it with each other right now in such a small space.

Eddie starts off the impromptu bathroom meeting. "Oh, pretty good I guess, at least for the person who just died. They went right in their door, all easy-peasy like, they must have known they were already dead. Most people who realize right of the get-go tend to jump in right away once that door is presented to them. Lucky ducks! Ehhh, Oh well, it happens."

"Makes sense to me, all of us here were pretty much instantly brought here, so that's the difference I'm sure," I said.

"So really, why are you in here bro?" Eric asks.

"Oh, you know, old memories and all, just checking out my old shitter here. This was my favorite place to um, *take care of my business,* if you know what I mean."

"So this was your office?" Austin asks.

"Uhh, no Austin, this is where I *took care of things* you know, Number Two? El Deuce? Droppin' the kids off at the pool? You know what I mean don't you?"

"I do, and that's nasty Guy!" Reannon says wrinkling her nose up, expressing her discomfort for being in a *men's* restroom right now. "That's it I have had enough of this." And with that we were all gone, and back in the middle of the detail shop again.

"I still can't believe you can bring four with you—that is fucking amazing," Eric said. "I have only been able to do me and sometimes one other person, I guess we all have our special talents in this shithole place. You still don't know what mine is do you Guy?"

"Well, not for sure. . .but if I had to guess, I'd say *mind control* would be your thing, am I right?"

"Yeah maybe. Could be, but here's the thing, if I'm good at the mind control stuff, then hows come I can't see in your head right now? By default, we all now know what yours is—it's *hiding things.*"

"Hmmm, guess it could be, that might be a good one to have being around you all the time then." I said.

"Geez, give it a break Eric. Who cares really? We all can hide things from each other, I can move us all around because I've been doing it for so long and you guys ask me to, you could do it too you know, just try a little harder next time. I really wanted to get out of that bathroom before someone realized there was a mirror in there and got curious," Reannon said.

So that must mean the mirror thing *is* common knowledge around here, I knew it! I'll have to act as if this is the first time I am hearing about it.

"Mirrors? What's the big deal about mirrors? I already kind of looked at one, sort of, but didn't see anything reflected back."

Reannon tried to explain it to me. "Well, it sounds easy, but it's a lot harder than you would think—it takes a minute or two or even longer than that, just depends I guess, but if you keep looking at a mirror some say that you can *start to see the real world*, which is the world we all came from, and at the current point in time that everyone else is living in it. You really have to concentrate hard when you do, and when you do, you open yourself up. . ."

"Open yourself up to what?" I asked.

"Anyone who cares to look inside you while you're all up into a mirror. It lowers your defenses, I only did it once. I looked at a mirror in a house, just to satisfy my curiosity, to see if it could even be done. I thought I could start to see some things after standing there for a while, it was a television and a couple of kids watching it. Obviously this mirror was in a living room. . .*no way would I stare at one in a bathroom,* all you would see are people *taking care of business.* Anyway, once it came into perspective it was like looking through a window, instead of a mirror, and you can't hear anything, just see, that's all. Very hard to tell what's going on but if you really want to look, you can. The only thing was, and this was my experience, I felt like total crap after, like I was drunk again and had a terrible hangover. Who knows what else it does to you, probably changes you. I never thought it was worth the crappy feeling afterward, and you really have to find a mirror in the right spot to see anything, so I never did it again."

"Talking about the mirror crap again?" Eric said. "I told you not to do that too much Ree, it's like cigarettes and crack, not only is it bad for you, once you're hooked you can't stop."

"I told you I only did it the one time, and even though I get curious anytime I see one, I haven't tried looking for quite a while now. Which I'm sure you do all the time with all your puzzle talk. . .why don't you let Guy in on all that. Tell him the story. . .the story of Eric LaRoche and the reason why you're the way you are."

"You ready bro?" Eric said looking at me straight in the face. I really didn't know if I wanted to see this—but why the hell not I suppose.

"Sure, let's do this, let me in—"

Eric LaRoche

I T WAS SEVEN-THIRTY in the evening—it was time.

Time for the newest member of the LaRoche family to finally come home for good. The adoption process was over for Eric and Layla LaRoche, the months of anticipation, countless hours of prayer, mountains of paperwork, and preparation have come down to this one moment. The doorbell rings, but Eric and Layla have already watched their new and now "official" adopted little girl walk up the driveway through the window with Ms. Beatty from the agency.

Layla LaRoche opens the door and looks down at the little girl who had previously stayed with the LaRoches—but had been away for about a week while the final hearings and decisions were being made in the court system.

"Well hello again little one!" Layla said with so much joy and happiness in her heart. It was the same feelings both Eric and Layla felt when that phone call came in with the good news about the permanent adoption. The little girl's biological father was still alive and well, but for some reason at the last minute was having second thoughts about the prospect of giving her up forever. But in the end, the decision was made in favor of the LaRoches.

Little Bean—that was the nickname Eric gave the sweet little blond haired and rosy cheeked girl that stood before him. She was wearing her favorite big flowered jumpsuit outfit, one that the LaRoches had bought for her a few weeks before on a shopping trip. The tears began to roll down both of the LaRoche's cheeks. . . *tears of joy.*

"Well come on in Lil' Bean! We sure did miss you!"

"It's ofish-a-wul I'm a La-woash now!" Lil' Bean screamed, ran in the door, and jumped into both of their waiting arms.

It didn't take long to get settled in, after all six-year-old Lil' Bean had been living there for almost three months before, taken in by Eric and Layla after she was placed in foster care by the State of Ohio. Everything was perfect, the LaRoche's, who were unable to have children of their own, now felt complete.

ON LIL' BEAN'S twelfth birthday, Eric had a surprise waiting for his daughter when she got home from school. Even though Lil' Bean wasn't so little anymore, Eric still called her by the nickname he gave her so many years ago, and to make sure she would never forget that, he had purchased a gold locket inscribed with these words: *You will always be my Lil' Bean, Love Daddy.* He planned on giving it to her as soon as she walked in the door. Most of her friends now just called her "Bean" but not her dad; to him she would always be his *Little Bean.*

Lil' Bean came home from school that day with a couple of girlfriends in tow, headed right to the fridge, grabbed a snack, and then on to her bedroom to do whatever twelve-year-old girls do after-school. Eric stood behind the door of the refrigerator, and when Bean closed it, there he was holding the locket up for her to see—but it also had one other little surprise—inside the locket was a picture of Eric and her on the day she officially became a LaRoche. She was wearing her big flowered jumpsuit and her big blond pony tails.

Bean had outgrown the flowered jumpsuit long ago. It did mean something special to her—that little shopping trip and getting the jumpsuit was her first memory of doing something together as a *new family*, even though it wasn't official at the time, it still gave her the feeling of togetherness that she never had experienced in her life before. The locket was a hit, even with the *Lil'* in front of the *Bean*. She didn't mind at all, she loved her daddy so much that she wore it every day of her life after that.

EIGHTEEN-YEAR-OLD Bean sits at her Paris High School graduation ceremony, awaiting her turn to walk up and receive her high school diploma. She would be going off to college next fall, to *The* Ohio State University. Eric and Layla were so proud of her. Not only for picking OSU instead of a school up north, but for overcoming all the adversity in the beginning of her life. The way she came to the LaRoches was an incredible story in itself, but Eric and Layla knew they did the best they could, and gave her all the best options in life that they could possibly give her.

Bean wanted to spend some time that night with her friends. Going from party to party. Some of the graduation parties were in one of the seedier neighborhoods in town, the Indian Heights subdivision. Paris High School was a *fairly* decent sized school and Bean was a *fairly* popular girl. With only one high school, all the kids are mixed together from all parts of city. Everyone got along (except for a few outliers, that is), and Bean wanted to say goodbye to all of her friends before going off to college next fall. Eric and Layla were reluctant at first, but gave in to the recent high school graduate and future Ohio State University student's demand. A decision they would later regret.

At one-thirty in the morning, police officers approach the front door of the LaRoche home. Just like the day their little girl came to them, Eric and Layla watched the officers walk up the driveway from a window. Both their hearts sinking, as they knew that this could not be good. Eric doesn't wait for them to ring the bell or knock on the door, he opens it, and lets the officers in.

"Mr. and Mrs. LaRoche the news is not good—I'm afraid, there was an acci—"

Eric stood there frozen. Numb. He could not believe the words he just heard. His Little Bean had been struck and killed by a drunk driver just under an hour ago over in the Indian Heights subdivision. She had been walking on the sidewalk, going to just one more house before heading home. The driver who was three times over the legal limit and trying to find his driveway had passed out, went up over the curb, and struck her from behind. There was nothing that they could have done to save her. She was killed instantly. One of the police officers standing inside the LaRoche home handed Layla the locket that Eric gave Lil' Bean when she was twelve years old. She held it in her hand. Eric joined her in an embrace and they both fell to the ground on their knees.

THE TRIAL OF Virgil R. Simms, the diesel mechanic who lived in the Indian Heights subdivision, and driver of the vehicle that ran over Eric and Layla LaRoche's only daughter, was about to go before the jury. The defense argued that Mr. Simms, who had two previous DUI convictions about ten years ago, was indeed drunk and well over the limit. But, on the same day as the accident, pain medication (that he had a legal prescription for) was erroneously filled with a higher dosage than prescribed. The pharmacy had made a mistake. Whether or not the miss-filled medication had been taken that day remains a mystery to Mr. Simms, as does pretty much the entire day as well, since he could not recall any memory from after the noon-time lunch hour. It was assumed that the memory loss may have been from the overdosing of pain medication *and* alcohol combined. Blood samples showed no signs of the medication in Simms's system, but the pharmacy records show Mr. Simms did pick up the prescription at around noon, at the beginning of his lunch hour, and on the day of the accident. Video surveillance footage backed that up as well. You could clearly see Virgil Simms, a burly man with a unique pot belly shape (from years of constant beer drinking) that was unmistakable—plus the blue mechanic shirt he was wearing with a name and logo on the front, although not readable, was clearly visible. Simms's defense council even claimed that you could see Simms open the pill bottle in the store, but Simms walks off frame at about the same time. It's still unclear if that happened or not.

This was a slam-dunk case the LaRoches thought. Justice will be served. This monster that sat just a few feet in front of them would be going away for a really long time. It was all Eric could do not to just jump up, grab the bailiff's side arm, and blow Virgil Simms away. Problem solved. An eye for an eye he thought. He was prepared to do this, for his *Little Bean*, for his wife, and he was willing to accept the consequences of his actions. Just as he got the courage to jump up and make his own judgement against Virgil Simms, the jury stepped out to render the verdict.

Guilty as charged, on all counts.

He would be going away for a very long time, Eric and Layla thought.

At the sentencing, the judge spoke at length about the little girl whose life was taken too soon by Virgil Simms. How she had her entire life ahead of her and how one bad choice can cause so much irreversible damage. Eric and Layla were allowed to speak as well, Layla did not last very long, becoming too upset to finish her statements. Eric didn't last much longer, but he managed to get out what he needed Virgil Simms to hear. *"You took her from me, and I hope to take something from you someday and not just your freedom. . ."* Which is probably something Eric should have kept to himself, since news cameras were recording everything in the courtroom that day.

The next thing that happened shocked both Eric and Layla. *Eighteen months in prison.* It should have been eighteen years! Or even eighty years as far as the LaRoches were concerned. It wasn't nearly the amount of prison time that they were expecting. "This is ridiculous! You call that JUSTICE?" Eric began an outburst in the courtroom that ended with him being thrown out of the building.

THE PHONE RINGS at a quarter past three in the afternoon, on a Sunday at the LaRoche residence. It was Captain Lee Owens from the Paris Police Department. Eric answers the call, standing silently and listening to what the Captain has to say. *"Yes, I understand,"* are the only words to come out of Eric LaRoche's mouth as he hangs up the phone.

"He's out."

Eleven months into an eighteen month sentence the State of Ohio releases inmate number 0018769 Virgil Renee Simms from incarceration. Not only for good behavior, but it seems that his attorneys had managed to get the overall sentenced reduced. The pharmacy incident played a huge roll. The attorneys filed a civil suit on Mr. Simms behalf and had settled out of court. The money from the settlement helped fund Mr. Simms sentencing appeal. . . and it worked. He was out, eleven months is all that Mr. Simms would serve in prison, *eleven months for a life.*

All this did not sit well with Eric LaRoche; his comments at the sentencing hearing were coming back to him. *"I hope to take something from you someday. . ."*

His feeling of not caring about what would happen to him if he just shot Simms dead while he sat in the courtroom began to come back as well. He was starting to unravel.

It only took about two weeks. Eric LaRoche found out everything there was to know about Virgil Simms. Eric, who was currently unemployed at the moment, had plenty of time to gather all the information he needed. He had been basically forced into resigning as the Finance and Insurance Manager at Bill Bradley Chevrolet about a month ago. The depression and distractions were just too much for his former employer to keep looking in the other direction, it was starting to affect the business, his face had been on all the news stations for the past six months, and people would just stop and stare at him *a lot.* Eric was fired, but he had told everyone that he was resigning due to obvious reasons. He had been given a very generous severance package and would be able to sustain his current lifestyle for at least a few months until things settled. But, really he could care less about all that. He only had one thing on his mind.

In a former life, perhaps Eric LaRoche could have been a detective himself. He was good at solving puzzles. Putting pieces together that didn't quite fit, turning them sideways, or upside down. He kept at it until he found the answers he needed. He knew, through his friends who still worked at Bill Bradley Chevrolet, that they were planning on interviewing Virgil Simms. The same man who was so drunk one night that he couldn't even find his own driveway, and ran over an innocent child in the process. They were going to interview this monster for a mechanic's job in the service department, and it was Eric's duty to make sure that never happened.

ERIC LAROCHE SAT in his car parked somewhere inside the Indian Heights subdivision. He sat there and stared at the remnants of flowers, little trinkets, and tributes that over a thousand people at one time had placed in this one spot. It was the spot where Bean had died. He sat parked for over two hours, sitting in his car just thinking about what she might be doing right now. Away at college, starting a new life as a young adult woman, maybe even meeting her future husband, but that was all taken away from her by the monster that was surely sleeping by now and not very far away.

It was almost four in the morning when he decided it was time. Eric grabs a black bag out of the back seat of his car, and proceeds on foot, one block over, to the street where Virgil Simms still lives.

This has not been the first time Eric LaRoche has been to Virgil Simms's house. He had been planning this for quite some time you see, he even had his own key to let him in when the time came. About nine weeks ago, when Virgil was still locked up, Eric had paid a visit to this very same house. There had been a magnetic key holder box placed behind the air conditioning breaker box, and inside the box, the key to Virgil Simms's house. Eric had figured that most black-out alcoholics tended to misplace keys more often than not, and sometimes keys are even taken from these chronic alcohol abusers on purpose so they don't harm themselves. . .or others. A friend or a taxi-cab drops them of at home, and the only way to get into their house is to have a key—a key that they could easily find in the dark while being completely wasted. It only took Eric about twenty-minutes to find the key holder box that Virgil Simms hid for himself, and when he did—he took the key out and had his own copy made. That was nine weeks ago and it was supposed to be in preparation for something he wasn't planning on doing for quite a while, that is if Virgil Simms had served out his full sentence.

But it was all happening *right now*.

Eric opens the back door, still carrying the small black bag from his car, and walks into Virgil Simms's house as if he were an invited guest. As soon as he enters the back foyer area of this little run-down and extremely neglected ranch style house, the smell of garbage and stale beer hits him hard. The stench almost makes him vomit right there on the floor. It wouldn't have mattered one bit. Looking over at the kitchen sink Eric sees a pile of dishes stacked to the top with what looked like a half-eaten hamburger bun with a crusty green horn-shaped mold spore growing off the top of it, and a half-empty bottle of *Yoo-hoo* with some sort of fuzzy green stuff growing inside. A little vomit would likely go unnoticed for months. The place is disgusting. This guy is just an absolute massive slob.

"This man deserves what I'm about to do to him."

Something else catches Eric's eye in the kitchen, laying on the countertop—a welcome letter from Bill Bradley Chevrolet's service manager congratulating V. Simms on his new job offer, it was a considerable pay cut from what diesel mechanics make at just thirteen dollars per labor hour, but a job was a job. Bill Bradley Chevrolet was certainly an equal opportunity employer, they'll hire anyone Eric thought, even a convicted drunk driver who has killed someone.

Walking down the hallway toward the bedroom, Eric could now hear a strange rhythmic sound, it sounded almost animal like, almost like—*animals having sex?* He thought.

"Oh my God, what have I walked into here?"

The sounds were getting louder, the high pitch sounds of a pig squeal, then something that sounded like a horse exhaling with its flapping lips, and then a human sounding grunt were becoming clearer. There was no doubt that some sort of bestiality scene was taking place behind that bedroom door.

"This guy <u>really</u> deserves what I'm about to do to him."

The bag that Eric LaRoche carried contained a weapon that he intended to kill Simms with. The bag also contained a letter explaining why he was doing all this, just in case something happened, and he didn't make it out alive. Up until this point he was sure he could do this. . .*kill another human being*, it would be retaliation and nothing more he thought. Eric LaRoche was not a killer, but Virgil Simms was. Or was he? Yes, it was a direct action of his that took Lil' Bean's life, but it *was just an accident*. V. Simms did not wake up in the morning and decide to kill a young woman walking on the sidewalk. But, Eric LaRoche decided at the end of the trial that he was going to *kill* a big monster sleeping in its bed someday.

The time came to open the door and finish this up. The noises had subsided some, but still a lot of strange animal like sounds coming from just inside the door. Eric pushes the door open slightly—he should have brought a can of WD-40 with him as well, since the door makes quite a loud squeak at the start when it's first opened. The squeak stops, and Eric can open the door up further without too much extra noise. The source of the strange sound is revealed. It's Simms, and he's all alone. He sleeps on his back, and the pressure of his pot belly against the rest of his body, especially his lungs and throat make him snore. His unusual body shape contributes to the weird sounds he makes while sleeping.

All the noise suddenly stops. There is complete silence for seven seconds, then it comes. A huge gasping for air, and at the same time a top heavy human figure rises above the sheets. Virgil Simms is now sitting straight up in his bed and looking directly at Eric LaRoche standing in his bedroom.

"What the fuck!" Simms yells. It is amazing how quickly he wakes, even just after his sleep apnea attack. Eric is equally surprised himself, and just freezes. He wants to grab the weapon he brought with him, but can't. He's frozen stiff. Simms jumps out of bed surprisingly well for such a large man, grabs the wood baseball bat that he sleeps with, and takes a swing at Eric's head—knocking him to the floor—knocking him out cold.

ERIC AND LAYLA sit at home. They have a few decisions to make. Eric, sitting on a chair at his kitchen table, is wearing a new ankle bracelet monitoring system that the court just started using for non-flight risk defendants. He just finished up reading the three-page complaint from the prosecutor explaining all the charges that were being brought up against him. The tables have certainly turned, Eric is the one now facing prison time, and it was time to make a decision on what he would do. His public defender was working on a plea deal, and they needed an answer by the end of the day.

After waking up at the hospital three weeks ago and seeing Captain Owens's sitting next to him, Eric knew that his plan had failed. He did not finish what he wanted to do to Simms. The fat ass surprised him by waking up so sudden and threw him off his game plan. It's funny that a thing that can kill you, like sleep apnea, actually saved Simms's life that night.

The one thing that was going for Eric, to counter the breaking and entering and pre-mediated attempted murder charge, was that the weapon he brought along to carry out the kill portion of his plan was not a gun or a knife, it was just an ordinary office stapler. It was the first thing he grabbed out of a box of personal items that had been sitting in the trunk of his car, still there from when he was fired from his job a few weeks before.

So, the stapler and all the pre-existing trauma in the LaRoche family's life that occurred prior to the B&E and attempted murder is why the prosecutor was willing to accept a plea deal. However, there had been a last ditch effort by the PD to get the attempted murder charged completely dropped, arguing that staples are very thin and at most would cause some minor puncture wounds and bleeding. The prosecutor countered that he did not think Eric LaRoche's intentions were to break into Simms's home at four-thirty in the morning, enter his bedroom, and start stapling him about the head—he was there with intent to kill.

The decision was made, Eric would plead guilty to lesser charges, but would still have to serve some time. It wasn't the most ideal situation, but he wouldn't have to spend years in prison and away from home.

The plea deal was done and the sentence was handed down. Twenty-four months at a minimum security prison camp, located within the same county that he lived in. How nice to be so close to home he thought, but the prison camp was not going to be a picnic by any stretch of the imagination. The thought that Eric LaRoche has to serve more time than Virgil Simms is absolutely astounding as well.

"It's just time, that's all," Eric thinks, "I'll be back."

PRISON CAMP IS not fun, and it's not really a camp at all. It's more like work. You do earn a small wage, but it's not much at all, enough to buy some shampoo, or maybe a magazine every so often. The first few weeks are mainly adjusting to prison life. Eric has had only one minor problem so far, some of the other inmates found out that the "weapon" he used in his crime was just an ordinary office stapler, and they were razzing him pretty good about it. Eric argued that a stapler is an underestimated weapon, and could do some significant damage if used in the proper way. Also, if he actually had the stapler with him at this particular time, he would show them how it works, by shoving it *up their asses*. A small scuffle ensued soon after that, but was quickly taken care of by prison security.

For the most part, things went well for the weeks that followed, and soon Eric was on the list for highway clean-up crew. Not the most glorious job, but you get to go outside, and are able to get away from the camp, at least for a little while. That really appealed to Eric. It was spring and getting warmer, he missed the outdoors, and if picking up trash is all he had to do to get out in the fresh air, well he'd do it, he thought.

The day came to go clean up a five-mile stretch of highway on I-25. Eric woke up that morning with a headache, this was his life now, and headaches were the norm. Ever since the night that Virgil Simms slammed a Louisville Slugger against his skull, things have never been quite right, and he would get a little zinger going every so often. It would sometimes make him quite dizzy. All he would need to do to remedy it was sit down for a few minutes, let it pass, and then he would be good to go. There was no way he was missing the fresh air, sunshine, and outdoors—he needed it today more than ever. The stench of Virgil Simms's house still haunted him every day.

He asked and was given some Tylenol before jumping in the van that would take him out to the highway that morning. He was starting to feel a little better now, just knowing that he would be outside in the sunshine, and pretty close to home too. Maybe Layla will drive by and wave, that would be so great he thought. She wouldn't be able to miss him either; he'll be the one wearing the hunter orange jumpsuit along with about four other inmates along the road picking up garbage.

Halfway up the five-mile stretch, Eric LaRoche stands along Interstate 25 at mile marker 74. The guards do not notice that inmate LaRoche has drifted off slightly from the rest of the group. They are too busy sitting in their van discussing the new prison camp policy regarding random drug testing for the guards and it's quite a heated discussion.

Eric's head is really starting to bother him now; the mid-morning sunshine is taking a toll. The concussion that doctors said may take years to go away completely is likely the cause, and he starts to get dizzy. Eric wanders off even more, crossing the white edge line, drifting onto the roadway and towards the oncoming traffic. At approximately 10:16AM, a grey BMW traveling in the far right northbound lane of the highway at a little over eighty-six miles an hour can see the man wearing the hunter orange jumpsuit slowly drifting into his lane of travel. The driver is unable stop in time nor maneuver out of the way. The Beemer slams straight into Eric LaRoche, sending his body flying up in the air almost fourteen feet high, twisting six times end over end before hitting the ground over thirty-feet away. Eric LaRoche was dead at the scene.

I FELT BAD. Hearing and seeing all that now made me look at Eric in a different light. I know now why he is so bitter. He lost his only daughter, and he lost the chance to avenge her death. I know what he is doing here, and it all makes sense now.

"That was an amazing story man," I said. "I had no idea."

"Well now you know, bro. . ." Eric said.

Eddie spoke. "If I had still been around, that Beemer would have been going a lot slower, nobody dared to speed on *my* highway back in *my* day."

Just like Mr. Tiny Face Trooper from my breakdown, these guys took pride in their duty to serve the public, I think it's great that they referred to it as *their* highway. Eddie's probably right too, if he had only been around, maybe the Beemer would have been going a lot slower and been able to stop in time.

"I had no idea you worked here at Bill Bradley, you must have left before I started, huh?" I asked Eric, we actually have something in common to talk about now, how about that.

"Yeah, it was a few years before you I would say, I never got back here to the wash rack too often, I worked up in the finance department—sold rustproofing, paint sealant, and a bunch of shit that nobody ever really needed, made a ton of money until—"

"Well did you know that V. Simms still works here? And that's how he has his name stitched on his shirt 'V. Simms,' probably so people can't make the connection right away about who he really is. Damn that fat fuck! I had no idea he did anything like that. The guy just kept to himself most of the time, I don't think I ever said one word to him. He came across as kind of a lazy ass though, always dragging his feet around. I would take my break at exactly three o'clock every day, I'd see him walk into the shop bathroom, and I knew what he was about to do in there. I only made the mistake *once*, I walked in *while he was still in there* polluting the place up. . .my eyes literally watered up. It was so bad I had to breathe through my mouth, or I would have barfed all over the floor. I got the hell out, and fast! I never went in there ever again, especially during his three o'clock shit breaks."

"That's interesting, three o'clock huh? And every day too?" Eric asked with a bit more curiosity in his tone. I wouldn't know why he'd care about a guy who takes a dump at the same time every day. It was the same guy who killed his daughter in a car, and the same guy who cracked a baseball bat against his head one night. So I could see why he would want to know every little detail about the jerk, which would probably include every time he took a crap. So it made total sense to me.

"Yes, three-o-clock, on the dot. You could set your watch to it."

"Yeah, set your watch. . .hmmm. It sure is too bad we can't keep track of time ain't it? I mean if we just could find out what time it *exactly is* at *this very moment*, we could—" Eric stops in mid-sentence.

"We could what?"

"Oh, nothing—say, have you ever tried looking in one of those mirrors? I mean a few of us at least tried it, kind of like drugs, you should try it at least once, it can't hurt you." Eric said, abruptly changing the subject.

"I don't know, won't it make you go crazy or something?"

"It won't make you crazy, but it does make you a little queasy, at least the first couple of times it does."

"First couple of times? How many times have you done it?"

"Oh not that much. Austin is the one you have to watch out for, that guy has done it more often than just a couple of times, and look at him—he's not *all that* crazy is he?"

"Well that's a matter of personal opinion I would think," I said. "I suppose it would be neat to peek in at someone, see what they are up to and all, even though you can't hear anything, maybe you could catch up on some television. Of course you couldn't hear any dialogue, unless it the closed captioning was turned on. Even then you would have to read it backwards like in a mirror's reflection right?"

"Not sure. Do you want to find out?" Eric said.

Do I ever, but I don't want to go nuts doing it. "Well I guess I wouldn't mind trying it at least once, can we get away from the others? We could go up to my private facility up towards the showroom, you know the bathroom where we were all stuffed into a little bit ago? It has a mirror and could be a good one to practice on. Can we do that?"

"Sure we can, everyone listens to me, I'm pretty persuasive," Eric said.

Oh yeah, that's right, let's not forget that extra special talent of *mind control and manipulation* that Eric LaRoche seems to have here.

20

WE STROLL DOWN to the end of the shop without the others noticing, and walk through the door that leads out into the showroom, courtesy of Eric LaRoche and his mastery of the mind and influence on others. This is where all the salespeople would usually stand around all day and wait for the next prospect to come through the door, so that they could all take turns jumping on them like prey—*except this is the dead zone remember*—nothing here but empty shells of inanimate objects that are somehow still here for us to do what we want with. Just inside the hall there are two doors, one marked *Men* and the other *Women*. These are the customer lounge restrooms. Nobody hardly used these, and that's what I liked about it. I can give this mirror thing a try, and hopefully won't see anything that will scare me too much, that is if this really works. I wouldn't want my first vision to be a customer standing there taking a piss, or even worse, that someone would be looking directly *in the mirror* trying to pick something off their face. That would be absolutely frightening.

We go into *my* restroom and stand inside.

"Well, there it is," I said looking at the rectangular mirror hanging on the wall above the sink. "Looks pretty harmless to me."

"Ok, well all you do is stand in front of the thing, and just start watching for stuff to appear, it's easy—sort of," Eric said. He wasn't looking directly at it at all, deliberately turning his head away in fact. Maybe because he was trying to avoid getting sick from looking at it is what I guessed.

"Ok, here I go," I start to stare at the mirror. It's weird at first, there is no reflection back at me, and there is nothing at all to see. I can't even see the urinal or shitter stall that should be reflected back, absolutely nothing. It's like looking at a piece of shiny glass of nothingness. I sit there and stare at this for all of three-minutes or so, at least it felt like three-minutes.

"How will I know if I see some—" I cut myself off, because well, now I can see something. It was coming into focus, like those 3-D posters that we used to hang up on the wall. Once your eyes figured out to focus farther behind the surface, the picture came into view very quickly. That's what this was like, I can see the urinal, the stall, and the door—it was cracked open a little too. Perhaps the last person to use this restroom needed to air it out a bit. There is no reverse image like you would see in a reflection either, it's more like looking through a window.

I can see some light coming through the crack of the door. Some real sunlight! The showroom is all glass windows basically, so when the sun was out at certain times of the day—it lit the place up, even down the hallway.

"Wow! Some crazy stuff here man! Guess what? It's daytime right now! Holy shit!" I said this like a vampire who was suddenly cured of the virus, or whatever makes him or her a vampire, and could now go outside in the daylight. It is unmistakable, the color is so much different than what I am used to in my current situation. It feels so good to see it too, it *is like a drug*—just like he said it would be. This looking-into-a-mirror thing is like crack cocaine in our world. I did some more surveying around. The place still looked the same to me, the sink, the weird sixties wood paneling on the wall, the soap dispenser; this was stuff you could see in my world now, but you really don't notice it since all the colors are the same and things tend to blend right in all together.

I look up, above the shitter stall, and I see something that I knew was there from before—something I thought was kind of funny actually—the whole reason why this thing is mounted above the stall was sort of a joke really, but now I'm thinking: *"Oh my God, I could give Eric something he really wants with that."*

"You see anything else bro?" Eric said. He was still looking down at the floor—if he knew what I can see hanging on the wall above the shitter stall right now, I'm sure he'd be right in here looking around with me.

"Just still looking around, it's pretty amazing man!"

"Well, remember it's just a bathroom, how amazing can it get? You better stop while you can for now, for each second you do that you're going to feel like shit way longer."

"Well Ok, how do I break free from this then? I feel like I need to be pushed off it or something, it's like an electric fence, when you touch it, you can't let go. . .and I feel like I—"

And here we are. Standing back at the shop now with the others. Eric must have poofed us back to the shop in one of those instant move things that I did only one other time by myself. Eric and Reannon are the only ones I know that can take more than just *themselves* when they want to move around fast like that. I wish I could figure that out. But for now, I'll take my special talent of *hiding things* over being able to take an extra passenger or two when traveling from place to place.

"Well, where did you two run off to?" Reannon said, looking at me and Eric, she was more motherly like than usual. I felt like we just got caught smoking a big fat doobie in the closet and were getting in trouble for it.

"Oh you know, just showing Guy here how to look into a mirror and see some cool stuff, he did pretty good, better than your first time Ree. He was in about say two and a half, maybe three minutes tops."

"What? Don't get him hooked on that Eric! You already got Austin doing too much of that as it is! You want to corrupt another one now?"

I was starting to feel what could only be described as a sick nauseating feeling starting to creep up on me. The bad thing is that there is no relief from this, a real live person would feel this way and just puke to get it over with. But, since we don't have any sort of digestive system anymore, I'm just stuck with the sickie feeling.

"And he's looking a bit seasick now," Reannon said. "How do you like that Mr. Guy? You better remember that feeling. The mirror is an awesome tool to have, but you better use it sparingly."

"How long do I have to feel like this?" I asked.

"How long were you in for?" Austin asked.

"I don't know, maybe a minute at the most."

"Oh well, I'd say since it was the first time, you have about an hour of that to look forward to. It does get better the more you do it. It's like starting to smoke, you have to build a tolerance up to the side effects before you can actually start to enjoy it."

"You always were a mirror-head weren't you Kimball?" Eddie Chapman said, now joining in on the conversation. "I'm glad I never got into anything like that, seems like that really makes you guys act all weird afterwards too—damn junkies."

"You should try it Eddie, it's not as bad as you think," Austin said.

"No thanks. Seems like every house we go by you're in there looking around to see if you can find any cats through the mirrors, and do you ever find any?"

"Oh yeah! All the time, dogs too, but I like the cats better you know, besides we don't have nuthin' else better to do, so why not."

I really feel like dog shit right now. I just start walking around in circles, hoping this feeling would wear off soon. I'm thinking about what I saw in the bathroom too. I wonder if I shared this discovery with Eric, what he would do with it? Is there a way to *go through the mirror* somehow, or be seen from the other side? I have no idea, but I'll bet LaRoche is working on it, and *if it could be done*, he sure would like to know a time when he could come face to face with V. Simms again, the man who had a part in both himself and his daughter's death. The information is my leverage, and why I would need leverage I don't know, but I just feel like I should. I get these feelings now, and they get stronger as *time* goes by.

I have no idea what day it is right now. I do know that it's currently daytime, because I just saw the real sun about twenty-minutes ago. I still have one more piece to add to my leverage collection; the parchment that Angel gave me. Or do I? Somehow I don't feel it on me anymore, that's strange. I thought *my thing* was that I can hold and hide better than anyone else here, but I can't seem to find it. What the hell?

"Looking for this?" Eric LaRoche said standing right in front of my face and holding up the parchment that once was hidden inside me.

21

HOW ERIC LAROCHE got my parchment is no mystery. He simply took it from me while I was wide open and vulnerable. Reannon told me that could happen, but I had forgotten all about it. I didn't listen close enough to her advice about the stupid mirrors and the side effects it can have on you. I was so busy taking in the sights of something I hadn't experienced in a while, which was just a plain old looking restroom, but one that actually had *real sunlight* coming through the crack of the door, and that was enough to let my defenses down. Kind of seems silly now, but it sure was amazing at the time. He must have seen it in my pocket and just took it from me. No police here to call and report a theft, there are no laws that I know of, so really nothing I can do about it. What is the big deal anyway? It's just a piece of paper with some general statements written on them, they don't really mean much. I guess I'll have to explain how I came to have it though. I could say I wrote it myself, but I really don't know how I'd do that without a pen. I'll have to let him in on my secret I've been hiding.

"How did you get this?" Eric begins.

"Someone gave it to me, a woman in the field where I was killed."

"A woman huh? Was it Ree?" Eric now focused directly at me, we seem to be standing there all alone now, he must have sent the others out on a shopping trip or out to run some errands, who knows.

"No, it wasn't Reannon, I actually never caught her name, but I think that's her initials at the bottom of the paper there, *LL*."

"So she gave it to you in the field? By the barn, or in that old farmhouse?"

"Oh, actually she gave me the paper here, in the shop while you were all trying to gang up on me with those questions and stuff, but I met her the first time in the barn, right where the crash happened. She is the one who gave me *the news* about all this."

"Well sounds like you better let me in your head so I can see what she looks like, might be trouble, you never know."

A request to get inside my head? Not so sure that would be a good idea. If it's anything like what the others were showing me before—with their *projections*—once you let someone in your head you can run around the whole time and do all sorts of things, that is everyone except Eric. He kept me, and I assume the others too, on a very tight leash while he projected his memory of how he ended up here, parts of the story and images were a bit fuzzy to me. For instance, I couldn't really see the face of his daughter or his wife Layla, they were blocked out, as if he didn't want anyone to see them. He is *the mind control master* here of the group, so he must have greater control over all of that. So far, I feel like he hasn't tried to make me do anything I don't want to do. All except for the time out in the field with that merry-go-round scene deal, but that was before I even knew any of these people, I feel I am a much stronger *dead guy* now than I was when, well whenever *that* was. I keep forgetting, there is really no time to keep track of.

"Eh, I don't think that's a good idea right now man, it seems so personal and we are really just starting to get to know each other, ya know? What I think we need to figure out right now are what these initials stand for *LL*, I got a couple of ideas to run by you." I call that *deflecting the request*, and I hope it sticks.

"Yeah, ok, well what ya got?"

"All right, check this out—the lady who was killed along with Eddie."

"Linda something, yeah. . ."

"Right, Linda Lyons was here name, she's an *LL*, Eddie said he never saw her after the semi hit them, so where is she then?"

"Maybe she didn't die?"

"But she did die, there were two crosses planted in the ground along the highway, I saw them myself, and not too long ago either—before I got here."

"Well what about this," Eric said. "Maybe she never died *at the scene*. You see that's the one common thing we all have and why we are all in relatively the same geographic area. We all were shot into this world like a cannon before we even knew what hit us. It's possible that she went to the hospital, knew she was going to die, and went right in her door—happens all the time out here. You see a fresh kill and they don't say one word to you, you can't even get the time of day from these newbies, and they just walk right in their door. . ."

"Sounds like it could have happened that way I suppose, but maybe she came back and is now like a manager, or supervisor of all the souls in this general area." I said.

"What? I think you are still messed up in the head from staring at that mirror too long bro. There's nobody like that around here. *Manager?* Now that's funny."

"Ok, I'll give you that, does sound a bit far-fetched—I do have one more possible scenario, but you might not like me telling you about it."

"Oh go ahead, I have an open mind, it's always open, like yours was in the bathroom back there. Sorry I took that paper while your head was in the sunshine, but my curiosity got the best of me, and it was just a hanging out there for the taking."

"Well thanks for apologizing, I guess, I'll try to be more careful who is standing around me next time," I said. "Ok—what about your wife Layla?"

"What do you mean? How can that be? She's not even dead."

"Well, and stay with me here, how do you know for sure? You don't. Layla LaRoche, think about it—her initials are LL too. We don't know for sure because we can't see beyond this place, we can with mirrors yes, but that does not give you a whole lot to work with, you can only look in the general vicinity. What if we could find out for sure?" I said.

"I think I know where you're going with this—your little paper there says if I put it on my heart, it will share something with me, right?"

"Yes, we could—" I started to say, but Eric cuts me off abruptly.

"I don't want to do that if it's going to show me what I think it will show me. I'm scared I'll find something out I really don't want to know about."

"Like what?"

"Well, if it's going to show me the future after I was gone, I don't want to, I don't want to know if—"

"You don't want to know if Layla is dead?"

"No, it's not that—I don't want to see how she's moved on without me, you know—if she has a new husband now or what. Then what if she *can* have kids now? We never really found out which one of us was having the trouble, we just figured we weren't getting pregnant for reasons beyond our control, so we just adopted instead. I don't want to know if it was me that was holding her back from having a child of her own. I *do* want to think she is happy though, It's just that I can't bear to look. . ." Eric said this with as much emotion as I have ever seen him express since I've known him this short time. The guy who seemed to have rubbed me the wrong way at the beginning of this journey, talked me into doing the equivalent of crack cocaine out here with the mirrors, and had stolen something that was given to me personally, has now touched my heart with the sweet devotion he still has for his wife. How the hell did that happen? *Mind Manipulator?*

22

THE REST OF the clan shows back up now, back from wherever they go to. That is, wherever Eric tells them to go. I don't even ask where they have been. I'm sure the master mind manipulator has his reasons for sending off his souls. Why we stay here and always end up back in this shop all the time is anyone's guess. Although, it is pretty comforting to me since this used to be the actual area where I worked every day. I can still see the time clock hanging on the wall, the same clock I used to slide my time card into and hit the lever to print the time I came in, and the time I would leave. It doesn't work or tell any sort of time now, but it's there nonetheless. A reminder of my old world, my old friend, and my old enemy—time.

When you exist on a plane that you never even knew was here, it makes you start to wonder, what's the purpose of all this? Who is really in control here? Is it God? Is it Jesus Christ? Is it Linda Lyons, the Regional Manager and Welcome Wagon Committee Chairperson? Who knows?

I have never had so much time on my hands. When you don't sleep, or eat, what else is there to do except look around and just talk to other people (if you can find any that is). The whole projecting thing is a lifesaver, not only telling someone a story, but putting their ass right in it with you—just as if you were there with them. Without that, I don't know what we would do to kill time. That's funny. *Kill time.* Just sounds strange saying it now, considering what I've become.

I decide to strike up a topic of conversation, maybe even one that they have had before, but how would I know, I'm just the new guy.

"So guys, what do you think happens when you actually walk through that door? And not the door right there at the end of the shop, you know *the door.*"

"You move on," Reannon says.

"Yeah, but to where?"

"What I'm hoping for, and you guys should be as well, is that we get to start over again, become a little baby embryo somewhere in some mother's womb—or if that is not a possibility, I am hoping to come back as a—" Austin says, but is suddenly interrupted by Eddie.

"A CAT!"

"No, but I wouldn't mind that at all! I am actually hoping to come back as a *black man*."

Ok, so now I start to think looking at too many mirrors *does* make you crazy, did he just say he wanted to be reincarnated as a black man? I think he did. The only thing stranger would be if he wanted to come back as a *black woman*.

"Ok, I'll say it," Eric chimes in. "What the hell for?"

"Well, in my *other life* I was treated differently, held in high regards, had just about anything I wanted, whenever I wanted it. My family had money and all that stuff. I really didn't need to go to college, my trust fund would have kept me fat and happy for many many years—I don't know, when you're brought up like that, it makes you jaded—I know it sounds strange but I was tired of being that way. So, if *the door* is a gateway to your new life, I really would like to be a black man, working my way through life, figuring things out on my own—becoming my own person—and a person of color at that."

"And the key is being a black man? I really don't get it. You can be poor and white too you know." Eric said.

"I know, I know—but see I always liked having a nice tan too—I never could tan—it always went to direct sunburn, then my skin would peel off in about a day or two and I'd look like I was some sort of burn patient getting ready to go in for a debridement. So coming back black—that would take care of that problem completely."

"You're weird Austin," Eddie says in his Eddie like tone, which is just as a-matter-of-fact as it gets. "I still love you like my own, but that is just bizarre, I guess there is nothing wrong with it though. If you want to come back as a black man, I'll support you on that."

"The door is there to help us move on to the next phase of all this and nothing more, so there won't be any coming back as a little baby, or a kitty cat, or even a black man. I suggest the next time anyone sees one, get in it!" Reannon said.

"Ok, will do Ms. Thirteen Missed Doors, that's good advice." I said remembering Reannon telling me before that she had passed up not one, or two, but *thirteen* doors in the fifteen years since she has been here.

"I know that too, and I'm working on it—it's just that something tells me to stay. I can't figure it out either. I almost feel like—" Reannon pauses, and gives a look as if she wants to say something else, but doesn't.

"Hey, Ree don't worry about it, we're all sticking around here for something it seems like huh?" Eric said. "You're missing her aren't you? That's what it is, isn't it?"

"I'm always missing her. My little girl, why was I so stupid? I'll never know the answer. I'm always thinking about her and what her life was like after what happened to me, I should have never gone out that night. Did she end up living with her deadbeat dad? Did my parents end up taking care of her? Did she at least grow up happy? You know I'd like to think that *the door* is there for us to move on, but what if it does take you somewhere else. . .and you forget who you are, or who you used to be? I'd like to keep on looking around in *this world*, to find the answers—to find the closure *I need*, even though this is not the best place to do that, I know."

"Just need to keep staying positive like you are I guess."

This sure didn't seem like a mind trick from Eric. He was very sincere and showed some concern, perhaps since he had dealt with his own loss of a child before. Another side of him I hadn't yet seen.

"Here, we found this." Eric pulls out a dark round object, looks to me like it's probably a coin. He flips it over to Reannon and she catches it, then takes a look at the object that was just thrown to her.

"Oh my, where did you get this?"

"We found it, Guy and I," Eric says to Reannon, but at the same time I hear words in my head—it sounds like just Eric's voice saying something like: *"Follow me on this bro,"* he doesn't even look at me when he transmits this now apparent private message directly to my head.

Yet, another trick of the dead I see. I follow along, just standing there listening.

"We found it up in the showroom, probably been there for a really long time and we just never saw it, looks like it, don't it?"

The dark round coin looking object he threw to Reannon *was* actually a coin. It was *my* coin. I could tell from where I was standing at, it was the same nasty old quarter that I had found in the blue mini-van, the day that I was killed. The day I needed some extra money to play the stupid Keno game at lunch with Cat and Joe. It must have still been in my pocket. That's crazy. Then why they would get all excited about a quarter that looks like it may have been riding around in that blue mini-van since the day someone obviously lost it down the crack of the seat is beyond me. Eric must have grabbed that out of my pocket too when he took my paper. I don't know why he wouldn't have mentioned it until now.

"It's a 1979, that's perfect, thank you guys so much!"

"Yeah, I know you died the same year, but it might have some good stuff on it." Eric said.

"I don't really get it," I said.

Reannon explains. "This coin has probably touched over a thousand human hands in its time. Yes, it's an inanimate object, just like everything you see around here. We found out, by mistake really, that if you put a coin up around where your heart used to be, it shows you little snippets of the people's lives it has touched. If they touched the coin, they left something on it. Most of it is boring, but every once in a while you see something fairly entertaining. It beats the same old stories I've heard from these guys. Pretty neat huh?"

"Kind of like a VCR?" I asked.

"A what?"

"A VCR, a video cassette recorder, you've heard of that haven't you?"

"My dad had a thing that played tapes of TV shows and movies, it was called a *Betamax player*? I think. Is that the same thing?"

"Well, sort of I guess."

"Well, it does have some limits, for instance you can only see things that happened within your own lifetime. You still don't get to see beyond your own death date. Someone or something is being very cruel to us when it comes to that. I'd give anything to see what happened after I died."

That brought up an interesting thought for me. Why didn't Mr. LaRoche tell her I had been given that paper? A paper that will allow you to see beyond the day you died. Once again, just as soon as Reannon finishes her sentence to me, I hear, via the private two-way radio that Eric LaRoche and I now seem to share *"Don't say anything just yet, trust me. . ."*

23

WILLIAM J. BRADLEY WAS born in 1932, the son of a farmer. He grew up on his parent's land learning all there was to know about farming—planting seeds, growing corn, growing soybeans, or sometimes even growing wheat. Making food for the people and even for the world is what he thought his ultimate purpose was; and for the first part of his life, he believed it.

But there came a time things began to change, something inside him said:

"There is more to life than this. . ."

This story was told to *every new employee* at Bill Bradley Chevrolet, no matter what position that you were hired in for. It didn't matter if you were a mechanic, salesperson, or just a low ranking wash boy. Some lucky someone from the HR department, whose turn it was to do the *orientation presentation*, would sit you down in the Big Conversion Van Showroom meeting area. They would have to present this pre-written, often long and boring (along with an accompanying slide show) presentation on the origins of William "Bill" Bradley—The founder and namesake of the dealership you now happen to be working for.

"The year was 1948, and William Bradley was just sixteen years old. Farming was his life, living in the rural countryside up until now, but Billy had loftier goals in mind."

That's about all I remember of that first day. After that bit about the loftier goals, I pretty much just zoned out, and started to stare around at all these conversion vans parked in this showroom. I remember thinking, *"I don't think you could stuff not one more van in here. How much money does this guy have just sitting in this showroom right now? Maybe a million bucks?"*

I was not far off, at least I don't think so.

Bill Bradley Chevrolet was advertised as the "MIDWEST FACTORY OUTLET" for van conversions. He even had his own van conversion factory in Indiana so that he could actually say those words legally in all his advertising. People would come from all over the place to buy a van from Bill Bradley, his reputation was outstanding, and he was known throughout the land as the *Van Man*.

If you didn't have the Bill Bradley logo on the back spare tire cover of your conversion van, you certainly didn't own the best. At the peak of popularity in the conversion van era, Bill Bradley Chevrolet would sell right around four-hundred conversion vans *a month*. . .these were just some insanely huge numbers for a dealership in such a small local market. The city of Paris, Ohio was on the map alright, and all thanks to Bill Bradley Chevrolet.

Mr. Bradley was a generous man, I met him a couple of times in the short six months that I worked at his dealership. The first time I met him, he handed me ten dollars and told me to go get a haircut—which I thought to be a little strange—but I went ahead and obliged and got it all trimmed up the next day. Then the last time I ran into Mr. Bradley, he was just strolling through the wash rack, one of the lowliest places in the dealership, and handed me a couple of tickets to a Bengals pre-season game. He says to me, "here you go son, have some fun!" Wow, what a nice guy! I guess he was ok with the haircut then.

In this part of the state, you're either a Browns, Bengals, or Dallas Cowboys fan when it comes to pro-football. On the college level, everyone except for a few flake jobs who were Michigan fans, were also Ohio State University fans, but for the most part in Ohio you either rooted for a big cat, a brown dog, or a silver star.

The two top salesmen every month for used *and* new car and van sales were Ronald "Opie Cunningham" Howard and Doug Lawrence. These two guys were neck and neck every month for sales and it was always a contest to see who could sell the most units. One month, Opie would win, the next it would be Doug. It would go back and forth all the time, they were always trying to cut the other's throat and cockroach each other's customers. If an open sales call came in, it was a race to see who could get to the phone first. There was no taking turns on the sales calls or a "who's up" system for them—it was man to man, and the best one won—whoever got to the call first, got the sale if the caller on the other end of the phone was buying. For the most part though, it was really just some good ole' fashioned friendly competition between colleagues.

The time had come to try something a little more fun. Since it was football season and Opie being a die-hard Bengals fan, and Doug a Cleveland Browns man; they decided to take it to the next level and place some bets.

For the next month, whoever sold the most units would be declared the winner. The loser would have to dress in either a Bengals or a Browns jersey (depending on which team you *hated*) every day during the *Battle of Ohio* week when the Bengals play the Browns, and also would have to hang up some sort of fan memorabilia on their office wall. Oh, and just to make it interesting, $100 cash to the winner from the loser. They almost agreed that they would go to the actual game dressed in the opposite team apparel from which they rooted for, but they both decided that might be taking it a little too far.

The results were in and Opie had lost. Opie tried to alter the deal at the last minute because he couldn't stand the Browns **at all** so the thought of having to wear their brown crap colored shirts all week long sickened him, but still, a bet is a bet.

Besides having to wear a Browns jersey, Opie would have to display some sort of Browns memorabilia mounted for all to see. That came in the form of a clock that Doug Lawrence, winner of the bet, *and* top sales leader for the month, had purchased especially for Opie's office. The authentic NFL licensed Browns memorabilia, bearing a dog's face and a brown football helmet void of a team logo, fit perfectly—right above the Top Sales Superstar for 1993 plaque that Opie proudly displayed in his tiny half-walled cube that some might think to be too small and cluttered at times.

The dealership had a longstanding policy about what you can and can't hang inside your office cubicle walls, there was to be nothing displayed that could offend a potential customer. This included political signs, comics, anything vulgar or distasteful, and also any type of professional or college sports teams. (Yes, people get offended if you root for the wrong team!)

An exception was made. Since a friendly wager between colleagues produced a sales increase of almost 21% for the month, the sales managers agreed that they would allow the Browns memorabilia to hang in Opie's office for exactly five days. After that, Opie would have to remove it and hang it up somewhere else inside the dealership. As long as it didn't distract anything or anyone, he was free to mount it anywhere he'd like. He agreed.

It was the last day for Opie Cunningham to wear the Browns shirt. Finally, Saturday and tomorrow, THE GAME. This time around it was being played in Cincinnati, at Riverfront Stadium. Doug and Opie planned to drive down together in one of the Bill Bradley vans, to do some tailgating and have some fun before the game. You see, it really wasn't all that bad, they always seemed to have a good time with the rivalry between them.

I happened to be working that Saturday as well, and was just coming out of my *private* bathroom up front. I saw Opie walking down the steps with the Browns memorabilia that had been hanging in his office all week. He saw me too.

"Hey Guy, hey buddy, you think you could help me out real quick? You doing anything?"

"Not really, just took my break. What do you have in mind?" I asked.

"You're a Bengals fan right?"

"Tried and true, been one ever since the first Super Bowl run in '81."

"Ok, well I got this piece of shit Browns thing finally out of my office, and I'm allowed to put it anywhere in the dealership, Perry said I could."

"Well if Perry said you could, I'm sure it's fine. He's the GM after all, the main man."

"Ok, well go grab a ladder from the wash rack and meet me back up here. Can you do that?"

"Sure, I'll be right back."

I bring back the ladder and we proceed to mount the Cleveland Browns memorabilia that was purchased by Doug Lawrence, and had been previously displayed in Opie Cunningham's office for all of his customers to see, directly above the stall where everyone sits and shits at in the men's bathroom. It was the only place in the dealership Opie thought the clock would look nice at, *in the shitter*.

"There, not in anyone's way and not distracting, that's what they said I could do and it's done. That should do it, thanks Guy, I'll buy you lunch next week sometime."

"No problem." He always says he will buy me lunch whenever we get his cars washed up quick, but he never does. It's fine, I don't really care either way.

"Now, when Lawrence goes in there and takes a dump after a long weekend of eating Chernobyl's from Toto's—maybe he'll melt that clock off the wall, I love it!"

"He eats Chernobyl's?" The thought of someone actually eating one is hard to picture, those things are not for the weak. I imagined the whole process from the point it enters the mouth, down the throat, to sitting inside the stomach. Then whatever chemical process takes place after that—surely some sort of toxic lipid is formed in the large intestine and expelled into the atmosphere at a later time. I don't think Opie is too far off from the truth, he may very well melt it off the wall someday.

"Oh heck yes, he eats them like they are candy! The guy is into all that hot stuff, he's taking a few with him tomorrow for the game, probably chow em' down while we're tailgating beforehand. I told him to keep those things on lockdown until we can get outside. The guy is just a freak of nature, but I like working with him, he keeps me pumped up and on my game, and me for him as well, I'm sure—we feed off each other."

Opie and Doug did have a serious rivalry going on at work, where the ultimate goal was to beat each other's sales records *each and every* month. Yes, sometimes they stole each other's leads, or *accidentally* misdialed a number on a customer that was not theirs to call in the first place. Those are just the little cut-throat tactics that every salesperson has up their sleeve, and nothing's taken personally. It was also nice to see them actually get along after work, when it was time to clock out and play nice together. Just like that Looney Toons Coyote and Sheep Dog cartoon—for eight hours they beat the shit out of each other, but at five-o'clock they punch out and are just like old friends again.

Sharing life experiences, sharing their passion for sports. (Even though they hated each other's favorite team.) It really didn't matter in the grand scheme of things anyway. Doug would do anything for Opie, and Opie the same for Doug. It was true, they needed each other to succeed. And, they proved it month after month.

That is why I intend to share my discovery of what I saw in the bathroom mirror with Eric, the one thing that will perhaps complete his puzzle. Just like Doug and Opie, Eric and I need each other to succeed. If I can do something for him, something that gives me nothing in return, an unselfish act. Then maybe, just maybe, I'll be rewarded with another door. It's worth the risk, what else do I have to lose?

Eric needs to know the exact time, an index, a starting point— and we can get it now—the Cleveland Browns memorabilia *was a clock*, and it's still mounted in the same spot that Opie Cunningham and I put it not so long ago; right above that shitter stall and in direct view of the mirror. Not only that, I intend to present a plan of action. A plan that will help Eric LaRoche come face to face with the man who was somewhat, if not totally responsible for him being where he is now.

24

REANNON WAS BUSY taking in the snippets of other people's lives with the quarter that used to me mine. All you had to do was hold the coin right at about your heart level, or about where your heart level used to be that is, and just flip through the scenes like a movie or a book. Once you've experienced a snippet and moved on to the next, whatever you just watched was wiped off the coin for good. If you wanted to join in on the fun before all the snippets were gone forever, all you had to do was jump in the person's head while they were looking at it. That's what Eddie and Austin were doing, they were going along for the ride inside Reannon's head.

I tried it for a few minutes, didn't seem all that interesting. Some of the snippets were of little kids playing with other little kids, and just being, well, stupid little kids. It really didn't seem like entertainment to me, more like a camera that had been left on and we were just watching the film roll on the screen.

There was one snippet that got a little more interesting though—one of the kids caught up to the ice cream truck coming through the neighborhood, and used my crappy coin to buy a drumstick. Now this guy, the Ice Cream Man, had some serious personal issues he was about to deal with. He had a wife and *two girlfriends* he was trying to juggle on the side, a real player this one was. Girlfriend-one was now pregnant, and it was just about to go down with the wife. She had just found out about everything that's been going on—it was apparent that Ice Cream Man couldn't keep his own drumstick inside his pants for very long, and he was about to pay the price for it. There was a real life soap opera going on here, and these guys had front row seats for all the action. I never liked soaps, and I'm not quite there yet to be *that bored*. Watching the life of Ice Cream Man with his love triangle *and* love child be presented in my head wasn't really something I cared to see at the moment, so that's when I decided to get out. At some point that same quarter will touch *me*, and they'll be watching *me* in a car driving to Toto's with Cat and Joe, playing Keno, and eating chicken wings. Who knows when that scene will be up, but when it does, they'll know that the quarter was mine. I really didn't want to be around for that. Eric stole the coin from my pocket and gave it to Reannon for whatever reasons, and I was asked to play along, so that's what I'm doing.

I jumped out of Reannon's head and got back to my own non-reality life. Eric was still there standing alone in the shop. I guess he just wasn't into any of that drama the others seemed to like. He was a thinker and a planner, you could see it. While the others were in there watching the trials and tribulations of everyday folk, I thought this to be as good a time as ever to present my plan to Eric. But, first I needed to see if I could find something we used to use in here, a tool *sort of,* back when I was still alive and worked in this very same shop we stand around in all day.

"Better be glad you're not witnessing any of that!" I said to Eric.

"Well, that's what they like to do to pass the time, everyone's got their thing. Thanks for playing along too bro, sorry I grabbed that old quarter off you."

"Well, I'm sure you have a plan. Speaking of plans, I have something I want to share with you, but first—can we actually open these cabinets and take things out? Like tools and stuff?"

"You should be able to, that's what I'll do sometimes around here, just start throwing around objects that aren't attached to the building and breaking shit. It helps me relieve stress, way better than watching some little snippet of some random person's life."

"Cool, ok so let me see. . .I used to work right about in this area, so should be this one here." I said putting my hand on one particular cabinet, I'm pretty sure it's the one we kept the loose junk in back during the breathing days of my life.

Eric points to the cabinet I was referring to. "This one?"

"Yep."

Instantly, the front of the cabinet was ripped off, looked as if it just exploded on its own. The wood just shattered into a million pieces and the contents inside were now exposed for all to see. Nobody even touched it, as far as I could tell. It was *divine demolition*.

"I'm pretty good at that, aren't I?" Eric said, he had obviously been the one responsible for getting the door off the cabinet like that in such dramatic fashion. "It's the little things that make this place more tolerable, I have been perfecting my demolition skills for quite a while now—I can smash things up pretty good huh?"

"Hell yes! That was fucking awesome!"

I start to root around in the cabinet. I was looking for a tool we used to use. It didn't take electricity, and I hoped it would still work in this world. But first I had to find it; I really needed it.

We used to have to mix up this special glue, it was for reattaching the rear view mirrors. Every once in a while we would get a little aggressive while cleaning the inside of the windshield, arms would flail around, heads too, and we would sometimes knock the rear view mirror off with these appendages—not just off the attachment point— the whole thing *including* the attachment. I actually knocked one off with my forehead once, let me tell ya, that didn't feel good at all.

There was a repair kit for these mirrors, but you had to mix up the glue, it came in two different parts. Once these two parts combined, the glue formed a bond that was so strong that it could hold up the weight of the rear view mirror attachment point and you could hang the mirror back up. The problem was always the timing, you had to wait exactly three-minutes, any longer and the glue became too hard, any shorter—too weak. It had to be just right. The one thing that Cat, the old school detail man, would often have in his stash of tools is things you would never think to use for cleaning cars. He had this plastic spatula, the kind you use to flip burgers with on the grill, which he would use to get down in the nooks and crannies of the windshield.

He could get things out that had been stuck *deep down* in the windshield crack for years with that thing, and he used it every day. If it ever came up missing, he would go crazy trying to find it. He once walked over across the drain and placed a newly hired employee into a choke hold (who he thought had stolen it) and said, *"where's my muffuckin' spatula muffucker!"* When you heard those *two* loud "muffucks" you knew Cat meant business. Turned out to be one big misunderstanding and soon things were back to normal, *but wow*—he sure as hell never liked losing that thing. That new guy never showed up the next day either.

One other item he converted from home to shop use, was an egg timer. The kind with the sand in it. He would use it to time the curing of that windshield glue perfectly. It was the right "tool" for the task. This sand filled, three-minute egg timer is what I was looking for, with that I can beat the system here, I could keep a pace, and track the one thing we can't track in here—*time*. Once I get my starting point, or my index, I'll be ready to keep track of time again. This timer doesn't take any batteries to work, it's just an object, one of many items still left in the dead world here. The glass, the plastic, the sand, it's just. . .

Well it's just—*right there*. I had finally found it.

"Here we go, now I got it," I said.

"Looks like an egg timer."

"Yep, we can keep track of the time now."

"Well, I hate to break it to you bro, but how can you keep track of the time with that little thing? Does it even work?"

I turned it upside down to start the sand moving. Hopefully, the gravity is the same as it is everywhere else on the planet, no matter what world you happen to be in. As far as I can tell *it's working correctly*. The sand moves normally and it seems to be about the right amount of time. Exactly three-minutes for every granule of sand to flow from one glass bubble to the next. Flip it over again, six minutes have passed—then once more, that's nine. If you keep doing that, you can count time for as long as you wanted. Need to be somewhere in exactly an hour? Flip it over twenty times—*that's an hour*.

"Looks like it works," Eric said.

"Sure does, now—remember when you asked me earlier—*if we could just know what time it is now?*"

"Yeah, I remember asking you that. Do you know how to find out?"

"What if I said I did?"

"I'd tell you to keep telling me about it, so keep going bro."

"What if we could time it just right, and go in that shop bathroom at exactly three o'clock, on a workday. Who do you think we'd find in there?" I asked.

"V. *fucking* Simms, that's who, that's his three o'clock high afternoon shit break, you even said you could set your watch to it, didn't you?"

"Yep, but there's more Eric, I can get *the real actual time too!* All I need to do is go back in that customer lounge bathroom up front where we were before, then look in that mirror. There is a clock in there, I know this for sure, I saw it there—it's a digital one and it even shows the day of the week! Hell, I even helped put it there! We go in and get the right time, then make Austin flip the timer for as long as we need it to be flipped. He's your goon right? He would do anything for you right? Well, just have him focus on that one task, and I'm sure he'll give us an accurate count of how many times he has turned over the egg timer. We just do the math in our heads and we got the exact time of the day if we want it, what do you think of all that?"

"I *really* like that plan. I'd also like to see that fat fuck Simms one more time too. I've got something for him."

"Like what? There's no chance that the real live people on the other side of that mirror can see us? Can they?" Eric stood there and stared at me. I could tell he was liking my plan and all, but he also had this shit-eating grin on his face.

"So, they can? See us? Are you serious?"

"Well, this is between you and me ok? I feel us connecting here and it's good. I think if you help me out here, you may even find another door to walk through for yourself."

"That's not really what I'm after, but if it happens it happens I guess."

"Ok, well, here's the thing—everyone is right about Austin—that goofball has been poking his head in just about any mirror he can find. We both have, I have him get his focus going, then I'll get behind him and look in too. We have been testing some things out, with just animals for now, you know like all the cats he says he likes? Oh he does like them, and they like him too. We think we've found a way to make these cats react to Austin's goofy little boyish face peering through the mirror—*we're getting through to these cats!* It's worked, I just know it has, they can *see him.*"

"Are you serious? Let's say it does work—what the hell do you plan on giving V. Simms once you see him, and he sees you?"

"I want him to see my face, he knows who I am, he knows what happened to me. I just want him to look into my eyes one more time, nothing else, that should be enough."

"Yeah, enough to send him over the edge."

"That's what I hoping for."

25

YOU WOULD BE surprised how many hands a coin will pass through in its lifetime. I don't know how long they were all just sitting there watching the little slices of random people's lives, maybe for an hour or more, who knows for sure. I was too busy using my newfound tool, the time keeping tool. I had flipped it over sixteen times, so they must have been watching for at least forty-eight minutes according to my egg timer. It was nice to keep track of time, even though it was a crude method by just flipping the timer over again and again. It was still a major achievement in this world.

Reannon, Eddie, and Austin started to come out of their weird little trances, so I had to put my new toy away for now. They either finally got bored, or they ran out of material to watch. If they ran out of material, then surely there would be some questions, and I was ready for them. It might be something like: *"Who was the guy with the black jelly beans for teeth?"* or *"Who was the man with the fuzzy head of hair?"* These could possibly be asked of me, especially when they find out that the quarter they were extracting all their entertainment from for the past hour, came from, and ended with a little snippet of me and my former co-workers one day at lunch.

"You missed a couple of good ones Guy!" Austin said.

Ok, so maybe they didn't get that far.

"It finally ran out, there is nothing left on that coin. We drained it!"

"Nothing huh?"

"Nothing, the last thing was a mother and her kids in some dirty blue mini-van going through a McDonald's drive-thru. The mom grabs the quarter and the thing just falls in the crack of the seat, end of story, end of all the stories."

"Sounds like it was one hell of a movie night," I said. "Whatever happened to Ice Cream Man? I bailed out right when the wife found out about the affair with girlfriend-one and the baby."

"She beat the shit out of him," Eddie said, "it was reverse domestic violence, at least the kind where the woman would have been going to jail instead of the man. She took a pan and hit him right on the side of his face, blood everywhere! Eric, you would have loved it!"

"Sorry I missed it, too bad the images are gone forever. . ."

Not only are those images gone forever, so are the images of the last person to touch the coin, which was me. I wonder if Eric can control that too? He must have done something to the dirty quarter that sat in that seat crack of a blue mini-van for at least a couple of years before being re-discovered by me. It's too bad they couldn't see any of my awesome Keno playing skills, or the Cat Man, or even Jelly Bean Joe, but at least I don't have to explain anything.

"So where is the quarter now?" Eric asks.

"Ree still has it, don't you?"

"Yes, I'm keeping it too, even though it's erased and ugly. I'll still keep it, as a gift from you guys, that was nice of you to think of me, really, it was."

"At least you can hold things better than Austin, he is a clumsy ass, drops everything. We still haven't found out what your unique skill is yet have we Austin?" Eddie said.

Reannon answered. "He just likes us and his cats, and if that could be a unique skill, then that would be his. You don't need to have a unique skill honey, I still love you all the same."

Well, I know what Austin's unique skill is, after talking to Eric earlier—it's focusing. He can focus so strong that he can break the barrier between our dead world, and the living world—at least in theory that is—the testing has only been done on animals (*they think they have made contact with some local cats*).

I don't think Eric is letting the others in on that secret quite yet either. The whole looking-through-the-mirror-at-the-other-side thing is still a bit controversial in this world, sort of frowned upon since it gives you such a good feeling. Touches your pleasure center, releases those euphoric feelings, that's why it's so controversial. Something that makes you feel so good *has to be bad for you*, it's just the way we are taught to think.

SO THE PLAN is this, go up into my executive bathroom up front, focus myself into the mirror, look up at the Cleveland Browns clock hanging above the stall, and get the correct day and exact time. That would be phase one, easy to do. We should at least go up and do a test run for this first part. What if we get a starting point, and its Sunday at 3AM? Well ole' Austin would be sitting there for quite some time flipping that egg timer back and forth. Hopefully, we can get a little closer to our target time than that. We then go on into the shop bathroom— and as soon as that last grain of sand falls out of the glass, we get Austin started focusing on the mirror. Eric will come up behind him, then just as V. Simms goes up to wash his grubby hands after making his daily three o'clock deposit, he'll look up and see Eric's face in the mirror and go completely mad. It's a brilliant plan, I really don't see how it could fail. Simms will see Eric, go crazy, be committed to an institution perhaps, then live out the rest of his life in an insane asylum. I can picture this all in my dead mind. There is no way he would ever come back to work, not to a haunted shop with an equally haunted shitter. Everyone is happy, and I can hopefully move on too. It's at least worth a shot. I'll also be thankful that we don't have to smell any of this, because Simms's shit smells like raw sewage, and I can testify to that. There won't be anyone else within fifty-feet of that bathroom, I guarantee it.

I try to do the one-way communicating thing again with Eric, to see when he might want to get all this started. Apparently that only works one-way, his way. After a while I settle into a hum-drum state of mind. I'm almost thinking about asking Austin to show me one of his cat stories. Now that's my definition of being bored right there. The words were about to come out of my mouth to ask, but the instant I thought that, Eric and I were up in the bathroom alone where this whole plan of mine started—he had moved us there. Were we about to start phase one of *the plan?*

I guess I'm about to find out.

26

I WAS STANDING. Looking directly into Eric LaRoche's eyes.

And it was kind of awkward.

There we were again in the strange little space that's usually reserved for personal matters, almost occupying the same area at the same time. I assume we are going to have a meeting of the minds here. I wait for him to say something first, I figured since he did the Tinkerbell thing and moved me and himself up here, that he would be the first to say something. But he just stood there and kept staring. After about a half-minute of this, I throw up my hands and finally say something.

"What the fuck?"

"Shhh—I'm trying to get in your head, but I can't. . . why can't I do that?"

"Because I'm special?"

"No, that's not it—your will is strong. You got some serious fight in you to keep us out. That's a good thing man, you don't want to end up like Austin, he was too easy."

"Yeah, but I'm sure he makes up for it in other areas right?"

"Oh, he has one skill that's pretty awesome, and maybe we'll find out for sure just how awesome."

That would be the focus thing with the mirrors, I thought.

Eric continued to look directly into my eyes, still speaking. "Listen, I want to tell you something first before we get into all this. I need you to keep it inside you and *under your hat* until the time is right. When we're done with what we're doing, I want you to take that paper you have, the one that can show your life after your death, and put it on Ree's heart. You think you can do that for me?"

"I can do that, why after we're done? Just curious?"

"Just do it after we are done ok? If you were planning to share that paper with anyone, she deserves to see first, she's been here for so long. I also have one other thing."

"What?"

"The quarter she still has—I figured out a way to skip over things—jump around *the scenes* you know. I was able to see the part with your friends, at some bar, the guy with the frizzy hair and the other dude. That's why they never were able to see it for themselves."

"I was wondering how that happened, makes sense now."

"Well, there is one last scene on the coin, make sure she looks at the quarter one more time, that's all I need for you to do for me, sound cool?"

"Sure, I got it—one more time, no problemo."

Just as our exchange of words finished, Austin's face suddenly was intermingled along with our own in the small bathroom. "I'm here!"

"Yes, you are *and hello!* Alright here is what we need to do—"

THE PLAN SEEMED simple enough, Eric pretty much said exactly what I was thinking earlier. One thing I suggested though is that we do a quick dry run on phase one, which is trying to set the actual time of day. Everything was coming together pretty damn quickly. I was really hoping when I get the first look at that clock, we'll hopefully have all kinds of extra time to think about how we wanted to execute *the plan.* Eric and Austin agreed, we should go ahead and make sure we can easily get our starting point in time, and to also see how far we are off. If it's too early, like three or four in the morning on a Thursday, we'll be waiting almost twelve hours, and worse yet if it's the weekend, even longer. The service shop is open Monday through Friday, and fuck-face Simms only works then.

Since we are all so fired up about this now, it would be nice to maybe have a few hours to kick back and prepare ourselves mentally for what we're about to do, plus Austin won't have to sit there and flip the egg timer so much either. The easier it is for him, the better off we'll be. I just hope he can stick to the task at hand, and accurately count each flip of the egg timer. He *was* in college before he was brought into this world, so I did have some hope that he could add by three's and count the flips with relative ease.

Even though Eric and Austin were well conditioned and probably don't experience the symptoms of mirror sickness anymore, I thought that I should be the one to do this, to poke my face in the mirror. This was pretty much my idea, I found the clock, and this was my bathroom of choice to use during my time of living, and I knew exactly where to look. Besides, I needed to get more used to looking at mirrors anyway. I don't know what the big deal is about them and I don't understand what it can actually *take from you*. I'm sure it will make me sick on this try, considering that it will be only the second time I've done this.

"Ok, well here I go fellas. I'm going in, wish me luck. . ."

"Ok, good luck!" Austin said being his cheery self. This kid never seems unhappy about anything.

"All right, so here's how we'll do this. Austin, take this." I hand him the egg timer. "Eric is going to make sure you don't drop this either, so don't worry about that."

"Looks like a little hour glass."

"Well, you're not far off. I really wish we had an hour glass, especially if we are way off on the time because it would make things much easier. This is just a way smaller version of an hour glass. Now, when I say the word, oh hell, I don't know. . .I'll just say GO, real loud like that. When you hear me say that, flip the timer over like this, you got it?"

"Got it!"

"Ok, so this is the trial run here, but when I say GO, you flip the thing over just as if we are really doing it, right now."

"Still got it!"

I start the stare down with the mirror. I'm actually looking forward to possibly seeing some real light again. It's making me feel all warm and fuzzy inside too, but that will be replaced with nausea here soon. I'll try to enjoy it while I can. I sit there for about a minute-and-a-half or so. I start to see some light, but it's not sunlight. That's still ok, it just means that someone closed the door behind them when they were done in here. Luckily, the lights stay on in this bathroom all the time or we'd be looking into a dark room. It's that shitty fluorescent lighting too that makes everything look pale and grainy, but it still beats the unnatural light here in this world.

Ahh, now that feels better, everything's coming into better focus now. Yes, yes—*here we go!* I can start to see the porcelain urinal and the stall doors. Ok, looking up above where the clock should be, here it comes, is it payday? It's payday! I mean it's really *pay-day*—it's Friday, and oh man look at the time!

"Ok, GO!"

Austin flips the timer over, and the sand starts to run down the glass tube. We have officially started to keep track of time. Something so crazy, but yet we're doing it in a world where keeping track of time seems impossible yet we *found a way*, and it feels good.

"Well, we have some decisions to make here." I said.

"What? What do you mean bro?"

"Ok, it's not the best case scenario in the world, but it's probably going to be workable. I just wish. . ."

"What!"

"I just wish we had a *little more time*. Austin, remember to flip that over when all the sand runs out, you still with me?"

"Yes, sir!"

"How long do we have before *show time* then?" Eric asked.

"It is 2:42PM on Friday, so we have about eighteen minutes or else we'll have to wait all weekend long before we get another shot at this."

"Guess what?" Eric said. "This is no longer the trial run, it just became the main event. Austin! The magic number is six, you hear me? Six! I need to know when you have flipped that timer *six times*."

"Ok, well it's about halfway done on the first one, so there you go!"

We just achieved something that, as far as I know, has never been done in this middle world. We can plan a future event to happen at a specific time of our choosing. Maybe others before us figured out a way, but I sure didn't see anyone else around here doing what we were doing. We are also about to make some more history here in sixteen-and-a-half minutes, *we are about to scare the shit out of someone!* Someone who's not even dead yet, and lives in the world on the other side of that mirror. A *real live* super-natural moment is about to take place in the *real live* world. A very rare event indeed, I would say. Nothing too outrageous though, just a standard spook job. It's not like we are trying to coordinate the second coming of Christ or anything.

It's the second coming of LaRoche.

"Ok, there's number one!" Austin yelled.

Fifteen minutes to go.

27

I HAVE NO idea where Reannon and Eddie are right now, if I had to guess I'd say Eric has them distracted doing other things. I'm not sure what that would be though. It's not as if we have to do laundry or any house cleaning around the shop. He just needs Austin and I right now, and nothing else that could possibly get in the way of *the plan*. The plan that was now in progress and beginning to move onto the next phase.

"That's three!" Austin yells.

"It's time to move, are you ready for this?" Eric said to me with that quirky smile he has sometimes.

"I'm as ready as I'll ever be I suppose. The question should really be *are you ready?*"

"I'll let you know in nine minutes. Austin and I will move over there now. I'd like to keep the dingle berry boy close to me, so that he doesn't drop the egg timer and break it. It can still break here, so we have to be careful with that. You just walk over, it's not that far anyway."

"Sounds good," and with that they vanished.

I walk over to the shop bathroom now, it's less than a thirty second walk, but why walk when you can just teleport there? I thought about it, but decided to just walk instead. I've only done the poof thing one other time, and I was worried that I may end up in Hawaii since at one time I had thought about going there permanently to live out eternity as a dead man. Come to think of it, since it looks like warmed over baby shit here, Hawaii probably doesn't look the way I remember seeing it in all the magazines anyway, so it was probably a wise choice.

I open the door and walk in. I have not really been in this particular bathroom for quite some time. Just the look of this place triggers a memory in my head and once again raw sewage came to mind. It didn't mix well with the nausea that was setting in from my episode with the other bathroom's mirror moments earlier. I tried to shake it off the best I could and continued to enter. Austin and Eric were already there. Austin still had the glass egg timer in his hand, staring at it intensely without looking away as if someone's life depended on him keeping a hold of this thing (which is exactly want we wanted him to think). Pretty soon he'd have to put it down and start to get focused on something else. Working the mirror, and the timer could get tricky.

"Let me know when you're on the last one, that's number six, don't forget." Eric said.

"Will do."

"You can set it right here on the sink when you get to that, then I want you to do your thing in the mirror. Be careful and don't drop it either. It will break."

Eric should have never said that, he jinxed it. Austin yells, "that's six!" At the same time dropping the egg timer. It shatters all over the floor. The glass and all of the sand were everywhere. The only thing left is the plastic frame, rendering my time tracking tool completely useless now.

"You dip shit! I told you to be careful! Oh well, I guess that's close enough. Start counting in your head like this *one Mississippi, two Mississippi, three Mississippi* all the way up to *sixty Mississippi,* then start over at *one*—do that *three times.* Then let me know when you're done. Go ahead and get going on the mirror too. Remember what I told you? About what I'm going to do when the time comes? You got that Austin boy? This is it buddy, this is what we've been waiting for!"

"Sure thing! Here I go, I'm going in *full throttle* too! *One Mississippi, Two Missi*—"

"Good luck fellas, hope this all turns out the way you're expecting it to. I really wish I could throw up right now." I said, the nausea was kicking in pretty good now. I didn't feel like doing anything at all except watch what happens here. Now this is something I definitely wanted a front row seat for.

28

THREE MINUTES SEEMED like an eternity. This was the most excited I've been since I showed up in this place who knows how long ago. If I were to guess, it feels like I've been here, maybe a week or more? The plan had been going flawlessly up until Austin, who can't even hardly hold a piece of paper because that's just not his thing, dropped the egg timer on the floor and it was now shattered into several pieces. Eric, not missing a beat, had him start to count Mississippi's for the last three minutes. The timing is not going to be perfect, but I know from seeing this day in and day out for the past few months that V. Simms, the man who destroyed Eric LaRoche's life, is going to be walking in that door any Mississippi now.

Austin, still counting in his head, has a look on his face of great intensity. This kid means business and he wants to serve his master well, you can just tell. I wonder if I should jump in the mirror too? Just like Eric plans to do? If Austin can really break the barrier between the living and the medium dead worlds, I wouldn't mind being a witness to that and seeing Virgil Simms's face when he sees Eric LaRoche in the mirror. If we could really record things on those coins, this would be something we need "on coin" for sure. It's going to be historic.

"Where we at Austin?" Eric said.

"Fifty-nine Mississippi, sixty Mississippi, ONE last-issippi, two Mississippi, three Mississippi—"

"Ok gotcha, last one, only one more minute and its three o'clock. I'm going to start getting into the mirror, Guy, you want to jump in as well? You don't want to miss this do you? You think you can stomach it? You feel up to it bro?"

"I already feel like crap from the last one, so why not. I guess I'll just stay nauseated for a few hours, I really don't want to miss this at all!"

I put my focus on the mirror, it barely takes thirty seconds to get inside of it this time and see the images on the other side. I must be getting better at it. Austin finally shouts out the last Mississippi and we now are at three o' clock in the afternoon on a Friday. Now onto the final phase of *the plan.*

After what seemed to be almost a whole minute of all three of us just sitting there waiting in total silence for that door to open and see V. Simms's pot belly walk through the bathroom door, I finally said something (I'm just not one to stand around in silence for too long).

"Hmmm, we must have been off a few minutes huh?"

"Well, maybe we're here too early. I mean he gets here at three, but how long does it take him to finish his business?" Austin said.

"Not long, as far as I can remember, he needed to turn his hours quick so he can make more money. When you take a pay cut to come work here, that's what you have to do, so I'm sure he was very efficient with his time management when it came to all his business here in the bathroom. What do you think we should do Eric, you want to abort the mission? Come back on Monday? We might be able to reconstruct the egg timer by then, you think? We should be able to scoop up all that sand off the floor, I'm sure it's possible."

Eric sat there in silence, not answering my question. He looked like a very disappointed man. It was either that or he was in one of his super-ultra-thinking modes where he just turns everyone off around him and tries to figure *it* out, whatever *it* might be. I'm thinking we might as well abort, I mean, I'm already in for a long bout of nausea as soon as this is all over. Each second I hang out in the mirror, just prolongs that feeling for me. When I'm about to throw the towel in and pull myself out, he pipes up suddenly.

"What's that right there?" Pointing to the ground, off to the side a bit, you have to really put your head almost right up to the glass of the mirror and look to the side to see.

"Them's boots!" Austin screams. "He was already in here doing his thing, holy crap!"

I don't really remember what Simms's boots looked like and there certainly was nothing holy about his crap. However, if there was anyone within fifty-feet of this particular commode at three o'clock during normal business days, it was Simms and only him. He had a reputation for being a sweaty, lethargic, lard-ass who decimated restrooms with his foul sewage like stench. It was his diet—the man exclusively ate fatty meats and starchy potatoes for practically every meal of the day, plus drank nothing but *Yoo-hoos* and beer, *lots of beer*.

"Well, we're about to find out for sure, the feet are moving and the pants are being pulled up. Get ready Austin to turn it up a notch if this is him, stand by my friend. . ." Eric said with more pep in his step and looking more like himself now.

The door to the shitter stall slowly opens and a porky little guy walks out. He waddles up to the sink, looks up at the mirror to examine himself, then runs his hand through some scruffy stubble on his face *first* before washing up—of which I found to be very unsanitary to say the least. There is no mistake who this is, and just in case we couldn't make a positive identification through other sources, his name was stitched onto his blue mechanic's shirt and it reads:

V. Simms.

"That's him Austin, go for it! Make him see me!"

Things go wild in here now. Austin looks like his head is about to explode, but in a pretty way. His face and body were turning into a rainbow of all sorts of colors, mostly blues and reds, but also a little magenta with just a tad of yellow to accent his eyebrows and lips. This must be Austin's *special talent* that nobody knew he had, and it's actually pretty to watch happen, at least for now.

"Look at me! LOOK AT ME MOTHERFUCKER!" Eric screams this as loud as he can while standing directly in front of the mirror and watching the man he tried to murder one night long ago. Simms is the reason Eric is here and he wants the fat bastard to look into his eyes one last time to send him over the edge—*the edge of his sanity!*

"You think he sees him Austin?" I asked, but Austin wasn't responding, all of his energy was going forward, into the mirror—trying to break the barrier. I wasn't even going to ask Eric the same question, he seemed to be doing just fine without any help from me and I didn't want to interrupt his mojo.

"Why can't you see me! WHY!"

I get a fairly good look into the mirror now. With all that was going on inside this tiny little bathroom, it was hard to do, but I managed to take it all in as best I could. This beat any snippet of a random life stored inside a coin, or jumping into someone's head to experience their own life right along with them—this was real, and in real time; not a memory of the past—and it was all going on right in front of me.

The mirror seemed to start turning brighter and brighter as the time went on. *Was Austin about to break through?* If he can, it would allow anyone on the other side of this mirror *to see into our world!* Even if it's just a glimpse, that's all it would take, just a quick fleeting look to make someone believe. Our target today was just one man, the sorry excuse for a human being who goes by the name of *V. Simms* on the other side of that mirror and he was now within our reach.

I can see Simms standing there—*did he see something yet?* I really couldn't tell since there is no audio portion to this spectacle, but his facial reaction—he sort of turned his head to the side like a dog does when it hears a sound it can't quite understand, squinting his eyes as if he was trying to pull something into focus. *He saw something, I'm sure of it.*

"Hey! I think it's working!" I screamed.

"That's right motherfucker, you look at me! Where's your baseball bat at now you cocksucker!"

Some pretty colorful language coming from someone who is trying to earn a door and move on, but I think it's actually justifiable at this point.

"Ok, Austin—here I go buddy—I'm going to do it NOW *three, two, one—!*"

What happens next is more than I could have ever imagined was possible in the world I live in now. I knew Eric was a strong soul, not only with the mind control he had over others here, but with his incredible strength too. The cabinet in the shop where the door had been ripped off is an example. That door had been shredded into a thousand pieces without him even touching it. I'm sure it could have been just opened up like normal, but he wanted to show me what he was capable of, and I'll admit I was totally impressed with the feat.

Eric raises his arms up, at the same time Austin moves out of the way, and he punches the glass mirror with a force so strong that the ground actually shakes under my feet, at least the place where my feet were when I had a human body for them to be attached to.

Eric broke the mirror.

The mirror shattered into tiny shards of glass that now lay all over the floor. It was impossible to see the initial impact from Eric's hands to the glass, the flash of light that followed was so brilliant that I was totally blinded for a few moments. Once I got my eyes back, my first look was of complete amazement. A gaping hole in the wall where the mirror once hung that you could see right through to the living world. I suppose you could say that Austin and Eric made their own *door* right there in the bathroom, only in this version Eric was hanging halfway in-between with quite a death grip hold on Simms's neck, trying to choke him to death; trying to end his life, his real life. Simms was resisting the best he could, attempting to pry Eric's hands away with his dirty little fat fingers. We were back in the living world with a vengeance now and the living world in ours too—at least Eric LaRoche was—I hadn't decided on what to do just yet, I still needed a moment to digest all this.

Austin was passed out, laying on the floor. We don't sleep here, but he was a totally spent soul now, so no help from him at the moment. I thought that I'd like to get up and help Eric out, but it looked like he wasn't doing too awful bad in the task of choking someone to death. I'd even say he was getting a leg up on Simms, if he would have had a leg to get up. When I thought about what I was witnessing in front of me, it really seemed impossible. Eric, Austin, and I are not human, no bones, teeth, or blood, just pure energy—that's exactly how I would describe our being—but here we were meshing the two worlds together, breaking the laws of physics and most likely several other natural laws in the process.

My former human rational side got the best of me though—I really should try to put an end to this violence before me, and just pull Eric back here into his own world where he belongs. Hopefully, that whole mess of a hole will clear up on its own since I would have no idea how to fix it myself. He doesn't need to continue this fight. What Eric

LaRoche has given Virgil Simms this afternoon should be enough to send just about anyone over the edge. I'd think the best options now for Simms—since he has seen and been touched by something not quite human, is to just go ahead and off himself or check-in to the insane asylum later on today (I think they are open until six), he still has time. Either outcome should be fine. Besides, this has to carry some sort of penalty for breaking these laws of nature. If there is any type of governing body in our world this *has to be frowned upon*, and the local authorities should be arriving any moment now. I sit up and start to walk over to him, but before I could reach Eric's being and pull him out, a couple of familiar voices shout out to me.

"STOP! Don't touch him Guy!"

Reannon and Eddie were back, and they looked like shit.

Eric's influence must have worn off since Reannon and Eddie were standing there with me now, and why did they look like death? (More than normal that is.) I guess I should ask them about that later. Austin was still passed out on the floor and unaware of anything that was going on around him. If I had got up just a few seconds earlier I may have been able to help Eric out of the hole. He looked like he was having his way with Simms at the time, but something else was happening as well—the hole was getting smaller. Reannon and Eddie arrived just in time to hold me back that extra second, if not I may have been caught up in it too with LaRoche as the hole was closing in on him. The scene was not something that any one of us had ever experienced before. Sure all of us had a door presented to us at one time or another, but it was covered up, you couldn't see beyond it, you had to open it, plus you felt like *you wanted to walk through*, like it was instinct. But, this hole thing looked like an open wound in the skin of our world, and it led back to the place where we all came from, where our former human bodies are no longer able to sustain life— unfortunately nobody knew what could happen if one of us actually went through. Would we vaporize and turn into nothing but a wisp of air? Then what? Do we become nothing? It certainly didn't feel like it wanted us in there.

"Stay the heck away from him, it's too late! He'll have to go all the way through!" Eddie yelled. "We have no choice here, if you get any closer it will probably suck you in too, stay back!"

Just like the moment of impact when Eric punched the mirror, a brilliant explosion of light filled the room, and all eyes were blinded by its tremendous brightness. Once it subsided, the place where a mirror once hung was replaced by a cement wall. Nothing was there anymore. Something else was missing too.

Eric.

29

AUSTIN KIMBALL, THE first soul I spoke to in this world, also the kid who desperately wanted to be reincarnated as a black man someday, and someone who we thought was capable of absolutely nothing extraordinary in this world finally sat up. He was coming out of his recent state of unconsciousness, something unheard of here. I think we were all curious on what he had to say about it, since some of us have been awake for a very very long time. Did he dream? If so, what did he dream about? You don't sleep when you're a soul. You're just here, all the time. The other more pressing matter at hand was obvious as well—where did Eric LaRoche go?

"Forty-two Mississippi, forty-three Mississippi. . ." Austin was still counting for some reason.

"Stop! No need to count anymore Austin," I said.

"What the hell guys!" Reannon snapped. "Who wants to explain all this?"

"What happened to *you* Ree? You and Eddie both, you look sick or something, never seen you like this before." Austin asked.

"It's a long story, but first one of you start talking."

"I'll explain," I said, "what you just saw here was all part of *a plan*. We found a way to keep track of a little time and we hatched a scheme to get some revenge, that's all."

"Ok, so what happened to Eric? Where is he at now?"

"I have no idea, you saw exactly what I saw. I'd say he is on the other side of that wall now, but who knows what happens to us over there. How would one expect to live without a living, breathing, human body, in a world for living, breathing, humans?"

"Ok, back up—revenge? Did you say *revenge?* Who could Eric possibly have a problem with here besides us? We don't see too many new souls here. You were the last one to arrive Guy, and so who would it be?"

"Virginia Slims, that's who!" Austin barks out.

"I think you're still a little fuzzy there Austin, Virginia Slims are a brand of cigarettes. We were after *Virgil Simms*, the man who wrecked Eric's life—we were able to figure out a time and a place that he would be. Eric and Austin must have been practicing what was really going to happen, but I had no idea it would turn out like this. I figured we were just going to see if we could get him to see our faces through the mirror and give him a good scare."

"The guy who Eric tried to kill?" Eddie said. "He's not even dead is he?"

"That's the thing, he's not dead, but did you know that Austin has a special talent here after all? And it's breaking through to the other side."

"The Doors! Jim Morrison!" Austin yells out.

"Why don't you go back and sit down for a few Austi boy, I think you may still be a little woozy there. . .you're saying some pretty weird things." Reannon said.

Austin sits down. We're all standing outside the bathroom where all the supernatural drama just happened. We still needed to talk all this out a bit more, and hanging out in the bathroom wasn't where I particularly wanted to be. Especially if Eric ended up actually killing Simms in there, you know what the next thing would be don't you? We'd see the fat fuck standing here, and most likely getting ready to go right on in his door. He knew he was being choked, so there was no instant death and the denial that comes with it afterwards, like we all had. We didn't know we were dead at first, but Simms would have seen it coming.

"What happened to you guys?" I asked. "Did you get caught in Eric's mind tricks or something? Where do you go when he doesn't want you around?"

"Well, sort of I guess. . .what Eric does is move us so far away from here that it takes us a while to get back. Most of the time we don't mind, it's actually kind of fun to see some of the scenery we haven't seen before. You know, walk through some nice houses, things like that. But this time, oh my gosh! I should have known something was up when Austin didn't come along. We were so far away and really lost. We had to resort to putting our faces into some mirrors to get a bearing on where we were. Eventually things became more familiar and we got back as quick as we could."

"Eric's influence must have worn off since he was engaged with something else and couldn't keep you guys away, like choking a *real live* human being in the *real live* world, I'd say that was it for sure."

"Yes, and since we had to actually resort to poking our faces into those mirrors, we're both feeling and looking like hell, more than usual."

"Your color is coming back, so I guess you're feeling better?"

"Yeah, I guess so. . .but—"

"You don't have to say it, I can feel it too Ree," Eddie said staring off with a blank look on his face. "He's gone."

"I don't feel him anymore, anywhere."

Reannon and Eddie stood there face to face, I don't know if they were talking to each other privately like Eric did with me sometimes or what, but you could see they were experiencing something real humans feel. The loss of someone close to them. Even though Eric was a manipulator and rough around the edges, he was a part of this family of medium dead souls for a long time. These people stuck together so that they wouldn't have to live in this place miserably bored and to have some companionship. Nothing is for certain here, and in the process of getting by, a bond was formed between them. Austin got back up and they all three stood face to face. I just stayed to the side by myself, I was new to the group and I felt like it was their moment to have by themselves.

30

I T WAS QUITE peaceful just sitting there by myself. I drifted off into a mode of reflection I guess, thinking about my old life. I wondered what all my old friends were doing now, thought about mom for little bit and then about dad. I hardly knew him, but I did get to see an image of his face not too long ago. It came from deep inside my head, and made me feel like I was really with him, so that was nice.

Am I here to replace Eric? I certainly wouldn't be exactly like him with all of his bad habits of course, but maybe I'm supposed to take care of these lost wandering souls now. They were all still standing together. I was alone, still reflecting back on my old life, when I soon felt a presence come near me. It was Eddie.

"There was nothing you could have done. It was going to happen no matter what, Eric was a determined soul to say the least. We just need to hope he's somewhere where he's happy now."

"I hope so too, I mean. . .I can't understand why he did that, but then again, I can. He wanted to finish what he started."

"That's probably right—that's probably right."

Reannon and Austin came over towards me now, things were a little more relaxed. But still, the mood seemed a bit somber.

"Did he say anything to you? Anything as to why he wanted to risk his being and do that?" Reannon asked.

"Not much, he had a countdown going on right as he smashed the mirror. Everything was well planned out really, I just helped him fill in the blanks and figure out some things, like a starting point on the time, and a place to find the man that he was targeting. That day we went up and practiced on the mirror in the bathroom by the showroom, that's when I found, or actually, I remembered, that I had helped place a working clock on the wall, and it was in sight of the mirror. That was also the time that he took my—oh yeah, I forgot he took my paper from me, took it right off me when I was all up in that mirror enjoying the sunlight, just like you said could happen too."

"Paper?"

"Yes, I almost totally forgot about this guys! This should help, check this out."

I pulled the parchment out of my back pocket, or the place where my back pocket would have been. It was still there too; nobody had taken it from me again. I held onto it even tighter after having lost it the first time, so it stayed put, even throughout all the action that just happened. I took it out and showed them the messages written on the front.

"Put this paper next to your heart, it will share something with you. It works on everyone." Reannon read it out loud. "What does that mean?"

"Oh, this looks just like the paper that strange woman handed to me, that I immediately dropped." Austin said.

"That's the thing that showed you some time after your death date wasn't it?" Eddie said.

"Yes!"

"Well, that's what it does then, don't hand it to Austin just yet, he'll drop it and we'll never find it again!"

"Oh my gosh! Oh my—you think that's true? You think it works like that?" Reannon said. "Did Eric do it? Did he see something after he died? Did he? Maybe that's why he did what he did."

"No, Eric didn't want to do it," I said, "he didn't want to know what happened after, he didn't want to see his wife with anyone else but him, that's the way he wanted to remember things."

"Makes sense to me, I can respect that. I think I'll do the same myself—I don't want to look, I'm fine." Eddie said.

"I'm ready, I'll do it, I'll do it right now too—and I'll let you know if it works, give it here." Austin said.

"I'm afraid the instructions were very specific from Eric, we talked about this, he wanted Reannon to go first. He said that she deserves to know what happened after her death *first*, since she has been here the longest—oh, and one other little nugget too, that quarter, do you still have it?"

"Yes, right here."

"Ok, well hold onto it—he said something about that too, but first are you ready to do this?"

"I don't know, I'm afraid, but I really would like to see my little girl again, even if she ended up with her deadbeat dad. I guess I want to find out she made it ok without me."

"Do you want us to join you Ree?" Eddie asked. "It's fine if you want the privacy, we understand. I'm sure it may get pretty personal and you have never seen it either, so you make the call little lady."

"Of course, I want you all there. Let's see if this really works, how do I do this?"

"Just put it on your heart."

"Like this?"

Reannon Banks – *After Death*

SIX WEEKS HAVE passed since the accident. Cherry Dearwester is being discharged from the hospital today. She had been the last of three women to leave since the night that the vehicle Cherry was driving failed to negotiate a very sharp corner, lost control, rolled three times, and came to rest upside down in a nearby cornfield. Reannon Banks, daughter of Joseph and Mary Banks, and a mother of one, was ejected during the rollover crash and was pronounced dead at the scene. Bonnie Millhouse and Wanda Hill were both released just a few days after the accident, and they remain at home recovering from their injuries.

The sheriff department's accident report stated that the contributing factors were a combination of several things including the prior removal of a stop sign that normally stood at the intersection (which was removed by unknown individuals the same night), excessive speed, failure to control, and alcohol. No charges have been filed yet, a review is still pending on the case. The DA's office is leaning towards *not filing* any charges, but no decision has been made so far.

This indecision with the district attorney's office is possibly what made sixty-eight-year-old Mary Banks suffer a heart attack just days after the death of her only daughter Reannon Banks. Her husband, sixty-nine-year-old Joseph, was not in the greatest of health at the time, but he seemed to be doing fairly well, all things considered.

Mary survived the heart attack, but was now on several types of prescription medication and really could not function like she did before. Life, as the Banks had known it, was about to make a drastic change.

The night of the accident, the elder Banks were delegated the responsibility of watching over their granddaughter, Lilly. As soon as the notification of the accident came, the Banks packed her up and took her over to the neighbor's house. It had been a very long night for the Banks to say the least. They returned in the late morning to pick up Lilly, and continued to grieve the loss of their only daughter. When Mary had the heart attack a few days later and was rushed to the hospital, it was decided that Joseph was in no condition to take care of Lilly on his own. The Department of Children's Services were notified, and Lilly was placed in foster care, at least until things could be sorted out.

CHERRY STILL HAS a long way to go in her recovery. She will have months of physical therapy ahead of her. She still can't believe what happened that night or that Reannon is gone. Even though they were not the best of friends, she still blames herself for what happened that night and has been in a deep depressed state of mind ever since. The therapy sessions are starting to help some, not only the physical aspect but the mental as well. She goes three times a week, and just talks. It's really helping her cope with everything. She has finally started to accept that all this was out of her control.

She thought she was doing the right thing by using the country roads to get back into town. She also felt that she could drive just fine. After all, she had walked the straight line in the parking lot without falling off to the side, not even one time. Her blood alcohol level, taken just after the accident happened at the hospital, was below the legal limit. But still, alcohol was listed as a factor in the publicly released accident report, and she had to live up to that. Including dealing with Mary Banks. Mary was very vocal in the press about Cherry, even though she was still in the hospital recovering. Mary made some pretty harsh statements, not all of which made it to print, but the sentiment was made known for all to read.

THREE MONTHS HAVE passed. Cherry has grown stronger and has been released by her doctor to go back to work. She doesn't have a job yet, but it's such a great feeling knowing that she can start looking for one now, and that things are looking brighter for her. She is getting back on her feet again and it feels good. The DA's office decided not to press any criminal charges against Cherry, even though the alcohol and high speed were factors, she was not legally drunk, and the ultimate cause of the accident was ruled to be due to the missing stop sign.

The phone rings at Cherry's mother's house, where she has been staying ever since she was discharged from the hospital. It's Mary Banks. After the phone call ends a weight is lifted from Cherry Dearwester's heart; Mary Banks called to say that she *forgives her*. The two women shed some tears over the phone for few minutes, and the conversation moves into an update on the Banks's lives—both Mr. and Mrs. Banks are now in an assisted living facility in Belle City and Lilly had been living with a very nice couple these past few months close by in Paris. The nice couple had already started the adoption process, and it was about to be finalized very soon.

Cherry's life was back on track for good.

THE DAY THAT little Lilly had to leave the Banks's house was hard for the six-year-old to understand, and so much had happened all at once. Her mother was gone forever. Her grandmother just had a heart attack, and was taken away in an ambulance. And, now she just sat there with her grandpa, who kind of talked funny sometimes. Ever since Joseph Banks had suffered a stroke two years ago, that's just the way he talked. Lilly thought he sounded like a little kid and she liked it. He also made her laugh out loud with all of the noises that he could make. The van pulls up to take Lilly away to her foster home, but little Lilly and Grandpa Banks still had a few minutes to say goodbye to each other. Mr. Banks hands Lilly her bag of stuff, and tells her that he put something special in there. Also, to make sure she looks for it when she gets to where she's going.

"They're magic beans," he says.

He went on to say that those magic beans hold her mommy's spirit inside of them, and every time she sees them shake around, that's her mommy moving from each bean to the other. Grandpa also explained that if someday the beans stop moving, it just means that her mommy is now up in heaven looking down and protecting her. Lilly was so excited to hear this that she almost got them out right then and there, but grandpa told her to wait—wait to find her *little-beans*—and make sure they make it to their new place with her safely, then she can get them out. She understood, and kissed him on the cheek.

Ms. Leona Beatty from Children's Services stood in front of Lilly now, ready to take her hand and head to a foster home for at least the night, maybe even longer, since things were still quite uncertain at this point. They both walked hand in hand down to the waiting van. Lilly looked back one more time at Grandpa Banks, waved her hand, and spoke loudly. *"Bye bye gran-pa! Thanks for my beans! Wuv you!"*

Ms. Beatty and Lilly walk up the driveway to the house where Lilly will be staying for a while. She asks if Lilly is scared. "No, I have my mommies spirt with me inside my beans." Ms. Beatty thought that was so cute and assured her that her mother's spirit will always be with her, no matter what. They ring the doorbell, the door opens up, and a man and woman stand in the doorway both with warm faces and huge smiles.

"Well hello there you!" The man says, "What's your name?"

"I need to get my little beans out! My name is Lil' Bean. . .I mean Lilly Bean..I, I, I mean Lilly Banks!" She said this giggling uncontrollably for a few seconds, her cute smile came out for all to see. All she could think about on the way over were those beans that she brought with her. She wanted to get them out and at a safe place, so she kept thinking the word *little-bean*, that's what her grandpa called them, and so when the man asked her name, that's just what came out.

It was such a great moment, the first time that this sweet young child who had been through so much tragedy in the past few days, said something so silly and funny that it just made everyone laugh out loud. It was the beginning of a relationship, and one that would last for many many years to come.

"We are the LaRoches, I'm Eric and this is Layla, come on in Little Bean!"

31

We ALL JUST SAT silently. Nobody said too much, a couple of gasps at the end there, but other than that not much else. It was a lot to think about after all, a lot to process in our non-living minds. The loss of one of their own, which was only a few moments ago, was still sinking in as well. Eric had been with this same group for quite some time. Even though he was not always well liked and could be very manipulative, they all considered him a member of their family.

Now this.

It became quite obvious as all of the pieces to the story came together in their heads, that perhaps their initial meeting and the reason that Eric chose to stay with them in this particular place was not random at all. He must have known that everyone in this group would somehow, and in some way contribute to his overall objective here, just another piece of *his puzzle* he would sometimes say. I don't think it was a puzzle at all, it was more like *his* project, or *his* plan.

Reannon still stood silent. She had a lot more to think about here. All of the questions she had about what had happened to Lilly after she died were answered when she placed that parchment up against her heart, but perhaps it only brought up more questions now after realizing that Eric was actually Lilly's adopted father. I'm sure it made her start to think back at all the stories Eric told her about his little girl; all of the fun things that they did together, all of the love that he had for her, and of course, all of the pain he felt when his little girl died. She looked back and cherished those memories now knowing that they were all about her Lilly, and she wished Eric was still here so he could replay them all, to give her one more look at her baby girl. There was a reason now as to why he always covered up her face when he shared his memories with everyone, he was trying to protect her identity.

I'm not sure why he never told Reannon that he adopted Lilly. It could have been so that she wouldn't have to go through the same pain that he went through when she was killed, eventually this would all come out, but I guess he just wanted to put it off as long as possible, who knows.

"I'm ready to look at the coin now." Reannon said, breaking the silence. Even Austin had been keeping his mouth shut all of this time (which was unusual), we all were. We knew this was something Reannon needed to think about on her own for as long as she needed to, without any one of us saying a word.

"Pull it out, I'm sure there is some sort of final message from Eric and I hope it explains all this. I'm really shocked Ree," Eddie said. "I had no idea that he had adopted your little Lilly, that blows my mind. He knew this entire time too."

Reannon pulls out the old tar and gum laden quarter from her being, holds it up for all of us to see, then starts to put it on her heart.

"I want everyone to join me on this," she said. She then placed the coin on her heart and the rest of us joined up inside of her mind to watch the final scene on the quarter. The image came up and it was that familiar face of Eric LaRoche, everyone looked at him differently now, the man who gave Lilly so much love when Reannon no longer could. It made all of the times he was just being an asshole to them for no particular reason, just fade away and be forgiven. She wanted so much to thank him now, but he was gone, and possibly forever. For whatever reasons that we may or may not find out here in the next few minutes, Eric LaRoche had completed his puzzle. His project. His plan. That's all that mattered to him this whole time. He wanted to finish what he had started before he died.

"Hello, Ree. . .it's me. If you're watching this, then Guy did his part. If you're also watching too Guy, thanks bro, it means a lot that you did all that you did for me, really man, it does. Can't forget my other bros too, Eddie and Austin, you guys mean so much to me as well. If I succeeded with my plan, I'm probably not around anymore, or I might be right there with you all and looking like a complete idiot right now, who knows right? To me, that's all in the future so I have no idea how it turned out. I'll just assume for now that everything went down the way I

needed it to go down, and now you know Ree, you know the secret I was hiding from you all of these years. Ok, here we go. . .man this is harder than I thought. Anyway, Ree, I'm sorry for not giving you everything I knew about my Lil' Bean, or Lilly—our Lilly. She was amazing Ree, she really was. Every time I looked at you, I thought of her. I wanted to save you the pain that flows in my heart constantly. Knowing that she was killed so young and by such an evil person, I just wanted to save you from all of that. It's was hard not to let you in, but I think I made the right choice, please forgive me if you think otherwise. I hope I succeeded. I hope I got him, and I destroyed the man who took her from us. There is one other thing Ree, I can still feel her around here! She's got to be close by! If you find her, tell her daddy still loves her, tell her she'll always and forever be my Little Bean—keep looking for her Ree, keep looking." That was it—that was the end of the message. The quarter was now completely blank, nothing else remained.

"Maybe that's what I'm feeling," Reannon said. "Maybe I'm feeling my little girl and that's why I can never go through my door."

"Could very well be," I said.

"Maybe she is here, close by, what do you think?"

Something comes to mind now. On the parchment it's signed with the initials *"LL"*, it's not Linda Lyons, the woman who was killed along with Eddie, and it's not Layla LaRoche, Eric's wife either. Little Lilly, Reannon's daughter! Her last name was changed to LaRoche after the adoption, so I'll bet just about anything that *"LL"* is *Lilly LaRoche!* Of course she wasn't so little when she died, so it's quite possible that she's the same beautiful woman who I call Angel, the one I met out in that barn on the day I was killed, the person who gave me that paper in the first place.

"I think you might be right."

32

SOMETHING WAS CHANGING in our world.

I don't know what was causing it for sure, but I was thinking of some pretty bad things. For one, remember what I said about us most likely breaking some laws? The natural ones? I'm not sure what happens when you break a natural law, but the atmosphere we were in was certainly changing. It seemed to be getting worse while we're still standing just outside of the bathroom door in the service shop area. I'm not sure how it could actually get any worse here, but it was. *It was getting darker*, and that's a bad thing considering there is hardly any light here to begin with.

"Hmmm. . .that's different." Austin said.

"No shit," Eddie said.

Nobody was moving. Just staring around the place, analyzing the situation. I wonder if this has ever happened before? I'd say by the vacant looks on their faces, it hadn't.

I sure as hell didn't want that Simms guy walking out here, then showing off to us by walking right through his door. But who knows, if he comes back, maybe Eric will too. All I know right now is that it's quickly getting pretty ugly here.

"Maybe we should go somewhere else, huh?" I suggested.

Still nothing from the peanut gallery, but something was about to motivate them. And, it came in the form of a new human shaped figure, standing right in front of us now. There is no face to be seen, just like the first time I met these guys. Souls really like to make dramatic entrances don't they? This was definitely a new soul, different than those I've been spending my time with. It's true, you get a feeling from being around them. You can tell who is who, just by the way you feel. Still, this one standing here has a bit of a familiar feel to it, and it should, as the face begins to get clearer now, it's Angel.

"*Heeey!*" I said real drawn out like, as if she was an old friend I hadn't seen in a while. I didn't really know how else to greet her. Last time I saw her, she told me that she could hide her presence from the others, this time I'm pretty sure she let them all see her pretty face, but it didn't last very long at all.

"We all need to move, take us to the field, and now!" Angel said without hesitation. This was something serious, you can tell by the tone, when she said now; she meant…*NOW!*

We move out to the field via Reannon Airlines (the thing where she can move multiple souls around with just a blink of an eye). She should really charge for this; she could make a ton of money. Angel was still with us. I look over at Reannon and notice here staring at Angel. The look is one that everyone has seen before; the look of a mother looking upon her daughter.

They both knew.

"Lilly?" Reannon asked out loud, "—is that you?" She started crying at the same time.

"Yes, mother—it's me."

The two figures combined as one now, a supernatural embrace I guess is what you'd call it. When they touched it was as if miniature fireworks had been set off or like sparklers all twizzling and dancing about on their skin. Come to think of it, I don't think I have ever seen any of us physically touch, so this must be the result of that action. It was pretty beautiful to watch. Not only the cool little light show, but the warm embrace that they shared. This must be how you really *get together* and get caught up on everything that's been happening in your life, once again a very effective and efficient way to communicate between each other. It was a mother and daughter reunion, a bond that never breaks, not ever, not even in death.

Even after the semi-long hug, they still held hands. I'm pretty sure Reannon didn't want to ever let go again. She looked as happy as I had ever seen her. Her smile said it all. They didn't say too much to each other after the embrace, they didn't need to. In an instant those combined souls exchanged everything Reannon needed to know about Lilly, her life before, and her life after, and she was now complete.

Why Lilly needed us to vacate the shop building so quickly was not quite clear. The more than usual drab lighting and overall doomy vibe that everyone felt was what I was thinking, but it also could have been just the aftershock of the ripped hole between the two universes—I mean that couldn't have been a good thing right? Certainly a plausible reason, however, more so than that perhaps was due to the pending evil that was about to join us for a few minutes in the shape of stench ass Simms. But, luckily it didn't matter now, as we were all safe out here in the field.

As I continued to think of all that *bad stuff*, something was happening right in front of us, something really good, actually—something amazing.

It was a new door, but only one. And, who was it for?

I'm not sure how they determine whose door it is when you are in a group like this. I assume they have some sort of system in place, such as drawing straws or maybe it's just taking turns.

"Who is that for?" I said.

"It's definitely for someone here, probably you Guy. You helped Eric get what he needed done, probably for you, do you feel it? If it's yours, you should feel the need to jump on through it." Eddie said.

"Really? Hmmm, I don't know, I guess I'd like to—"

"No *guessing!*" Eddie said quickly. "If you even think of not wanting to walk through then it will go away, even quicker than it appeared—*this one is for you kid!* Get in it!"

"Ok, ok . . .I want to go through, I do! But—"

"No *buts* either man!" Austin yells.

"No, *I want us all to walk through it!* We can do that, can't we?"

"I never thought about it, but I guess we could try." Eddie said. "What do you think Ree?"

Reannon looks at her Lilly. She stares at her grown up face, taking in every little detail, still holding her hand and asks her "will you come with me?"

"I can't—*I've already gone through my door.*"

Lilly now starts to fade away. . .

"I love you!" Reannon yells out to her, Lilly's last image fades off, not in the fast poofy way like before either, more like a fade to black, way more dramatic (these souls like dramatic entrances *and* exits). The last image now gone, she is no longer standing there with us.

"Did she say she already went through her door? What does that mean? We go through and come right back? What?" Austin said.

"She was different, had to be, she could go wherever she wanted. Don't worry Austin, let's do this—let's all walk through this door!" I said. After all it was my door right? So I should be able to invite whoever I want to walk through it with me.

"*I want this door, I want this door!*" I keep saying that under my breath, just in case any wild thoughts sneak by and the door thinks I'm not interested.

"Time to go guys, let's all do this now!"

"I'm scared!" Reannon said.

"Don't be, trust me, trust Eddie and Austin—maybe we'll find Eric, all of us together."

I stand up against the door now, so far it has still stayed there. This is going to work, I can feel it! We line up, I'm first and then Reannon, Eddie, and Austin line up right behind me.

"Here we go!"

I open the door, nothing but blinding white light, you can't see anything at all. You just have to take a leap of faith and take that first step in. "*I want the door, I want to walk through, I want the door. . .*"

I take the first step, my footing still intact. That's a good thing, no sudden drop off. What a cruel joke that would be, a huge drop off right when you step inside, but that's not happening now. I take one quick look behind me and still see the others, and they are still right there. This is going to work! We are all walking through the door! The second step is just like first, solid ground, but now I can't see a thing. Complete white out situation, absolutely no forward visibility. Wow, this is amazing, I even feel a little different now too, I feel like. . . I feel like I have a really bad headache?

Yes, that is pain, I'm sure of it, just one of those garden variety headaches, but a headache it is. I haven't felt like this since back in the good old days, when a nasty hangover was setting in. If all I'm getting is a headache out of walking through this door, then I'll just march my happy ass out. But I can't. I can't make myself go backwards. I keep moving forward, I guess I've gone past the point of no return now. I should check behind me to make sure the others are still there, but I can't even turn my neck now, it's completely stuck, locked into place. This doesn't feel like a happy ending at all, *this door is broke!* Feels like I'm starting to fade away into nothing, *but wait. . .*

What's that smell? I haven't smelled that since. . . *just a second*, has Cathy Barlow been here? I know that funky funk anywhere. I worked with that woman for six months, and for all six months that's the smell I was exposed to, it was that unique. The light is still blinding me, but now coming into more of an elongated shape, like a couple of shitty grey fluorescents, just like in the bathroom. Why am I back in that place again? I hope not. I'm supposed to be moving on, just like the beautiful woman promised me at the very beginning of this journey. And, I want to move on—not end up in a bathroom with shitty fluorescent lighting and the essence of Cathy Barlow permeating the air. I'd rather go back and take my chances in the middle again than have to go back to that.

But I can't. I'm here now and I realize just where here is. I'm not even standing up anymore, I'm laying down. I see another familiar face, it's my mother's. She is standing over me, along with some other unknown person, and the look on their faces seem strange to me, it's a look of amazement or maybe even shock.

"There we go now, he's coming around Mrs. Bishop."

I need a drink. Not a drink, drink—I'm just really thirsty, just like what Cat said before we wrecked in the car, and I think to myself:

My mouth dry as-a-muffucker!

33

I HAVE WATCHED the shows on television before. The one's where someone was clinically dead for who knows how long, usually just enough time *not* to get brain damage, and then miraculously come back to life. After all that's done, they write a book about the experience, and then talk about it on these stupid shows. Some of them are very convincing, some are just making the shit up, you can tell. Most of these freaks were only *dead* a few minutes and they have all these elaborate stories to tell. I do find it quite entertaining sometimes but to me, it's just that—entertainment.

As I lie there, things are starting to come back to me, my brain is getting back on line again. The first thing that I become aware of would be exactly what you would probably think, *what the fuck happened here?* I'm still alive, I know this now. I'm breathing on my own, I'm extremely hungry, and I'm really really thirsty.

My headache is getting better, the fluids being pumped into my body are helping. My senses are starting to come back as well. I can start to focus on things around here with my eyes. It's a hospital room, there are flowers all around, planters, balloons, all kinds of knick knack crap. This can't all be for me can it? I hate knick knack crap. It just looks like a bunch of clutter spread about the room. This stuff must be for mom, speaking of which she is still sitting next to my bed. The other guy must have left, I don't see him anymore. The funk of Cathy Barlow is still here though, and I'd say with some confidence that she's been in the room recently.

"Sweetie, can you hear me?" Mom says. "The doctor left and is going to be right back with some other doctors. He said you're the miracle boy!"

I can hear all this, but can't seem to craft a response. I try to at least give a groan or a moan, or even a small grunt, but that's not happening yet either. Just then mom grabs my hand, and I muster up a squeeze for her.

"That's it honey, squeeze my hand, oh Guy—I'm so glad you're waking up! I thought I had lost my little boy!"

I wish I could say something, it would be something along the lines of asking my mother to stop calling me a little boy, I'm almost a grown full-sized man now, but I guess it's ok, just a few minutes ago I thought I would have never seen her again. The feeling is coming back in my legs now, my arms too, my neck is still immobile, I must be wearing one of those neck braces to keep it from shifting. Overall, recovering here nicely I think, all things considered.

A couple more people show up now, nobody that I really know or even recognize. They start looking at the machines in the room, then look at me, then look back at the machines. I might be part cyborg now for all I know, the sixty-million-dollar man or something. I can barely hear them speak, all the words sound like medical jargon anyway, so I can't understand anything they are saying. One word did stick out though that I have heard before, the word *coma*.

This very scenario went through my mind at the very beginning of all this. I thought that if I at least stayed active in my head, that hopefully these doctors would see that, and not give up any hope on me.

One of the doctors now starts shining his little flashlight thingy right into my eye, both of them, one after the other, it was very annoying. Then someone else ran some feather thing down my leg, which didn't tickle at all, it made me want to itch it, but no way to do that all bound up like this. I was starting to get pissed. This time, I was able to push out something, a nice long grunt of say about three seconds in length, and the place went wild with excitement.

"Guy, can you hear me? Say something—anything—can you do that grunting sound again?"

I not only was about to produce another sound for this asshole, but I was ready to form a complete sentence that he could write down in his report as the very first words I said after waking from my comatose state: *"Stop fucking with me!"* But what came out was something that was just as incoherent as the first grunt I made, but maybe with a little more volume.

"All his vitals are stabilizing. We'll need to do a few more tests but all his motor functions should come back with time, including his speech," one of the white-coats says to my mother. How does he know everything will come back to normal? Everything isn't normal inside here, inside my head, I still have all the memories of what I just went through, and *that was not normal.* I was in another place, one with other people just like me, who had passed away, but had never moved on. How did I get so lucky to come back?

For now, I just lay here and try to think. Remembering how to talk again would be a good start, I'll need to tell my story. Or should I? Not so sure anyone would believe me, even on one of those stupid television programs devoted to this very subject. I'll have to really think about that. I zone back out for a while and when I zone back in, the sun is shining through the window. Oh man, what a sight! It must be morning, and here I am alive again, how cool is that? I look around the room and see my mother sleeping in the chair beside me. I try with all my might and power—I pull back and really try to get this out, I can do it, just like being a baby again, really dig down in the head and pull out the baby words, worked before, should work again right? I take a deep breath, the air flows over my vocal chords and out of my mouth—
"Mommy!"

My mother wakes up out of a dead sleep, looks over at me, jumps up and gives me a hug. I actually formed a word, probably one of the first words I ever said as a little baby, but that's where we are at now.

Baby steps next.

34

THE MORE TIME that went by, the better I got. I guess that white-coat dude was right, things did start to get better. Every day, new people would come visit me, and each one had a special talent. It was just like when I was dead—the people on my trip beyond this known universe— each had special talents there too. But, the talented people here now are helping me to sit up, stand, walk, talk, and even how to use the bathroom again. I guess for the record (I may not have been able to talk a whole lot, but I was a great listener), I was not actually *all the way dead*, just in a really deep coma. I got little tid bits of info here and there from the docs when they talked to each other. When my communication skills fully come back, I'll ask the serious questions and hopefully get some real answers.

I have been peeking at some things as well, one day one of the white-coats had left his little note pad beside my bed, I could pick out some of the words, even within the medical jargon and sloppy penmanship. *Head injury* and *seven minutes* were the only words that made sense and stuck out the most. The seven minutes was underlined twice, so that must have meant something really important to these people. Is that how long it took me to get to the hospital? Doesn't seem that long at all, maybe it was how long it took for them to bring me back, *maybe that's how long I was really dead for—ewwwww . . .creepy.*

Seven minutes dead? Hmmm, I certainly felt like it was longer than that. As the days kept ticking by, the more I was able to think back at my little adventure there being medium dead. I started to question if it was even real. It sure as hell felt real to me, as soon as I was able to focus my eyes and speak coherent sentences again, I asked my mom to grab something for me. A phonebook.

She thought it to be quite an unusual request, but did end up bringing me in a phone book from her house. I immediately flip to the white pages and start looking up names. The one I thought of was Kimball, there were three in the directory, and one had a Spruce Avenue address. That's what Austin asked me the first day we met, if I knew any Kimball's up on Spruce Avenue. This could possibly be his family, but a random call from a stranger asking about their dead son is not something that I think they would appreciate, so I decided against it. There has to be other ways to find out, to see if the stories they told were true. If they were, my little adventure was real, all I needed to do was look up the stories, surely they were recorded down somewhere. There's always an official record of death right? And surely there would be at least a little newspaper story about it. Some of the stories I sort of half-assed knew about, like the kid that stole the car and killed Austin, and the two crosses planted on the road for Eddie Chapman and Linda Lyons, so it's possible that my active brain could have just made up the stories around the stuff I already knew. I needed more information, and it wasn't going to happen until I got out of this place. This hospital room.

I'm ready to blow this popcorn stand, I need out.

Who do I talk to about that?

35

I THINK TODAY is the day. The day I get to go home! Has to be, they are taking all the flowers, planters, balloons, and knick knack crap out of the room. So this must be it! As they pull some of the other planters out of the way—something is revealed, it's quite a peculiar looking plant to say the least.

"Where is that one from? That weird looking red plant there, never seen anything like it with the whiskers sticking out, kind of looks like a cat or something. Who gave us that?" I ask my mother.

"Oh, that's from your friends at work. The one lady with the red hair stopped by and I met her out in the waiting area, she brought that over."

"Red hair? From work? Oh, well that's got to be Cathy Barlow." I *knew* she had been here, but sounds like she never even came in the room.

My mother grabs the planter. The plant growing out of it has thin stem bottom with very vivid and colorful petals, and the cat whiskers sticking out make it look pretty unique too. As she swings it over so that I can read the card and take a closer look, something hits me hard. It's the smell. That's *the smell*—the tang of Cathy Barlow, but not quite to the point of spoiled rotten fruit just yet, it was getting there, maybe a couple more days in this low humidity hospital room and dry heat, then it would be just about a perfect match. (I asked my mother to just go ahead and get rid of that one.)

The card read: *Hey Guy, hope you start to feel better soon! We all miss you! The gang at Bill Bradley! P.S. These are my own special prayer plants I grow in my greenhouse, they will help your spirit heal as well as your body, God Bless…Cathy.*

That explains a lot there, at least I now know the source of Cathy's funk, it makes it more palatable knowing that the source is from organic plants and not actual body odor. If I ever get back to the shop again, I'll feel better knowing that.

I GET ALL set up at my mother's house, she had the neighbor help her get my old bed out of the basement and set back up in my old room. I have to stay with mom for at least three months or so, since my walking was still not so great, and I needed help moving around. I don't think my mom cared either, she felt needed again, and that made her happy. There was a small fund helping with all these extra expenses now, and the insurance company was paying for most of the medical bills. I hadn't been to work in almost two months, so I don't even know if that job is still waiting for me.

So much mail and crap to go through, most of it is from attorneys. The ambulance chaser types, trying to solicit my business, they'll take my case on for free and will sue everyone imaginable if needed. One of the random letters I had opened up even wanted to sue the property owner who had put the garage up beside the road. I'm really starting to think that most of these lawyers are fucking idiots. I threw most of that crap away. Another random letter I opened was from the hospital, even though I don't have to pay a dime of this, and anything I do pay for out of pocket can be reimbursed, this statement has the most numbers I have ever seen on a bill. The amount due is *six digits long*, yes—*six*. It is amazing how much it costs to get put back together. Even though this stuff is wildly overpriced, they did a great job, and I am eternally thankful to the staff at Big River Valley Hospital, they saved my life.

Now, you ready to hear some gory stuff? I thought so. The eight weeks in the hospital was a time of reflection for me, and also a gathering of information. Mostly from mom and a couple of the nurses who said they saw my story on the news. I have finally put all the pieces together of what happened just after the crash.

Since I was the only one not buckled into the car, I was the one most seriously injured. It wasn't the impact of hitting the outbuilding that did all the damage, it was the sudden stop. Cat and Joe survived the accident. They actually walked away relatively unharmed. The seat belt law has been enacted in Ohio for about eight years now, and Cat, who was one of the most law abiding citizens around, required all the front seat occupants to wear safety belts. I didn't wear mine since I was seated in back, but really I should have been. The sudden stop thrust my entire body up and over the seat, and my head directly hit the windshield, fracturing my skull. I had hit so hard that my heart stopped beating and I had stopped breathing. If I had been in the front unrestrained, I'm sure the result would have been more like, I would say—permanent death.

Now, death did have something to do with all this. It was true, I had been *technically dead* for seven minutes, that's about when the ambulance arrived and was able to get my heart beating again.

Now, the gory part is coming up.

For those seven minutes that my body lay there dead, there was someone who didn't give up. Someone who refused to see me lay there and die. Someone who, that until a few days after I had woken up in the hospital, I had no idea could even do this. It was Joe, he was able to perform CPR on me at the scene. Joe Meadows kept the air flowing and the blood pumping through my body. He never gave up. Ok, the gory part is this—*he gave me mouth to mouth!* (Yes—*think about that one,* but make sure you have not eaten your lunch yet.) The jellybean teeth and dirty ashtray mouth right up to my lips—makes me want to gag right now thinking about it, and I believe I just did. But really, I shouldn't be complaining about anything at all. The man helped save my life, preserving it, he never stopped until the professionals arrived and could finish the job—I owe him big time.

I had not seen anyone from work since the day of the accident, mom said they were at the hospital while I was still in the coma, but had not actually come in the room to see me. Today, that would change. They would be here in about an hour, my mother had set this all up. It would be the first time I have seen them in almost two months, it will be the first time I get to thank Joe Meadows for saving my life. It would also be the first time I get to see his black teeth again and be reminded that they were up against my mouth for almost seven minutes. (I'll try not to think of that so much.)

The doorbell rings and my mother answers the door. It's the gang from work, well actually just Joe and Cat, Cathy is not here, she is probably going to be late. My mother walks them into the living room where I'm set up for the day, and their eyes light up. Mine too, these guys are a sight all right. Cat, who wears dentures anyway, has a huge white big tooth smile a mile wide, and who could forget that frizzy gray hair sticking straight up. It looks a little longer than usual today, but that's because I have not seen it for a couple of months and it's grown out some. Joe, unfortunately, is smiling too and all you see are those black things stuck there, quite the contrasting smiles, but I just take a quick glance and then it's back up to his eyes, big blue ones, and they are welling up with tears. I instantly get all choked up too, this guy saved my life.

"Got-Damn! Guy—you look good muffu—"

"Language!" Joe interrupted. "Remember, we're invited guests at Guy's *mother's* house, watch the m-f's Cat!"

"Ah rah, sorry. . ."

"Thanks, guys—thanks for coming over! This is awesome!"

"Well we're still missing one, the late one, she said she'd be here, she said she had to go..."

"Go take her old man somewhere?" I said interrupting Joe.

"Yeah, probably! She did say she wanted to see you, we all miss you man, how you feeling? You're still slurring your speech a little, you been drinking already? Just kiddin'!"

"Oh, yeah—I've been getting wasted all day long, nothing else better to do. No really, it's a lot better, all I could do before was grunt, so since I'm actually able to communicate with you now, even with this slur, it's a thousand times better than when I first woke up. Everything else is coming back together too—finally!"

"You need to get your ass back to work now. We told muff—I, I, mean we told Perry we ain't gonna be hiring anyone new back in the rack till' you said you ain't comin' back! So we'll hold these muff— we'll hold them off hiring anyone till then." Cat said, shaking his head side to side each time he almost let out his two favorite words, or I guess it's really just one word the way he pronounces it. I had to hand it to him, he was doing a pretty good job of controlling his profanity.

"I'm up for it, I love working with you guys—it might still be a while though. I'm talking a few months at least, if you guys need the help, don't worry about me, you can hire someone else if you have to. You can tell Perry that too, I know he is the GM and will do what he wants anyway, I get it."

"Well, if we do have to hire someone, we'll kick them out as soon as you want your job back, won't we Cat?" Joe said.

"Oh hell yeah we will!"

We talk for a few more minutes, I get through my heart felt thank-you to Joe, for saving my life and he gives me a big hug after that, and of course he still smells like a big ashtray. It didn't matter to me—if it wasn't for him, I'd still be—*dead*. Well, technically *medium dead*, or was that even real? I still have not done a whole lot of research on that yet. It's not as if I haven't been thinking about it, it's been on my mind this whole time. I do have a way of confirming an event that happened while I was away in that world, the day that we broke the mirror, the same day Eric LaRoche went missing in our medium dead world and the day he tried to kill Virgil Simms. There was finally a lull in our conversation so that I could ask the random off topic question.

"Hey, you remember that short stubby mechanic that worked up in bay 2? I think his name was—"

"Muffucker's dead! Ooops—sorry!" Cat interrupts, I guess just me mentioning something about the short stubby mechanic in bay 2 recalled an exciting event that happened while I was away. I knew the profanity free hour would be over soon, but this was a big deal. I don't think my mother could understand him anyway. Really, the way he says it so fast like that, I think it was ok. Cat tries to contain himself by sort of whispering it to me. *"That big ass dropped dead in the bathroom, the one he stink up every day too."*

"Are you serious? How did he die?"

"He had a heart attack." Joe said. "He just got done doing the thing that he does every day at three o'clock, and then just drops dead. You know how nobody will even go near that area, especially at that time of day right? Well, I guess Smitty over in bay 6, which is at least fifty feet away from the door, hears this loud crashing noise, I guess it was crazy loud too. Nobody wanted to go in and find out what it was either, the smell you know, pretty funky and all. Well I guess someone decided that in the spirit of human nature that they would go in and investigate, so they put some shop rags over their nose and mouth and went in to see what had happened."

"So what did they see?" I said.

"Just saw that Simms guy laying on the floor dead. He must have fell straight forward too, the mirror was shattered, pieces of mirror all over the floor. They called the squad, but it was too late. I could have gone in there and tried to do what I did to you with the CPR, but did you know that guy killed someone? A young woman, few years ago, dude was a drunk. I know I'm one too, but I ain't never killed anyone. I just acted like I didn't know what was going on, looking back I kind of feel bad, but—"

"Don't," I said, "I knew about that too, he wasn't worth it, trust me." I didn't elaborate any further about how I knew, as far as he knows, I found out the same way he did, just through the normal gossip channels at work.

"So, they confirmed it was just a heart attack that killed him?"

"That's what the news said, just a plain old heart attack, at least he didn't take anyone else out with him."

"Yeah, no kidding, man. I never went in that bathroom before and I'm definitely not going in there now, probably haunted now, you know?"

"Eh, I'm glad the dude is gone actually, and I can use that bathroom again. It still stinks, always has, but it's a lot closer to us and way more convenient. I don't believe in any of that crap anyway, that haunted crap. When it's time to go, you just go—and it must have been his time to go."

"Yeah, I guess so, but I'm still not going in there—that just creeps me out."

Well that's either quite a coincidence, or—

I decided right there, that my adventure was real. The things Joe described as happening match up to what I already knew. The reality was setting in, I had been dead for only seven minutes and that must have been enough to get me there, but the coma *kept me there on the other side the whole time*. It really did happen as far as I was concerned so this changes everything.

WE FINISH OUR catch up time, I was starting to get tired, and the doc said not to fight the fatigue and just to get as much rest as possible. Cathy never showed up, but that's ok, I'm sure we will run into each other soon. I would really like to go back to work with these guys, they almost seem like family to me now. It will be a while though; I still have a long road ahead until I'm fully recovered. Until then, I plan to keep on searching for the answers I need. I'm working on my own puzzle now. The one where, if I solve it I may find an old friend waiting around for me to show up and say hi.

I might just find Eric LaRoche.

36

I T'S BEEN ALMOST eighteen months since I walked through that door in one world and woke up in the hospital in another. Did you hear what I just said? It's amazing isn't it? Eighteen months, I can track the time very easily now. The sun comes up, it goes down, and then comes back up again. The clock on the wall tells me the time, all I have to do is look at it. These are the things that were void in my little extracurricular adventure into a completely different universe—and to this day I have not told another soul about it living or dead.

It turns out the wash rack gig at Bill Bradley's was not going to work for me after all. I went ahead and sent in my resignation just a couple of days after the guys stopped by to say hi and see how I was doing, I think they actually knew that when they saw me, I mean, I had just learned how to walk, and talk again. I'm sure they just didn't want to say anything at the time, and I sort of knew as well that it was probably going to be the last time I saw them for quite a while, but it was nice that they came over that day. I'll try catch back up with them soon if I can, at least I hope to.

So with not having a real job to go to every day and simply collecting free money from the taxpayers in the form of short term disability checks, I ended up having a lot of time on my hands, probably too much time on my hands.

I have at least tried to make good use of it. I tracked down everyone's story in the newspapers, which was a pain in the ass to do. All that searching and searching, my eyeballs were severely strained from trying to read all that tiny writing. The library has every edition of newspaper since the early 1900's on this stuff called *microfiche*, but you have to read through them all on these tiny backlit screens—only if someone could figure out a way to put all that information onto a computer or electronic storage device, then have a way to search it with one or two words, the whole time while you sit at a desk in your own home. Now, that would be an awesome invention for sure, it would save *so much* time—maybe someday.

Then, as I sat around watching television, which was a part of my normal daily routine, something inside my bruised brain clicked. I don't know where it came from either, but it was very clear to me. *Why not just go out and learn something new?* I can't really do physical manly labor to make money, at least not anytime soon, so I just did it, I had mom take me to the community college and I enrolled myself into a few classes. I wasn't going for a full blown degree or anything, I just wanted to get a few credits in, that's all.

Today that would hopefully pay off, as I had an interview at Bill Bradley's at one o'clock, for a position that has come open. In a totally different department from where I had been working before.

I'd like it to be known that laying around collecting money from the government is certainly not my first career choice. I do still need it while I continue to get better, and I'm thankful that I live in a country that can provide that, but now I'm ready—I'm ready to get back and actually become a productive member of society. I'll leave the professional bumming to all the Frank Barlows in the world (that's Cathy's husband and he is all that and more).

My interview was at one o'clock in the afternoon, but I was ready at nine in the morning, I'm so ready to get out of this house. I love my mother to death, but once you've tasted the freedom of living on your own, it's hard to go back to living with someone else, especially a parent. Just something about being able to walk around naked in your own place that has a bit of an appeal to it, not that I ever did that sort of thing while living on my own, but it was nice to know I could if I wanted to.

I ARRIVED EARLY for the interview. I was meeting with Bruce Westfall; he was the current F&I manager at Bill Bradley Chevrolet. This is the department that handles all the financing, insurance and extra crap you buy for your brand new purchases that you may or may not even need. I got the idea of applying for this position, once it became open, from someone I met, someone who is at this time missing from the universe (at least that's what we are led to believe).

Eric LaRoche had been the F&I manager here for many years, way before I even thought of working at this dealership. He talked extensively about his job sometimes, with nothing else better to do in the medium dead world that's just what you did, and I thought it sounded like something I could at least give a try some day. So that's what I'm doing here now.

The job opening is right up my alley for what I had been studying for in those college courses—*business stuff*—but also it had an element of sales, and that's really where you made your money. It would be my job, if I actually get the job that is, to convince people who just got a loan for twenty-thousand bucks or more, to just keep adding to the balance owed by purchasing a package. They had all kinds of packages to choose from, like rustproofing, paint sealant, scotch guard, security etching, extended service contracts—you could buy them à la carte, or bundle up and save big. No worries either, they just add it to your loan so you can go into even more debt. The shit will practically sell itself, how much easier could it be?

I was about thirty-minutes early so I decided to wander around the van showroom for a while to kill time. Thought I'd check out some of the new models that had come in since the last time I had been in here, which was probably the day of my orientation, and that was almost two years ago by now.

Maybe it was the standing up and walking around that was building up fluid in my neck or something, but the tie I'm wearing was starting to feel too tight. I used to wear one of these back when mom and I went to church every Sunday, but I'm beginning to think it must have been a clip on. I don't ever remember it getting tighter as the day went on. This was a real one alright, and if I got this job, I'd have to wear the thing every day. Luckily mom knew how to actually tie a real tie, because I couldn't get it right at all, it looked more like a fancy knot whenever I did it.

I had thought about going over to the wash rack to check in and see who might still be working over there, but that would mean walking through the service shop and past all the grease monkey mechanics. I think a few of them still worked there that I used to say hi to every now and again and who would probably recognize my face if I walked by, and that would have slowed me down. They all knew the story of what had happened with the accident and all, I'm sure it was a topic of conversation every day for a while there, so if all of a sudden the kid they sort of knew from work who was killed and then resurrected again is walking by, well then they might want an autograph or something, or at least want to chat it up for a minute or two, and I only had about thirty-minutes to spare until my interview. It was probably better just to hang out here in the showroom for a while, so that's what I did, maybe if I have time later, I'll head over there.

Now, if you don't work at a car dealership and you stand around too long, eventually someone wants to sell you something, no matter if you're buying or not. I had to keep this in mind as I had been wandering around aimlessly for about ten minutes. I was most likely being staked out and sized up too. That's how these salespeople work. They watch you from afar, study your body language, maybe even try to read your lips, not trying to decipher personal communication or anything, just wanting to see if certain key words come out of your mouth, the words that tell them that it's okay to approach you, and if there is any indication that you're interested in the product—*you were buying it today!*

I walk around a brand new Mark III conversion van, which was strange why it was even in here because this indoor showroom usually only housed *Bradley Designs*, that is of course the conversion line that Mr. Bradley owns, so wouldn't it make sense to push your own product? Especially when you have to pay to heat this place.

I remember these Mark III's and how I hated cleaning the interior side windows. But, it looks like they have actually changed the design of them, how about that? It looks a lot easier to clean, too bad I'm not back at my old job, we'd probably have to celebrate that.

As I admire the truly brilliant design change for this conversion van line, I notice a figure approach me from the left. I don't bother to look over or acknowledge the presence, this is probably just a salesperson who has finally caught up to me and decided that my time has come. Perhaps they are noticing the look on my face, I suppose I am displaying some sort of pleasure, I mean, I'm finally here, out in the *real* world, looking for a *real* job, and I'm very confident things will go my way today, I just know it.

"Hey bro." The figure says. What a way to greet a customer I thought, but then I also thought of someone else who greeted people like that. Used the word *bro* all the time—surely this can't be that person, right? I look over and it is someone I know.

"Oh, hey Opie! How's it going?"

The face was instantly recognizable to me, it was Ronald Howard. This guy has been here for eternity, probably ever since Bill Bradley opened his doors in the 1960's. He is the number one sales guy in this place, a real people person, he never forgets a face, had a firm handshake, and he knew me, how could he forget? I'm the one that helped him hang the Browns clock up in the bathroom that one day.

"Wow, it's Guy right? You remember me don't you?"

Well of course I remember Opie Cunningham, he must think I had amnesia or something. I did sustain a brain injury in my accident, but it really only affected my motor skills, not my memory, and besides I just said his name back to him.

"Of course I remember you man, how can I forget Opie Cunningham?"

"You look great! You back in action in the wash rack? You sure aren't dressed for it I see, you in sales now?"

"No, no, I'm interviewing with Westfall in a few minutes. I'm looking to get into the F&I department. I've been off for about a year and a half now."

"Oh okay, getting into the back end product—yeah, yeah, good idea. Way to expand the horizons for sure. Damn, has it been that long? Just seems like yesterday seeing your picture in the paper and on the TV news, you were the poster child for the religious folks for a while there, coming back from the dead is a big deal, but you look fantastic now and it's good to see you standing here."

"Thanks, I hope I can pull this off, I'm sort of nervous."

"Ahh, nothing to worry about, you got this. I will tell you this though, if you want to make the big bucks, sales is where it's at my friend. Last year I pulled down *a hundred-grand* from this place, and this year I'm on track for the same, how about that? That's some serious coin, ain't it!" You got to love these sales guys, they have no problem disclosing their annual income, and to just about anyone who wants to listen to them gloat about it. I get that sales is one of the higher paying jobs around here, but there is also a lot of throat-cutting activity involved, these guys practically kill one another for a sale, and I'm just not that way. I would get swallowed up by all the bigger fish around here and would end up out on the street, I need stability, that's what I need.

"Well I do hear you are the best, and it sounds like they pay you well for that. I'm hoping to get into something with a little more room for advancement, and an opportunity to help people get the right product to protect their investment."

"See, you got it Guy, that was great, you just go in there and blow Westfall's socks off, say that shit right there that you just said, and you're in man!"

I guess that did flow off the tongue pretty nicely, it felt good coming out too. You know I think I might be ready for this.

"Well hey, I gotta go, I'm actually on my way over to F&I to check on one, I gotta a five pounder in the works. That's *five-thousand-dollars gross profit bro!* Yee haw! Drinks on me at Toto's if I get them rolled— you want me to let Westfall know you're out here waiting?"

"Nahh, I still have about ten minutes until the interview, I'm cool— but thanks anyway. Good luck on the five-pound thing too, I really hope you get that done."

"Allrighty man, hey and good luck to you too, maybe someday I'll be headed over here to talk to my ole' bud Guy about some deals, can't wait man. . ."

Ole' bud huh? That's who everyone is to Opie Cunningham, you're his good ole' bud until you get in his way and he needs to cut your throat to make a move that will only benefit himself. That's how you really make over a *hundred thousand dollars* a year as a used and new car salesman in this business. I can't blame him for being good at what he does I guess, everyone has their talent, and selling cars no matter what, that was Opie's.

I T WAS FINALLY time to head into the F&I department and find Bruce Westfall. This is a man who I never really saw a whole lot when I worked here before, but I sure did hear his name all the time being blasted over the public address system loudspeakers around the dealership.

Just as I think that, the page tone goes off and then you hear some desperate sales manager scream over the phone paging system, probably trying to find out what's going on with his five-pound deal and needing to talk to the man who can make it happen. *"Bruce Westfall dial extension three-three-two, Bruce, three-three-two, customer waiting. . ."* Followed by the sound of them struggling to hang up the phone. It's never a clean hang up, the sound of the handset hitting the phone cradle is so annoying and it just echoes all over the place, you can even hear it bounce off of Mabbit's Carry Out's brick wall, a quarter mile down the road. Then not ten seconds later, another page goes off: *"Ronald Howard you have a call parked on sixty-one, Opie, pick up sixty-one..."* It's all part of the ambient sounds of a real live working car dealership, eventually, you get used to it.

Bruce is still on the phone when I get to his office. He waves me in and so I just sit down in one of the chairs until he is ready for me. The phone conversation is very interesting, at least this side of it, the one I can hear. It's not quite heated, but you can tell someone didn't get approved for a loan, or maybe they were having to change a deal up, and Bruce was hearing all about it.

"Well if you would put more into the trade-in, Dave, this deal would probably work...what do you mean? Do you want me to come over there and do your job too? Ok, then...that's what I thought, send them on over..."

That was about the end of the call there. I liked Bruce, he didn't seem to take any shit at all. He kind of reminded me of Eddie Chapman in a way. He was a numbers guy too; he knew his stuff. Bruce was also part of the Bill Bradley mafia, not the real mafia, that's just what we called them when they would be strolling around the dealership, it would always be the same three guys, Mr. Bradley, Perry the GM, and Bruce Westfall—so he was definitely in Mr. Bradley's trusted circle, and that could possibly mean something down the road, maybe I could someday squeeze my way into that circle, you never know.

"Sorry about that Guy—just a minute." Bruce picks the phone back up again and dials a number. "Yes, they are on their way over now, ok then—yep—good luck." He hangs up the phone, stands up and shuts his door. I guess the interview has now officially begun.

"So, you're the *Miracle Boy*."

"The what?"

"*Miracle Boy*, that's what they were calling you in the newspaper. It doesn't offend you does it?"

"Oh, no, no—I must have missed that one, I don't really read the paper too much. I think my mother mentioned that to me before though, I didn't know they were calling me that, but I guess it does fit."

I wasn't lying, I really didn't keep up with the current news, I did read some articles about the accident in the *Daily Call*, but never heard of this *Miracle Boy* thing, that must have been published in the Christian newspaper that the Lutheran church puts out, and I never read that one.

Bruce continues. "Yeah, that was crazy, I remember the day it happened. That was a big shocker around here, I heard it on the radio. They hadn't released any names, but once they said the people involved in the accident were Bill Bradley employee's, we were all like—what the heck!"

"Oh, wow, yeah I guess it would have been something to hear."

"We had a prayer chain going on for you in our church, and well, looks like it worked! Here you are, right in front of me, praise the Lord!"

I started to think, is this guy going to go all *Holy Roller* on me now? Was this interview just a way to get some face time with the *Miracle Boy*? Listening to Bruce on the phone earlier and the way he talked to people, he didn't seem the type at all, he seemed like a very direct man, borderline hard ass for sure. Most Christians I know are pretty laid back and have a tolerance for everyone, including people that irritate them. The sales manager on the other end of that phone conversation was definitely irritating Bruce the way it sounded. Then as soon as that door closed, Bruce Westfall the Christian man turned on, and Bruce Westfall the asshole turned off.

I just sat there with a deer in the headlight kind of look, so maybe he caught the vibe.

"Oh, my wife would have killed me if I hadn't said something to you about that, when I told her I was interviewing you for a job in my department today, she was excited to hear about it, she just loves a happy ending to a bad situation."

"Oh, that's fine, I totally understand that—and uh, thanks—I guess—for the praying and all, that's cool that you did that, you didn't even really know me then."

"You're welcome. Do you mind if I ask you something first before we get started?"

"No, I guess not." I said.

I bet I know what this question will be. . .*wait for it.*

"What was it like to be dead for seven whole minutes? Can you tell me what you saw, if anything—I mean wow, it's amazing that you're here right now isn't it? Aren't you grateful for what the Lord has done for you? Giving you another chance?"

Bingo! There it is! The number one question that people ask me ever since I came back from the dead, at least the people who know my story that is. One of these days I am just going to unload on someone and tell them the truth. The truth being that when you die, as long as you know you're dead everything will be fine, but if there is any doubt as to your demise, well then you have a lot of work ahead of you, and in a place that has no sense of time, no natural light, no sleep, no food, nothing but yourself, and if you're lucky enough, other lost souls to share the pain and sorrow with. It's not as pretty a picture as they paint it, I guess the Catholics are pretty close to figuring out what that middle death experience is all about, they call it Purgatory. Well, I got one for the Catholics, or anyone else who has interests in the supernatural community—*you have someone unaccounted for*—and he may very well be walking among the living.

I think about it for about a second, but decide that Bruce Westfall is not the man to hear any of this. He seems like a perfectly decent closet Christian man, and I don't want to take that away from him now. I just give him my standard prepared response anytime someone asks me that question.

"No, I sure don't. I don't remember a thing."

37

THE INTERVIEW WENT quite well I thought, we were able to cover just about everything I could think of. I gave him some good solid business minded answers, and if I were him I surely would hire me. I was impressed with myself too, I sounded like a pro.

I was also able to ask *him* a question about Eric. I have not been able to really talk to anyone that knew the souls I was with, who knew them directly, so it was interesting to hear Bruce talk about Eric LaRoche when Eric was *a human*.

Bruce Westfall had taken over as manager when Eric was let go, and he remembered him well, talked about what a great man he was, adopting Lilly, then how depressed he was in the final days. He tried to get him to go to church with him and his wife or at least talk to someone about it all, but he was just too stubborn to do it. It sounded so much like the medium dead Eric I knew, but of course I had to just say he was a friend of my mothers, and that's how I knew him.

The holiness wore off Bruce as the interview went on too, he spoke and acted more like a business man rather than a pastor at a church. I might have even heard him almost drop an f-bomb, it was close, he caught himself, but I knew what he was going for. He wanted to lay one out there, but he probably thought he'd better not use such heavy language in front of the *Miracle Boy*.

We finish up with the small talk, and I head out the door and back into the showroom, Bruce walks out with me, didn't really expect that, but I thought that was nice of him to do.

"Well, I hope I get the job, I'm sure I'd make you proud, but no pressure, you need to get the right man or woman, and I understand if you—"

Bruce cuts me off, just as the door closes behind us and we are standing in the indoor van showroom alone. "Oh, shush—you got the job, congratulations! You know your stuff and I can't wait to get you going. I think you'll do great here—can you start next Monday?"

"Well, uhhh, yeah sure, only thing is I still don't have my driver's license back yet, I have to take the test again, so I need to make sure my mother can bring me but I'm sure it's no problem at all, man this is great! Thanks so much Mr. Westfall!"

"It's Bruce, and you're welcome."

"Bruce, ok yeah sure, no problem."

"Ok, great, next Monday, eight-thirty, just come here, same place and I'll have your office all ready to go. It's not really an office, more like three walls and no door. You have to get to my job first before you get any doors, but you never know—maybe someday!"

It's strange that he talks about doors like that, like I need to earn it, and I hope to do just that one day. I will need to *earn that door* on my office.

"Oh, one more thing, I don't have to do that silly orientation thing again do I? You know, the one where they do the slide show and tell you all about the Bill Bradley story?"

"I'll tell them to skip that for you since you already had to go through it once before. I can save you the pain of that again."

"Great!"

"Ok, we'll see you next Monday, congrats again Guy!" Bruce shakes my hand one last time and then heads back through the business office door. At the same time, the page tone goes off and its Opie Cunningham's voice over the loudspeaker: *"Bruce Westfall, dial extension two-one-two, Brucey, two-one-two..."*

That was an interesting sounding page, I don't think I'll ever call Westfall *Brucey*, that sounds like something only his mother would say to him. No wonder he doesn't like Opie all that much.

I STILL HAD some extra time before mom came and picked me up. I told her to give me at least three hours so she'll probably be around in, I'd say about another hour. All I have to do is look at that clock right there on the wall, or just look at my watch and make sure I'm standing out in front of the showroom at four. I never used to wear a watch, never thought I needed one, time is easy to keep track of, at least it is now. I wear the watch now so in case I ever find myself in the supernatural situation I was in before, at least I have something that shows the current time. I don't know if it will work there, but it certainly can't hurt to wear it now.

I stroll over across the street to the detail shop, my old work area, I'm wondering who still works there and who they replaced me with. Should be interesting to see. This will also be the first time I have shown my face in the place since I was on the other side of that mirror, the place where I roamed around as a lost soul trying to find my way back, even though I had *no idea* I'd actually be coming back.

I get through the service shop undetected, which was nice, they probably didn't recognize me wearing a shirt, tie, and dress pants, I'm sure they just thought I was a new salesman, which worked out great. I also walked right by the *scene of the crime*, the shop bathroom. Before I leave, I might just suck some fresh air into my lungs, hold my breath, then walk in there to check it out one last time, see if there are any clues that may have been left behind, maybe see if I can *feel anything* in there.

I walk through the door for the detail shop and right off the bat, I see two people I don't recognize, but over on the other end of the shop I see a familiar one, Cathy Barlow.

I head down that way, in the center of the shop, right along the drain, the same place that Joe Meadows would deposit three-hundred or so cigarette butts per week and twenty pounds of hacked up lung butter each and every morning. This grate covered drain always had a sour tangy smell coming out of it, not like the raw *ass-sewage* you would expect, more like a muddy field after a rain storm. It brought back memories of when I worked here. I got about halfway down through the shop and I hear Cathy scream.

"Ohhh my God!" Cathy recognizes me, even in my white collar business attire, she drops the hose that she had been spraying a car off with and heads over to greet me. She gives me a big hug. She looks different too, something about her has changed. It's quite obvious too she looks like she has lost a few pounds for one, and something else—*the smell*, her signature foul scent, it's no longer present.

"Oh my God!" She says again. "How have you been Guy! You look great! Oh my God!"

"Great, thanks! You look great too, you lost some weight haven't you?"

"Oh, thanks for noticing, yes—almost thirty pounds!"

"Awesome, good job! Looks like you're still here working hard at it too, where's the rest of the old crew?"

"Well, Cat retired about a month ago, Joe got another job, and now it's just me and those two clowns over there. I'm still here, plus I'm important now, they made me the supervisor! Can you believe that?"

"No, I can't, that is actually *unbelievable*, how do you manage with you know, the late thing and all?"

"Oh now! I wasn't late all the time! I'm much better at that now. Wow, look at you! Oh my, what are you into here? You a salesman now?"

"No, just had an interview today, and I got the job, over in the business office, the F&I department, I'll be working over there with Bruce Westfall, I start next Monday."

"Dang! That's great! You're moving up into the big time! You going to be part of the Bradley mafia now? Rubbing elbows with upper management?"

"Oh, probably someday, that's my goal at least."

"Well good luck, sounds great, don't forget to come back here and say hi every so often, or I guess we'll see you when you mafia guys stroll through here every month."

"Sure thing—so you said Cat retired huh? He wasn't that old was he? He could retire?"

"I think he just had turned sixty-five. He came in one day and said he was going to go *grab some hairy* for the last time, just got all his trinkets, his spatula, all his personal stuff he hid here from his wife, you know all the letters from his girlfriends over the years, and then headed out the door. Haven't seen him since."

"That's crazy, and Joe?"

"He got a job at Hartzell. He had been trying to get in there for months and he finally got the call. Now he makes airplane propellers and gets a decent paycheck."

"Good for him, I don't blame him—maybe now he can afford to fix his teeth, you know?"

"I think he did that already. I saw him at the festival last weekend and he has nice white teeth now, just like Cat had, a big mouth full of dentures. Hartzell must have a great dental plan."

"Good for both of them. Well then that just leaves you, and look what you've accomplished since I've been gone, you were chronically late for months, called in at least once every two weeks, and they still made you the boss of these wash rats, now that's pretty good right there Cathy, that's quite an achievement."

"It's stressful though having to deal with the sales department, and the body shop wanting to get stuff done in here too. I've had to really try and make it here on time, plus I still have to work just as much as I did before. That's why I've lost all this weight, plus I can't grow my prayer plants anymore, just not enough time in the day."

"Oh, yeah, hey thanks for the plants and the note, I just remembered you had sent those over to the hospital, geeze that was almost two years ago—time sure does fly, don't it?"

"Sure does, speaking of which, I better get the suds off of this one, it was great seeing you Guy, I really mean it, you better stop over and say hi, now that your back."

"Oh, I will!"

I say goodbye and Cathy gives me another hug just before I get out of there. It was weird not smelling *the smell* from her anymore, but at least it wasn't body odor all that time when I worked with her, it was those things she grew at her house, what did she call them? *Prayer plants?* What the hell is that?

WELL, ONLY ONE last thing to do on this side of the dealership. I'd like to go inside that bathroom and see the exact spot where it all happened. The place where a natural law of the universe was broken. That law existed to keep these two worlds apart, the living, breathing, real flesh and blood world, and whatever we were on the other side of that mirror. I walk by Smitty's bay, he's the mechanic who heard the loud crash coming from the bathroom in the first place on that day. He had his head buried inside the hood of a van, so he never even saw me walk by. I open the door, and this place still has a bit of an everlasting assy odor to it as I push the metal door and go inside. Once in, I look around and see that the mirror has obviously been replaced, looks like they might have even given this shithouse a fresh coat of paint too. I look down at the ground, then back up at the mirror. I wonder if I stare at it long enough, could I see into the other world? Just like what we did the day Eric LaRoche disappeared? Nahh, that's just silly, besides I have already tried that at home, and I never got anything out of it except a headache from staring at the mirror for so long. But, this one might be different since it was the same one that we used before, or is it? The original mirror shattered into a thousand pieces, but still...this is the same exact place, and this is exactly where Virgil Simms died. We should paint a cross right here on the floor so everyone knows that, knows that some fat, potbellied, convicted vehicular homicidal ass-clown, died right here.

And I wasn't so sure it was from a heart attack either.

38

"DAD!"

This is how I wake up now.

My weekend days usually start with my youngest daughter screaming that word at the top of her lungs, and almost directly into my sleeping face. It is quite an eye opener to hear that. I no longer enjoy the semi-dream world right before I officially wake up for the day, the place where I could be whatever I wanted to be and do whatever I wanted to do for that brief moment in time. The sandy beaches and nice soft dreamy waves have all been replaced by an eight-year-old little woman with a natural bullhorn attached to her mouth—it's eight o'clock in the morning and she is hungry, and only one thing will do. Timbits. Those delicious, sugary donut holes that you can only get at your local Tim Horton's.

"Dad! We need Timbits!" This is a small but very demanding little person, and as much as I'd like to just stay under these warm covers, I will comply with her request.

It's funny how I feel about time now, I keep an eye on it. I never lose track *ever*. I am on time anywhere I go, and if I'm going to be late, I know just how late I'll be. Time will not be my enemy anymore, not ever again, I am in control now.

It will take me exactly nine minutes to drive across town to Tim Horton's, and at this time of the morning on a Sunday I can expect to wait for at least six minutes before I can even pull up to the speaker to order those forty assorted Timbits with no chocolate, extra strawberry, and two large black coffees.

We named this little girl with the veracious appetite for small donut holes Emily Lynn Bishop. We have another daughter too, Holly Rae, she is three years older, and is more into cereal and milk for breakfast. She'll even get up and make it herself, and that is just fine with me.

I have been married now for almost fourteen years to Christine, who is the love of my life. Remember that job interview I had? Well that was seventeen years, eleven months, and twenty days ago, and for all these years, almost twenty of them total, I have only worked for one person, Bill Bradley.

Christine Adkins was just another customer coming in to sign paperwork for her recent automobile purchase from Bill Bradley Chevrolet on a Wednesday evening back in May of 1999. I sort of knew what her situation was ahead of time, it was pretty easy to do since I had her credit application laying on my desk. I sure didn't see a Mr. Adkins listed anywhere, and she was cute to boot. I felt like I cheated in a way, already knowing she was single, had great credit, and no children, at least no dependents were listed and that pretty much meant the same thing. Most guys trying to meet women at a bar or anywhere else for that matter don't have the luxury of a fully filled out application, so I really felt ahead of the game in that regard.

From there it was your typical love story, I asked her out—she said *yes*—I asked her to marry me—she said *yes*—she told me we're having a baby, I said *a what?*

No, actually it was the best thing that ever happened, Holly Rae Bishop was born and life as we knew it changed forever. Then just a short three years later, a Timbit eating, loud mouthed, and highly demanding little lady followed. It's just me and three women in the house these days, and we're living the *American Dream*—a big porch, a big yard, and a big mortgage.

One other good thing for me about having two daughters is that I don't have the pressure of naming a son after me, like my grandfather and father did before—so as far as I can tell, there will be no Guy Bishop *the Fourth*, sorry to all the other Guy Bishops before me, it's just the way it goes sometimes fellas, luck of the draw, a flip of the x or y chromosomes; fate. I guess it's still possible to have another Guy, but seeing as I just turned forty-six years old and had the ole' boys downstairs retired two years ago via an easy outpatient procedure called a *vasectomy*, that's probably not going to happen.

To think that none of this could have ever happened is quite scary. Nineteen years, eight months, and one day ago, remember, *I was dead.*

I sure have never forgotten. Over the years other memories have faded some, but I still remember the faces, and the stories they told. My search for Eric LaRoche has hit pretty much a dead end, I'd say for at least the past ten years, I haven't even thought of trying to look for him.

So maybe, it's time for him to find me?

The technology these days is amazing, this thing called the Internet is without a doubt the greatest invention of all time, and we have Al Gore to thank for it. I can now sit in my living room, my den, even my bathroom (you knew that was coming), and I can communicate with anyone in the world if I wanted to. No more big cell phone bags either like the tiny faced trooper had the day I was stranded on the highway (I'll never forget that either). You can actually fit a phone *in your pants now*, who would have thought that would ever happen?

I had hoped to use this new way that the world communicates to reinvigorate my search for *the missing one*. In fact, I had been thinking of a plan for a few years now and was about to plant the first seed.

Tomorrow when I get into work, I'll get into my normal Monday routine, voice mails, e-mails—you know, the usual—but at ten-thirty, a news crew is set to arrive in my office, and one of those hot shot reporters is going to interview me: *The Miracle Boy of 1994*.

It turns out, the piece that the Lutheran church put out *did* get picked up by the mainstream newspaper way back when. There had been quite a rash of accidents as the years went by, and a lot of it had to do with those twisty and windy roads. The people demanded that action be taken. Someone wrote a letter to the editor of the *Daily Call*, they published it, and a shit-ton of people wrote back. The next thing you know my story was right there for all to see, *again*, but this time with a much bigger audience. In that story, I was just a wash-rack-dude that worked at Bill Bradley's or I think the actual wording may have been that I was a *service department employee* or something, you know since we wear the same kind of uniforms and *service department employee* sounds way cooler than *wash-rack-pion* when you put it in print.

This renewed interest in my story occurred shortly after I was hired in at the F&I department as a loan closer, so I wasn't even working in the same area anymore. You would think they might have wanted to actually update the story before they published it again, but I guess they forgot. My story of being dead for seven minutes only to be revived and brought back from the dead was told again to the mass reading audiences around the entire metro and surrounding areas. Shortly after, I did get a few whack jobs that dropped by to see if they could have a word with me. They wanted to know what I had thought of the other side of life, specifically the part where you're dead—they wanted to know what I saw, heard, and what I felt. I could have really just made up anything with these dip shits and they certainly would have believed it, but that would've only make things worse, so I just stuck to the basic facts.

That was about it. Throughout my entire fifteen minutes of local fame I still maintained the same response since the accident happened, and stood by it every time—*I don't remember a thing.*

I was surprised these people had even found me. That's back when Cathy Barlow still worked here, she must have just been sending them on over from the wash rack. I didn't really mind this too much, after all I was still in search of someone at the time. It also made me think— if Eric LaRoche was anywhere nearby and had read that article, *he would now know.* He would know that I'm here, and he would certainly want to come talk to me about it, wouldn't he? He disappeared before I made it back so he had no idea what happened to me. That would surely stimulate his curiosity, that is if *he* is even here at all.

This had been around '96 or so, the Internet was nothing like it is today with the super-fast speeds, streaming video, and 24/7/365 news coverage. So really if you didn't see the story in the actual paper edition of *The Paris Daily Call*, which only had a subscription base of about twenty-thousand or so at the time, then you probably still had no idea who the *Miracle Boy* was.

The days wore on after the second run of the *Miracle Boy* story in the *Call.* I was really expecting to see, or at least hear from LaRoche. This was huge exposure I thought at the time, there would be no way he could resist trying to contact me, to find out how I made it back, and with my original body.

But, he never showed.

Or did he? He may have disguised himself as one of the whack jobs that showed up in my office area days after the story ran in the paper, or maybe he just stood by in the shadows, watching me. I guess I had no idea of what to expect, what would he even look like? He had no physical body here in this world to come back to, the original one was cremated, I found his obituary in the paper, that's what his family decided to do with his body when he died. So no chance of walking around as a corpse for him, of which I thought to actually be a good thing.

I GUESS I'M a bit nervous about doing this interview. It's been almost twenty-years since I had my first job interview in this same office. I just try to think of it as another job interview. I really shouldn't be this nervous, I of course am the one in charge around here now, and have been for about ten years. Well, actually nine years, eleven months, and two days to be exact. I remember the day Bruce Westfall handed over the keys to his old desk, saying how proud he was of me taking over the F&I department. Bruce was moving onto greener pastures, I felt a bit sad on his last day, he was my mentor and friend. But, that sadness wore off pretty quick once I inherited his office and his salary. I had finally earned *that door* on my office.

The conversion van boom is all but finished, the days of selling four-hundred conversion vans was now a thing of the past around here. A lot of things are *a thing of the past* around here, even Mr. Bradley is gone. He passed away two years ago, about a month after he turned eighty-years old, he had lived a full great life and his legacy is passed on. Opie Cunningham is gone too, he is retired—mowing grass all summer long in Ohio and then spending winters in Florida is what he does now. His retirement money is tight, so he has to have a summer job, so much for a hundred-grand a year huh? It's the circle of life I guess. Mr. Bradley's grandson now runs the day-to-day operations at the dealership, and there is a new breed of Opie Cunningham's working here, with the entire world at their fingertips with more reach than ever thanks to all the new technology out there.

Things sure have changed, Id' say.

The news van pulls up right on time, ten-thirty, I can see them pull up as I sit in my office and look out the window. A little jolt of electricity goes through my entire body when I see the big double-deuce numbers on the side of the van, News 22. It's just a case of the shakes, that's all.

My daydream reminiscing ends as the reporter, whose real name is Marty Feldenbacher but goes by the name of Mark Baker on the air, pops in and introduces himself to me.

"Excuse me, are you Guy Bishop?"

"Yes sir."

Mark extends his arm out and we shake hands. "Glad to meet you Guy, we spoke on the phone, I'm Mark Baker from News 22, I'm sure you know that though." I really hope he didn't mind touching my clammy palms.

"The big white van you just hopped out of with those huge 'twos' on the side gave it away. You sure do look a lot smaller in real life." I said to hopefully get a small chuckle out of him, and me as well, I didn't want to come off as looking nervous or anything. I wanted to do good here, after all, I wanted to make sure they put this on the air. I hope he doesn't mind the short reference either, but it's true, he looks so much bigger on television. He did at least smile, it made me feel a little bit more relaxed, and I don't think he could see that both of my armpits were pretty soggy right now.

"That's the camera for you, always adding something, whether it's pounds or inches!" He tried to be polite about it, but I did see him wipe his hand on his pants from just touching my clam hand. "Mind if I sit down, and we can go over the outline for this?"

"Absolutely, have a seat."

"Great, thank you. Ok, well just like we spoke on the phone, I'd just like to ask you some questions about your accident from 1994. We've been working on this story about tax dollars at work, and since they just finished up the multi-million-dollar project there on County 25A, buying up the land and straightening out most of the roads, we wanted to add in some back story, get some real faces on the screen you know? So are you ready for that?"

"Sure, I guess I'm as ready as ever."

"Great, ok, here's how it will work, I'll get my guys in here to set up the cameras, we have two we like to use at the same time, using slightly different angles and I'll sit here and just ask you some questions, then all you need to do is answer them, just like you're talking to someone, don't look directly at the cameras either, look at me—just like we're having a conversation here. Sounds easy enough huh? Piece of cake, right?"

"Well, I'll admit, I'm just a bit nervous, I hope it doesn't show through to the audience."

"Oh, you'll be fine Guy, we're just two guys here talking to each other." He said reassuring.

"I think I'll be fine once we get going."

"Great, I'll get my guys in here and we'll be ready to go in about ten minutes."

The next ten minutes seemed like an hour. It wasn't that I was regretting doing this interview, I was just wanting it to either get started so that I would calm down, or hurry up and get it over with, and hopefully I don't look and sound like a complete buffoon on television. I had to excuse myself to go urinate before they were done setting up, even though I just went not ten minutes ago right before they got here. I hadn't even taken in that much coffee this morning, I was just nervous that's all, and I have a strange way of showing it. I sweat, my heart rate stays high, and I always have to go pee.

"Ok, we're about ready here—check test, one, two, three—how's my level there Sam?" Sam, who I guess is like a stagehand, gives Baker the thumbs up sign then starts turning on lights, big bright ass ones too, they flood my entire office with white light. It reminds me of the day in the bathroom, when Eric vanished into the big open portal hole in the wall. My eyes finally adjusted and I hadn't even noticed someone had attached a lapel microphone to my shirt, but there it was, and that meant we are about to start. Hmmm….do I have to take another piss? Damn nerves.

"Ok, Guy—can you go ahead and say something there so we can check the mic level, that'd be great—just talk in your normal tone and volume."

"Ummm. . .Hello? Checking—one, two, three. . ." I look over at Sam and he gives Baker a nod and another thumbs up—so that must mean it's show time. I do have to pee again, but fuck it, I'm just going to hold it.

"Ok, rolling now, and *three, two, one. . .*"

39

THAT ACTUALLY WENT well. Once I got going, I couldn't stop, I was on a roll. I didn't rehearse either, I just said what came out of my mouth, which was just about everything I remembered about that day back in 1994. How the accident on the highway had forced all the big semis onto County 25A, and how those eighty-thousand pound trucks shook the ground and moved the air each time one of them went by. It was a major distraction, that and the hairpin corner coming out of a fifty-five mile an hour zone were the major contributing factors in the accident.

I did leave out the parts just after the crash—all that stuff in between like not knowing that I had been killed, walking around for a week in death-land limbo, meeting other dead folks like me, chatting them up, seeing all their stories in vivid life like color, and then being a participant in something that was most likely *naturally illegal* when we ripped open a portal hole between worlds. Oh, and then proceeded to lose someone who was technically a semi-permanent resident of this said death-land limbo.

Yep, I skipped over all that. I picked it back up when I awoke in the hospital, saw my mother's face and heard her sweet voice. That part I'll always remember as being the best, I enjoyed talking about that. Also, my renewed look on life, and my quest to become something better than just a kid who washed and vacuumed your new car. I don't know if they'll use any of that, but I got to tell the story again, and in my own words. It sure did feel good.

We finished up, and the stagehands were now gathering up the camera gear and lights. Me and Marty Feldenbacher, a.k.a. Mark Baker, still had a few minutes to chat off camera, I tried to think of something to start off with to get a conversation going. I had already razzed him about how much smaller he looked in real-life off camera, so I thought maybe I could ask him how he got the name Mark Baker out of Marty Feldenbacher, I guess there is a bit of the same sounds buried in there, and I couldn't imagine having to say "Feldenbacher" every time I signed off the air, so it's pretty obvious why he changed it. I just went ahead and asked a few questions about how this story would look, and more importantly would it be available on the Internet anytime soon.

"So, do you think you're going to use any of that?" I asked.

"Oh, heck yes, couldn't even tell that you were nervous, maybe the leg shaking side by side would have been a sign, but that's going to be off camera, so yeah—good stuff there Guy."

"Great. The leg thing, yeah. . .I can't even control that, it just does that on its own. Say, do you put all your segments like this on the Internet too?"

"Sure do, pretty much right after they broadcast, maybe a couple of hours after."

"You know I was thinking, if other people want to get a hold of me, you know to maybe talk about and go into more detail on the whole accident thing and stuff, you think we could put an e-mail address somewhere so they can contact me?"

"You sure? You'll be surprised how many people will literally come out of the woodwork and you will probably get a lot of unwanted e-mails. We can just put a small crawler on the bottom showing your e-mail address, plus we can put it on our website right next to the story, that's all you really need if you really want some feedback."

I give Mark Baker my e-mail address to put with the story, I know what he means by people coming out of the woodwork too, that happened the last time I did this sort of thing with the local newspaper almost eighteen-years ago, except the people coming out of the woodwork just showed up at my place of employment, back when you couldn't hide behind the anonymity of an e-mail. This has to work, if Eric LaRoche or the person formerly known as Eric LaRoche is in my world, this will get him to contact me, I just know it will. If it doesn't, then I'll hang this quest of mine up forever, this will be the last time I try to find him, after this I'm done.

A few days go by, and I receive an e-mail from Mark Baker:

TO: guy@billbradleychevrolet.com
FR: MarkBaker@news22.com
Guy,
Thanks again for your time on Monday, the story is ready for air. I wanted to send you the final cut now so you can watch it first. I think it came out really good. I used a lot of your story. There are two other people that appear in the segment as well, you will see them when you watch. We were able to use the "wild dream" you talked about too, I think that will give the story a bit of a humorous edge, makes it more human, it turned out great! Video is attached, this will air at 5:30, 6, and 11 tonight....so make sure you watch!
    Thanks, Mark

Yes! That is exactly what I wanted to hear. I didn't know if it would work or not, but it did. You see, all these years I have told the same story, everyone wants to know what I *saw* or *felt* while I was *dead*. So instead of just saying I didn't remember anything, this time I wanted to plant another seed. A seed *inside* the seed if you will. The whole reason for me doing the interview was to get a message out on the *World Wide Web*, with the intention of getting someone's attention, specifically *the missing one*. But, this was another little something extra that I hoped would get into the story, and it looks like it made the final cut.

I open the attachment and it starts to play. The standard disclaimer pops up saying that this is the property of News 22 and all the legal mumbo-jumbo in small print, but as soon as that goes away, *there it is*.

My big fat huge head.

Jeezus! That is ugly! And, does my voice really sound like that? I don't even remember saying what I just heard me say, but I must have, it was my face saying the words— *"I woke up and saw my mom's smiling face back at me and I knew I was home..."* Then the shot goes to Mark Baker, a much better face for television I might add, he starts on his story about the big multi-million-dollar project that just finished up out on the county roads, turning three hairpin corners that had a history of fatal accidents into safe, straight line roads, even the one that the locals called *Dead Man's Curve*. There were two other quick shots about survivors that had been mentioned, and also all the tragedies that had accumulated over time around these three corners—thirty-seven souls total—over a period of about fifty-years. One of those souls, a woman named Reannon Banks, someone who I never knew as a living person, but knew so much about, was one of them.

I hit the pause button and turned down the sound a bit because I'm still in my office and I didn't want anyone to hear this just yet. I decide that I'll just wait to watch the whole thing on live television tonight, when the rest of the community does. Then I'll check out the version they put on the Internet a few hours later. I did scroll through, to the one part that I wanted to make sure is there and it is, just like Marty-Mark said it would be.

It was the answer to *the question*, the number one question asked of me in regards to my whole dead-time experience:

"What did you see or feel when you were laying there clinically dead in the field that day Guy? Can you tell us anything you might remember?"

Insert bullshit here: *"Well, it was like a dream…a really wild dream, I'm not sure why, maybe the radio had been playing right before the crash, but all I can remember is that I was at a rock concert in Austin, Texas….and Eddie Van Halen was playing that Fleetwood Mac song, that one hit they had in the seventies…uhhh Rhiannon I believe it was called, which is strange because Eddie Van Halen is not even in Fleetwood Mac…"*

Planting seeds.

You see what I just did there? That is some serious deep embedded code shit there. I just mentioned a group of names that maybe only one other person might recognize in that particular order. Three names, Austin, Eddie, and Reannon. I think that will be enough. My face is older looking, but not that much older—I still look basically the same and I sure sound the same. If Eric LaRoche's soul is still around in my world, he'll see my unusually large head on the television, or see the story on the Internet, he'll hear me talk—then those names that I just mentioned should do it—he'll know I'm speaking to him.

Where you at big boy?

40

I WAS ABLE to get home early that night. Usually, I'm held up at work for sometimes it seems hours after we actually close, always trying to get that last deal sold and rolled. That's the name of the game you know, but today, I left early. I wanted to catch the first run of this story about to air on the local news, and watch it with the girls at home. I think it will be better if I watch it with them—one of the main reasons being that I was hoping they'll reassure me that my head is not really as big as it seems on TV.

I roll in the front door of my house, it's about a quarter past five, and the news broadcast is just about to start. I turn the TV on and flip over to News 22, it's a commercial break at the moment—right in the middle of this break I hear a promo for the upcoming news broadcast. It was one of those voice overs that went along with part of the video of an upcoming story, *"coming up at five-thirty, a Paris man tells his tale from beyond the grave…"*

What a great teaser! If I was sitting there just doing nothing and that's all I had seen, I'd definitely stick around to watch it! I love the way these news programs hype the hell out of everything. It's supposed to be a story about well spent tax dollars, and the benefits and possible future lives saved, but no—it's all about the spook factor isn't it? Beyond the grave, yeah ok—if you only knew the truth!

My cell phone rings, and it's my mother.

"Yes, ma…yep…that was about me!" Just then I remember that I probably should have called mom and mentioned my News 22 television debut, I could have at least texted her, she's not really that old, she can still read, even though she doesn't really text back a whole lot, just those one word texts like "yes" and "ok"—she's does pretty good for a seventy-five-year-old woman living on her own.

"Sorry! I forgot to say something last time we talked, yes that Mark Baker guy came and interviewed me on Monday, I know—I've been busy at work like always ma. . ."

I finish up the call with mom, she'll be watching with everyone else in Paris, but just at home by herself with her cat named Wiggles. I call in the girls, and we all sit down on the couch—it's time for the five-thirty news broadcast to start.

"Ok, now tell me what you think when you see me on the television." I ask the girls.

"Were you scared dad?" Emily asks. "Did you pee your pants?"

It seems that the little one there pays attention to things that I say. I have never peed my pants before as an adult, but I have told stories to Christine about how I feel when I get nervous.

I smiled and answered the cute little donut hole eater. "No honey, but I was really nervous!"

"Ok, it's about to start!" Holly, my older daughter, the more intellectual one, wants to have full attention and no distractions while she watches this. I just want to hide behind the couch or go stand in the kitchen, I don't know if I can take seeing that thing again, that head of mine.

The story is about to begin, but not after we have to watch the first three main stories of the day. Paris was a small town, and the television station broadcasts from the big city of Dayton. The first three stories were about an ongoing unsolved murder, an armed robbery at Benny's Kwick-n-Kold drive-thru on the west side, and something about pot holes on the highway. All important things for folks to know about, but now here it comes—the story.

They do a great edit job for a local news station. Mark Baker did a lot of research on this, or at least someone who works for him did. All the facts were there, about how the county back in the forties tried to buy all the land to make the roads straight from the get-go, and how nobody would sell the land, so the county just gave up trying. They didn't think it would matter if the roads were straight or not. Just think if they would have been able to do that—how many lives would have been saved. Thirty-seven people's lives had been taken total over fifty-years' time, one of them a friend of mine, and one of them me. I was lucky, and somehow survived, but most were not.

My strategically placed embellishment is about to come up, this should be good to see the reaction of the girls. I never told them I was going to say this—*here it comes. . .*

"Well, it was like a dream...a really wild dream, I'm not sure why, maybe the radio had been playing right before the crash, but all I can remember is that I was at a rock concert in Austin, Texas....and Eddie Van Halen was playing that Fleetwood Mac song, that one hit they had in the seventies...uhhh Rhiannon I believe it was called, which is strange because Eddie Van Halen is not even in Fleetwood Mac..."

I look over at them and they all slowly turn their heads towards me.

"What?" Christine says. "Where did you come up with that?"

"Hey, just a little tiny embellishment, wasn't it funny?"

"It's doesn't even make sense, and it's kind of dorky sounding and not really all that funny, I'm surprised they even put it on the air."

I didn't tell her what it was really for, I've never told anyone the real story, so why start now.

"Oh well, I guess it's no different than anything else, with all the stupid reality TV shows on these days," she said.

"Yeah, I was just going for the entertainment value, see, no harm really right?"

"Well, just wait, was that your e-mail address there flashing by? You're in for it now mister, every fruitcake nut job who sees that will try to make contact with you. There are people out there that want to know and take this after-life thing serious—well anyway, it's your e-mail that's going to get blown up, so you better be ready!"

We finish up watching the story, it turned out really nice, very informational. My cell phone rings and it's my mother again.

"Hello ma. . .so what did you think? What did Wiggles think?"

41

THAT NIGHT I sat in bed just thinking. Wondering. What do I do if I actually find him? What do I say? Is it my place to put him back where he belongs? How do I even do that? Maybe I can report him to the supernatural authorities? Yep, all I need is the phone number for the proper agency that handles that, and I'll contact them the minute I see or hear from him. You see where I'm at on all this? I should have really thought it out a little more before I launched this half-assed mass media campaign to seek out the *missing soul*.

I now realize it's three in the morning, and I'm still laying here just thinking. It's one of those nights where your brain can't turn off. There are other little miscellaneous sundry items I'm thinking about, intermingled with my current dilemma of figuring out what to say and do if Eric LaRoche steps into my world again. So, along with all that, I am also currently thinking about a finance deal that I need to follow up on first thing in the morning for Jay Lubke. Jay is a next generation superstar salesman who does 90% of his sales on the Internet, with basically no human contact other than chat rooms and e-mails, and very minimal talking on the phone. Sounds crazy, but there is an entire generation of people who prefer to communicate that way. In between all that, I am also thinking about getting another snow blower, the one I have now is on its last leg and will soon need to be replaced. That last item with the snow blower does not factor in at all on the priority list of shit to think about at night, but somehow it gets thrown in the mix. Those are the three items that are fighting for my time, and it's keeping me awake.

Then the alarm goes off.

I don't even remember falling asleep last night, but that's how it usually goes. The way I wake up now, other than the weekends with that donut hole eating little monster that personally wakes me up, is with a very low volume alarm that sits on my side of the bed. You see, when you get married all things change. You think everything will be the same, but in order for things to properly merge together, to live a peaceful and cohesive life, there are some compromises that need to be made. The first thing is Christine, my beautiful wife, does not like to hear radio music first thing in the morning, or jokes, or stupid comedy bits about reindeers in space. Nothing. Really, it is amazing to say but she does not require anything to wake her up in the morning. She is a freak of nature and I can testify to this, all she has to do is tell herself, out loud before she goes to sleep, what time she wants to wake up in the morning, and she wakes up at that time, some people just have great internal clocks, not me though.

It's Friday morning. Here recently I have been trying to wake up thirty-minutes earlier than normal so I can go downstairs and run on the treadmill for twenty-minutes or so—this is *not* one of those mornings. I do get up earlier than normal, but I go sit down on my home computer instead. I attempt to login to my work e-mail, sometimes it has issues when I try from home, but it looks like it's getting ready to connect. This is the e-mail address that was included with the story on television last night, and by now I'm sure it's been on the Internet too.

Hmmm. . .I must not be as important as I thought.

I connect to my work e-mail, but there are only twelve new e-mails, not twelve-thousand like I was thinking might happen. I scroll down through them, there is one there from a lady named Mildred Sumter, from Port Jackson she says she loved my story and is praying for me. That's nice. I give a quick reply back to thank her for the message. Just as soon as I hit the send button, another incoming e-mail arrives, this one is from Terry Westfall, that's Bruce Westfall's wife, my old boss— she must have caught the story on the television too. She says basically the same thing as Mildred from Port Jackson says—*enjoyed your story, going to pray for you.*

I go through the spam folder to see if anything may have ended up in there by mistake, nothing except the usual garbage, so I decide it's time to go get ready for work. I must have forgot to log off the e-mail server before I got up from the desk, as I'm halfway down the hall I hear another sound from the computer, it's the sound you get when you receive a new e-mail. For a second, maybe two, I thought I'd walk back and see if it was another response about my story on the tube last night, but I'm already three-minutes past my shower time, so I just continue on down the hall and into the bathroom, remember, *I'm never late.*

I make up the three-minute deficit—didn't skip a thing wash wise either—the three majors were all covered—*pits, butt, and balls,* all three areas were thoroughly *and* properly washed—clean undies, talcum powdered up, and standing tall. Ready for the day's activities and whatever adventures may lie ahead. Back on track now—I'm glad the days of wearing a suit and tie to work are over. I did get pretty damn good at tying a tie, after about a thousand times doing it, I could do it in my sleep. It's just so much easier now, throw on the tan khaki's and the Bill Bradley logoed golf shirt and I'm ready.

As I walk out to the kitchen, the girls are up and eating breakfast. My usual thing is that I don't eat breakfast, but I do drink some coffee. Thanks to getting back on track time wise from my very efficient *pit, butt, and ball* washing technique, I can enjoy the last seven minutes I have with the girls before they head off to school and me off to work.

"You sure were tossing and turning all night," Christine said.

"I know, I couldn't get my brain to shut down, one of those kind of nights, plus it's almost time to get another snow blower."

"Snow blower huh? Did you get up and work out at least?"

"No, but I did think about it, and that should count for something."

"Just because you thought of it? Well if it were that easy. . ."

"I know, I know, I got up and was checking some e-mails, I thought I might get some from people who wanted to know more about the story from last night."

"I saw, your e-mail program was still up on the screen when I walked into the office this morning, I was thinking you would get all the crazies trying to contact you, but really not all that much."

"Did you see Terry Westfall sent me a message? That's Bruce Westfall's wife."

"I saw her name, I didn't read what she wrote. I still don't see why you wanted strangers to e-mail you, do you even know that Mildred lady? Or that Linda person?"

"Ummm, Mildred, no, Linda. . .never heard of her before."

That must have been the e-mail that came in when I was all the way down the hall headed to the shower, I didn't catch the *Linda* e-mail, but I'm sure it's just another random person.

"Yeah, well the name sounds familiar—*Linda Lyons?* Why do I know that name? Is that one of your ex-girlfriends who saw you on TV and is now trying to make contact?"

First of all, never had a girlfriend named Linda that I can recall, and I can tell you where I have heard the name Linda Lyons before, back in the day of my medium dead experience, that's who Eddie Chapman pulled over the night they both were killed along the highway by the sleepy trucker. I never met her in the after-life, we all figured she must have just went right to and then on through her door. I try to think of a response, it takes me a second or two, but I thought of something that seemed plausible.

"Oh, I know, those two crosses that are planted up between Belle City and Paris on the highway, one says *Trp. Chapman*, the one beside it says *Linda Lyons*, you probably see that every day when you drive by it going to work honey, and that's why it looks familiar to you, must be someone with the same name, that's all."

"I don't try to read those, you know that."

"I know, but your eyes look at them, you might not read it, but you see it, just natural to do, I'm sure that's where you've seen the name before."

"Oh, probably so, I guess. . ."

Now that I got that handled, I need to take a look at what *Linda Lyons* e-mailed me. I'll bet you it's not the *Linda Lyons* who died that night along the highway with Eddie Chapman either. My bet is that my message made it out into the mainstream, and now someone else is trying to respond back to me. I try not to show it, but I'm shaking inside from top to bottom, this has got to be it. As much as I want to go in there and log back into my e-mail to find out for sure, I can't—I need to get going. I have to look at Jay Lubke's deal and get that all done first, I don't even know how I'm going to do that with all this excitement and anticipation built up inside me. I'm getting that nervous feeling again. I think I have to pee.

42

I GET TO work, but I can't focus on a thing it seems. All I can think about is that e-mail. Somehow I manage to muddle through the paperwork needed to get this deal finished. It took a little longer than normal because every four or five minutes I would stop what I was doing and just stare off into space, it's something I typically do on any given morning, but today more than usual for obvious reasons. *I need to read an important e-mail!*

I do need to get this deal finished and sent off to the bank before nine-thirty, Jay Lubke like all these aggressive salespeople, are always on the finance department's ass when it comes to their loan approvals. It doesn't take much longer to finalize what I need to do and I can finally have some *me time* in my office. I go grab another cup of coffee, take an obligatory piss, and go sit down in my chair—it's time.

Hold on to your hats, here it comes.

As usual, this thing takes its time logging on, of course it seems longer than usual now, always does when you want it to hurry up and work. Finally, there it is. Sure enough, the name of the sender is *Linda Lyons* and the subject line says: *Your Story*.

TO: guy@billbradleychevrolet.com
FR: Linda Lyons (Lyons777@aol.com)
Subject: Your Story

Mr. Bishop,

Very interesting story. I too share a very similar story, I was clinically dead for several minutes in a highway accident many years ago, I remember a dream I had very similar to yours and would love to see if we could talk about it over coffee someday. Please see attached file below for my contact info, I look forward to hopefully meeting you and sharing our experiences together.

L. Lyons

This is interesting, I thought this would be the answer to the question I've had for the past twenty-years—*where the hell did he go?* But, now it's starting to look like one big coincidence, just a fluke, someone with the same name that just so happens to be on one of those highway memorial crosses, and one that I am familiar with. Just a random thing. I guess it's possible, considering how many millions of people are in the world, have access to the Internet, and saw that story of mine. Maybe this person did have a similar experience like I did. But, really? And, her name just happens to be Linda Lyons? I guess it wouldn't hurt to try and make contact, sit face to face, or maybe just a phone call to feel this person out. After all, it still might be him, but he is just being careful not to bring too much attention to himself—he might be hiding from *someone* or *something.*

I click on the little attachment, it's one of those zip files, and its asking for a password. Now that's odd, why would I need a password? This is just supposed to be a phone number or an address or something. How the hell am I supposed to get this to open? Why didn't she give me the damn password?

After sitting there, re-reading the e-mail, studying the context, and then stepping back and putting myself into Eric LaRoche or a.k.a. *Linda Lyon's* shoes, I come up with something—*he wants me to put in a password that only he and I would know*—then this file will open up and the *real message* will pop out. If so, what a brilliant idea he has here—that way his message reaches the intended target—me, and only me. It's either that, or Linda Lyons is just an idiot for not including the password to her file attachment that is supposed to contain important contact info. I guess I could e-mail her back right now and ask for it, but I'm not so sure I'd get a reply. I'm pretty sure it's up to me to come up with it on my own.

Only one thing to do now, and that's figure out this password. This might take a while, and I'm at work right now, luckily not a whole lot going on at the moment so might as well try a few passwords to see if anything is easy to guess. The first one I put in, *LaRoche,* is not it, that would have been *too easy* I guess. I then put in everyone's first name we were with during the time we were all together. *Eddie, Austin,*

Reannon, Guy, Eric, still not it. I try just about every combination of names I could think of, mix-n-matching them all up, first, last name, then vice-versa, caps on, caps off, still not getting this attachment to open up. He's really going to make me work for this isn't he?

BEFORE I KNOW it, it's noon. Geesh, have I really been sitting here trying to figure out this password for three hours? So much for guessing an easy password, that's three hours of my life I'd like to have back. Time to get up and go get something to eat and stretch the legs. I'm sure it's something very simple and only something he and I would know. I just need to think it out. *Think, think, think!*

I decide to head over to Subway and get a sandwich, that's what you do when you're almost fifty-years old and are trying to watch what you eat, right? But the thing is, Subway is no better than McDonald's after you add all the junk to the sandwich, especially the cheese, mayo, and a heaping pile of meatballs. It's just loaded up with the fat, and no better for you than a Big Mac, but damn if it isn't good all jazzed up like that.

The whole time I'm driving, I think about that after-life experience again, this password I'm trying to figure out has to be in those stories somewhere. Most, if not all, of the memories are still there in vivid detail. I remember all their stories, and how they were told to me, via the direct-to-the-head method. I always thought that was the coolest part of it all, just being right there with them while it was happening. I had always dreamed of being a cop, pulling over someone and giving them a ticket, so when Eddie Chapman shared his story, it was like I was him. I loved the fine minute details that came with it too, the challenges of figuring out a new radar gun, the boredom, the crossword puzzles he did to kill the time. Those little details in the story was what made it unique and special to me, and I'm sure to all of us that got to join in on those memories with him.

I finally get to Subway and go stand in line, thinking of what I want to eat today—probably the same thing I ate last time I was here which was just a couple of days ago. A foot long maybe?

No, you fat ass!

How about a six-inch turkey on wheat? Should I skip the cheese today? Nahh, since I'm doing a six-inch, that more than makes up for the fatty cheese right? To me that makes complete and total sense, and I justify that in my mind.

It's finally my turn to order up, I go for the six-inch turkey on whole wheat bread, then it's decision time as the Subway sandwich artists asks me *"what kind of cheese do you want on that?"* As if this is a mandatory item, but did you know you can say *no cheese?* For just a second, well probably less than a second, I'm thinking I'd do this with the *no cheese option*, how proud would my wife be when I tell her I skipped the cheese today on my sandwich? But like I said, it was less than a second to decide this and if you haven't noticed yet, words tend to just come out of my mouth unabated at times.

"I'll take pepper jack today." If I'm going to get cheese, might as well have a kick to it. I realize what I just said and something hits me.

I get my sub to go, I need to get back right now.

I just figured out what the password is.

43

FROM THE TIME I paid for my sub, to the time I walked back into my office, I couldn't tell you anything that happened. My mind was on autopilot; I don't even remember the drive back to the dealership. The last thing I remember was the cashier handing back my receipt and telling me I had enough Subway points to feed a college student through one, possibly two semesters (I apparently eat a lot of Subway). But, if it wasn't for my appetite, and an internal discussion inside my head: *To cheese, or not to cheese.* I would have never remembered, or maybe I would have, but it would have taken a lot longer, and a lot more Subway visits before it hit me again.

It really was everything coming together at the right time to get this epiphany. My whole thought process during the ride to the restaurant, I was trying to recall all the stories those souls told me, so long ago, but still so vivid in my mind. Seems strange, but it's like the memories are set in there for good.

I bring back up the file that was attached to Linda Lyon's e-mail, at this point I'm not even hungry, I've lost my appetite for the moment. The little box to put the password in pops up and I start to type. If my hunch is right, it's the same word in Eddie Chapman's story about the night he saved that family on the highway—he was working on a crossword puzzle right before it all happened—it was the answer to twenty-six across, and in his words:

The only word that it could have been, the only word that fit, PEPPERJACK. That was it!

The file opens up, and at the same time that feeling shoots through my body just like the day I died so long ago, that jolt of electricity, it's those crazy nerves again, I almost lost my breath, I'm sure my heart stopped for a second too.

I was right, there is more to this message, *a lot more. . .*

Guy,

Congrats, you did it bro...not only did you figure out how to open this attachment, you somehow managed to get back to life as we used to know it, and I envy you, I'm jealous! I'm sure you have a thousand questions about what happened in the bathroom the last time we were together, it must have looked pretty bad on your end what I was trying to do that day. I'm sorry if I misled you, but just know that what I had set out to do, worked. First of all, I need to be clear on something, I was not directly responsible for Virgil Simms's death, so don't think I'm a murderer like that ass fuck was. Yes, it didn't help any that we broke through the dimension that day and showed him something he wasn't supposed to see, I'm sure that had a little to do with it, but the man just flat out was scared to death, and in the literal sense too. I was never really able to get a good grip on him, I was actually holding him up from falling onto the ground, and well, you know what happened after that I'm sure. I suppose the number one question you might have is what happened to me? And also, what and where I am? Well, it's hard to explain but *I'm nothing*. That's right, *nothing*. It's very hard to describe what I am now. I am basically a snail without a shell, a freaking slug, nothing more. The day I broke through that mirror? That was actually a big mistake on my part, and now I'll never have a chance at another door *ever*. I am stuck in your world now, with no chance to move on. I am basically your garden variety spook, phantom, apparition, poltergeist, or whatever name you can come up with for a freak like me which is just a soul without a *real* body in the *real* world. I'm *the thing* that you thought you saw, I'm that cold chill going up your spine. Ok, I'll say it...I'm just a *ghost*, there I said it, are you even surprised or scared? Hell no you're not! You were once like me too, remember? I'm telling you it's not all that great knowing you're stuck here forever. At least in that crappy no color, no light, shit-box world we were in before there was at least a chance to get out and move on. Ok, second question I'm guessing is how am I even sending you these messages? Well, around 1995 or there about, this thing called the Internet started to go mainstream, and all of us in the *ghost community* (yes, there are more here than just me in the same situation) soon found out that we could easily jump right into it, and become part of it, we could become someone again! Why not? You all do it! Hide behind a keyboard and a mouse, take on an identity, even if it's not your own! A *digital soul* if you will. Then once that Myspace and Facebook thing started, holy shit! Even better! Now a nice picture to go along with the name! But let's be real here...nothing beats having an actual living and breathing body, like what you have. At the end of the day that computer can't go out and have a family, or go for hikes, or just enjoy life. I know I say I'm jealous Guy, but *I get it, I made my choice and did what I needed to do, and I can "live" with it.* I know you have been trying to look for me all these years too. Thing is, I found you first a long time ago. I was there, right with you the day you met Christine, the day your first daughter was born, and even the day your second daughter was born...I was standing right there with you man. Hell, I even cried with you! You have an awesome family bro, so don't let them down ever! Ok, let's talk about moving forward here, I must say—I am impressed with the way you have answered the one question everyone has when it comes to that seven minutes you were dead, and keeping *our kind* in the shadows. Well at least until that news story came out...But I totally see what you were doing there. You were reaching out, trying to touch someone, namely me! So, since you've done that for all this time, I'm doing this—I have a little pull in this supernatural community, don't ask how...remember, like you said, in your words—I'm the *mind manipulator* and here is what I propose. *How would you like those seven minutes back?* Yes, I'm talking about the seven minutes you were dead, I can arrange to get them back for you. It sounds crazy, but all you do is think like you did back in those medium dead days— you know, like when you wanted to move somewhere? You just thought of the place where you needed to be, and you were there? Well, that's how it works. I'll get you those *seven minutes* back, and you just say, *or think*, and it will happen. Time will turn back however many minutes or seconds you need, of course only up to a total of seven. That's all we really owe you right? Once you've used those seven minutes up, we're all even, you can go on living your life and I can go on *not* living mine. So are you in? Just think, you have a traumatic event happen in your life, who knows, an accident, or maybe a wrong turn down a road that ends up in a tragedy, I don't know—they are your minutes to use for yourself or someone else. All you do is think, how many minutes or seconds do you want to turn back and do over again? But this time, you know what to do to make things right. Oh, I guess you could go out to Las Vegas or any one of these casinos along the coast and just tear it up and make a bunch of money by using those minutes up, cheating on those gambling games or whatever, but do you really think it's worth that? Think about your family. Think about yourself. This is a huge thing Guy, if I had seven minutes back I would have changed a lot of things. For one I would have turned around and walked out of Virgil Simms's house that night. Use those minutes wisely my old friend. This is something you don't want to screw up. I know you won't, you're smart. All I ask in return is you keep doing what you have been doing all these years and if anyone asks...you don't remember a thing that happened when you were dead way back when. Just keep on saying *"I don't remember a thing"* and we got a deal. So are you in? Just let me know, all you'll need to do is reply to Linda Lyons's e-mail here—a simple "I'm in" will do. Make your choice bro. Maybe someday we'll talk more—but for now this is adios—Oh, also, one last thing. This message will erase itself as soon as you close it, never to be retrieved again, so make sure you read it as many times as you need before you close the file. That's just the way we do things around here, I'm sure you understand. You have until the sun goes down today to claim those minutes, or else they'll be gone forever. Make your choice!

EL

Ok, am I still breathing? I check my pulse and I'm still here. I'm still alive. I read the message at least eight times. I'd like to keep a copy of it, but it sounds too dangerous to keep. I re-read it a ninth time so I can try to retain as much as possible, then close the file. There, it's gone forever, but the message still clear in my mind.

What do I do?

I only have until sundown to think about it? There isn't much to think about is there? Any sane person would just hit the reply button and type *"I'm in"* without thinking twice about it. Is he really going to give me back my seven minutes? How is that going to work out? How does one have the authority to do such a thing? What happens when I want to cash some time in? All those thoughts go through my head for at least another hour while I sit alone silent in my office.

I really need to start doing some actual work, but I'm not quite all here mentally. I go ahead and pass on a couple of deals to the other underwriters, they really didn't need my attention anyway. What needs my attention right now is *me*. I begin to wonder, is there something else hidden in that message I need to worry about before I accept his gift?

So, the whole time he's been gone, he hasn't really *been gone*. . . he's been right here. Or at least pretty close by me the whole time. That's creepy. Especially when he admits that he's just your basic everyday run-of-the-mill ghost now. I never really believed in ghosts. Once I had my experience though, I knew there was something else beyond this world, so I definitely believe they can exist today. They obviously do, and they enjoy trolling around on the Internet it seems. That's even more creepy.

The customer that Jay Lubke talks to exclusively over the Internet? That could just be an old trapped soul, trying to get a good deal on a used car, even though they have no intention of picking it up and driving it off the lot. They can't, not without proper identification, and oh, I don't know, an actual body?

Beyond that craziness, I still have to decide on something here. Do I take the minutes or not? If I take them, is there a trade-off that comes with it? You know, other than a space-time continuum paradox, which is something that has to be considered for sure. It does sound like a sweet deal for me, for my family, maybe even for the entire world. If I had the right connections, I could stop a terrorist attack, or stop a train from going off its rails, or save someone's life. Seven minutes doesn't seem like a whole lot of time to go back and do over, but it's surely could be enough under the right circumstances.

I could choose to just use them for myself, just me and my family exclusively. God forbid something terrible happens to my kids or my wife. I could turn back the time and make everything right, and that alone is worth it. Of course the other option is to make myself rich, just like he said, I could just go to Vegas and tear it up, I wonder how much money I could win before they threw me out of town forever? Probably not as much as I think.

It's starting to get late now and the sun is about to set. I start to wind things down in the office, it's about time for me to go grab some hairy (I still say that to myself when it's time to leave for the day, and I still have no idea what it really means).

As I sit in my chair, I think about it all one last time and the decision is made in my mind. I bring back up the e-mail from Linda Lyons and hit the reply button. In the body of the message I type two words, and two words only.

I'm in.

THE END

Author's Notes

Sometimes the gentle roads we travel on are not so gentle. We are reminded of this each time we drive by a roadside memorial, or a cross planted in the ground on the side of the road. Something happened there, at a different time, and it wasn't good. Someone died.

As my family and I would travel to our vacation spot in South Carolina from Ohio, I would see many of these along the way. I never counted how many, but it sure seemed like quite a lot. What happened? I always wondered. What if these souls were still out here, wandering around? That was part of the inspiration for this novel.

I have never written anything that resembled any kind of story that I can remember in my life. So, I have no idea where any of this came from. I just tried to write something here that I'd enjoy reading myself, and I hope you enjoyed it as much as I did writing it.

I hardly have any time in my *real* life to read *real* books. I even flunked out of a reading class in high school because I tried to "fake" the teacher out by giving a book report on a book I had never even read. Unfortunately for me, the teacher did read the book, and then proceeded to ask me questions I couldn't answer! Shame on me! That cost me another half semester of high school, all because I decided not to read something. So hopefully this novel I wrote makes up for it Mrs. Wildermuth. (Sorry that it's been almost 30 years!)

Oh, and as far as grabbing some hairy? Well, that's something real (I think) I used to work with someone that said that phrase every day at quitting time. I just figured it was something he did on a nightly basis, and really didn't think too much of it. It sure did sound funny though! I hope it's nothing too vulgar or some sort of slang that I totally missed the real meaning of, if so I apologize for that!

Thanks for reading!

Richard Kennett

If you enjoyed this book I would be very grateful if you would post a positive review. Your support matters, and I do read all reviews.

If you go to the books Amazon page, that is where you can leave a review, you can also go to my website to find a link to the review page.

You'll see a big button that says "Write a customer review," just click that and you'll be good to go.

Thanks again for your support.
Richard Kennett

RichardKennett.com

www.facebook.com/rickroy111

www.ingramcontent.com/pod-product-compliance
Lightning Source LLC
Chambersburg PA
CBHW050928120626
46552CB00001B/100